The Cannonball King

Tyler Anderson

This book is for

My son Mason
This summer has been the time of my life
I love you
Dad

Welcome to
FOSSIL
We're glad to know ya!

Prologue

Do you remember when you were thirteen? The first half of summer is great, no school of course…; swimming every day till your dry skin itches so bad that it's almost impossible to sleep at night; camping at your favorite spot and wolfing down barbecued marshmallows till you can't stand the sight of another melted blob and keep feeding them to grandpa's *dog*? Maybe a family trip somewhere new; on the drive you eagerly listen to your dad's old time stories and the crazy things he did when he was a kid, but your mom stops him with sharp poke in the ribs every time he gets to a really cool part. But then surprisingly, when the summer has been streaking past like a good book, the days suddenly begin to slow until they drag by in never ending boredom. You find there's nothing to do and even school begins to sound interesting, almost inviting. It's hard to forget those times and it's comforting to close your eyes and draw yourself back into the strong memories and relive some of the best days. This is the story of a close family in a small town where an easy going boy and his friends find the simplest escapade interesting. They wish summer could go on forever. It is nineteen-sixty-eight and although much of the world around them is in turmoil, Logan's days are full of laughter and endless adventures, each morning he bounces from bed ready for the day's fun to get underway.

Until the ordeal, or as Logan puts it, "The mess started. The really bad mess."

One

With the wind whistling in his ears Logan chases Stoney and Ballsac down landslide hill on his rusty Schwinn. Both of them are heavier than Logan and gravity gives the bigger boys a considerable speed advantage. His pedals flying around so fast that his legs can't keep up; Logan stops pedaling and patiently watches his friends as he coasts over the smooth asphalt leaning forward with his chin resting on the handlebars; the front tire hums lightly; small vibrations from the cracks and stones rattles his teeth together as he bounces over.

Where the street flattens at the bottom of the hill the tables turn to Logan's advantage. In the lead, Stoney starts pedaling before Ballsac gets to the bottom. They still have the entire block to race before they reach Logan's house and Logan has more endurance than both of them combined. A confident smile covers his face as he starts to gain.

Logan passes them two full houses before they reach his yard. As he jumps the curb he raises his arms over his head in celebration, locks the back tire then skids his bike sideways across the grass of his front yard and watches Stoney come in second, and Ballsac sulk as he coasts in last.

The smoky aroma of a barbecue grill reaches Logan as he tosses his bike against the house; it slides down the wall on its side, the seat squeaking over the painted bricks, the back tire spinning away. As usual, his Uncles brand spanking new Corvette sits in the driveway beside his brother's fifty-eight junker Pontiac Chieftain.

Satisfied with his victory he spins in a circle while pumping his fists over his head, "Won again." As he runs into the back yard he laughs over his shoulder, "Losers."

Thick gray smoke is billowing around his dad's head as he bends over the barbecue. Logan calls out, "Hey dad, I'm starving!"

Rob looks up at Logan's flushed face and replies in an irritated voice, "It's gonna be a while buddy. This d..., darn grill is givin' me fits."

Logan's Uncle Larry waves a beach towel over the grill. Pretending to make smoke signals, he's poking fun at Rob as the smoke bubbles from under the towel. Larry holds his throat and fakes a choking gag as he playfully squeaks, "This thing needs a mechanic."

"Dad *is* a mechanic," Logan indignantly rolls his eyes at Rob.

"Yeah, I know. His Ford smokes just like this too," Larry prods, trying to get Rob to react.

An ace mechanic Rob built a thirty-four Ford coupe hot rod two years ago and keeps it covered up in the detached garage. "Dad's car doesn't smoke."

Running his fingers through Logan's bleached hair Rob notes how it's almost turned green from the pool chlorine and makes a mental note to reduce the chemical levels as he happily banters, "It'll smoke that new Corvette of Larry's."

"Sure, when hell freezes..." Larry begins but Rob cautions him with a warning frown and shake of his head.

Logan waves his friends to the pool without trying to disguise the annoyance in his tone, "C'mon guys. My dad's coupe is cherry."

Logan thinks the world of his dad and can't stand it when his uncle plays around like this. Larry acts like he knows more about cars than his dad and it really gets under Logan's skin. His dad makes a good living with his repair shop and people come from all over Fossil and sometimes all over Arizona, confident they'll get their car fixed right the first time. Rob opened Fossil Auto Works before Logan was born and he knows his dad works hard and doesn't like Larry smearing him, even in jest.

After draping his sweaty shirt over the fence Logan closes his eyes and drops backwards into the pool. When his head breaks the surface his spongy pool football floats right in front of his nose. With an evil smile at Stoney he squeezes and ducks the football under the water. Then aiming carefully, he throws it in the *general* direction of Stoney, but it flies over his outstretched hands and bounces off his Uncle's ear with a splat.

At the last second Larry spots it out of the corner of his eye and tries to jump out of the way, but his heel nicks the picnic table and he stumbles sideways, his arms wheeling like a humming bird until he catches his balance. "What the heck," he complains as he rubs his ear and dries his hair with his shirt sleeve.

"Knock it off Logan," Rob orders. He knows how Logan dislikes the way Larry torments everyone for his own amusement and shakes his head disapprovingly at him over the barbecue.

It's not that Logan doesn't like his Uncle. The spitting image of Rob, it's impossible not to love him. Rob and Larry are brothers with only two years between them. Six foot two and athletic, they played on the high school basketball team together. Larry can be a lot of fun at times, but his constant pestering tends to wear everybody thin. Every family has one and tolerating them day in and day out can be pretty tough—Larry is a master pest—chuckling with pleasure when he thinks he's artfully got under your nerves. Whenever a victim reaches the point of no return, completely fed up and snapping in frustration; Larry holds his hands up defensively, adopts what *he* thinks is a gangster tone and mischievously says his standard tag line, "What's the matta now?" Logan always ignores him before it gets to that point.

Stoney jumps in feet first but Ballsac, knowing the pool is too shallow, waits for Rob to look the other way and dives in. Dunking him until he sputters for relief, Logan warns him not to do it again with a harsh whisper, "What are you thinking? You know my dad will kick you out again."

"Whatever," Ballsac grunts carelessly as he splashes Logan in defiance and retreats.

Logan's Aunt Ginger slides open the back patio window and slides a tray of hamburgers on the bar as she calls out, "Hey Rob here's the burgers."

She's the saint that puts up with Larry twenty-four hours a day and Logan likes her a lot. She's tiny in comparison to Rob and Larry, barely five feet with flaming red hair she keeps Larry in line with her quick temper. She spends most of her time at the house with Logan's mom, Carol. When they're not together planning a party, they're together shopping. Clothes shopping, grocery shopping, shoe shopping, it doesn't matter; they're just always together and always talking.

Stoney tosses the floating toys out of the pool and shouts, "Let's make a whirlpool."

Round, four feet deep and twenty-five feet across the above ground pool is almost always filled with neighborhood kids, bouncing and screaming at the top of their lungs. The barbecues at Logan's house are legendary and the neighbors flock to their afternoon festivities.

The water reaches their shoulders and the boys run around the wall of the pool; pushing the water faster and faster until the flow carries them around floating on their backs; the sun reflects off their sun-tanned faces as they spin in slow circles. His ears filled with water, Logan could float in the silence like this for hours contemplating and planning, unlike Stoney.

Stoney covers his own eyes as he splashes water in Logan's upward turned face, "You need to put a shade over this thing, the sun's burning holes clear through my eyelids."

Logan dives to the bottom of the pool, finds a set of swim goggles and tosses them at him. "Here ya go pansy waist."

The sun is getting ready to disappear behind the tree in the front yard. Shadows trickle across the yard as the limbs sway in the breeze. Grease in the grill catches fire and Rob covers it with the lid as Uncle Larry laughs with delight.

The burger's aroma fills the air and Logan's stomach rumbles. He hasn't eaten since lunch and they played flag football for over two hours this afternoon. Drooping his arms over the side of the pool as if dying, he asks no one in particular, "What's taking so long?"

Carol answers, "By the time you dry off they'll be done." She watches him slouch back into the water and swim to the other side—both of her boys look so much like Rob it's uncanny. Josh's hair is darkening as he gets older but Logan's is still light. Josh is already as tall as Rob but Logan, who's more of a thinker, is a little smaller than Josh was at his age. Easy going and getting good grades without seeming to work at it, he enjoys life. Josh gets straight A's too but has to study harder, which seems to be his style anyway, focused and direct—She brushes her blond hair over her ears and rubs lotion into her delicate hands hoping the upcoming school year will go as well as last year did.

As Logan climbs out of the pool Stoney swings a pool floater into his head knocking him back into the water, but as he falls Logan grabs Stoney's ankle and wrenches him into the water.

Tangled in headlocks they dunk each other. Every time they surface Ballsac cracks their heads with a pool floater until Stoney yells, "Stop hitting me with your noodle ball... *sack*," emphasizing sack with a dramatic pause.

Of course this only makes Ballsac swing harder. The noodle resoundingly thumps into Stoney's ear as he growls a short mean laugh, "I've *got* your ball sack."

His name isn't really Ballsac, it's Robert Bolsic, but Stoney started calling him that in the third grade and somehow it stuck. For some reason the PE teacher even calls him Ballsac, which probably hasn't helped him to shake the moniker. He's taller and a little on the heavy side for a boy his age and quiet most of the time. Wearing his dark black hair longer than the other boys he's comfortable with himself, and his mom calls him her little man because of his quiet and seemingly serious nature around adults.

Stoney is always making up nicknames for people. He probably gets that from his dad. Stoney's name is Steven Tony Wilson. When he was a baby his parents called him Steve and his grandparents called him Tony after his uncle who died in a plane crash in Korea, so his dad compromised and started calling him Stoney. Stoney's a big jokester and Logan's best friend.

"Stop hitting me with your noodle, ball sack," Stoney dodges under another swing and grins happily, knowing that he's hitting a sore spot.

After throwing the floater at Stoney in disgust, Ballsac climbs out of the pool and dries off with his back to him in silence.

"*C'mon man*, I'm just messing around," Stoney pleads apologetically.

Glaring at him over his shoulder Ballsac continues the silent treatment.

Without drying off, Logan runs down the stairs to the picnic table then snatches a hamburger bun with his wet hand. His fingers sink together as it soaks up the water streaming from his elbow. Frowning at the soggy mess, Larry pretends to gag and says disgustedly, "You're gonna have mushy soup for dinner if you're not careful."

Logan holds it out for a burger and smiles back knowing that if he reacts in any other way Larry won't drop it and will happily torture him. Hoping to catch a hint of their daily ventures, Carol and Ginger seat themselves at the picnic table with the ravenous boys, but they eat in silence. Stoney and Ballsac don't talk much if they think an adult is listening; Ballsac sometimes won't even respond to an adult. It's not that they're bad kids; they just don't want the adults to know what's going on in their lives. Whenever an adult finds out any little thing they always ask too many questions; bugging the boys if they find out they've been talking to a girl; or endlessly asking them how school is going.

Logan's older brother Josh is the worst though. He's only seventeen but can't keep his mouth shut, as if he forgot what it was like to be a kid. He hears anything and it never fails, he tells Logan's parents and they hound him with their stupid questions to no end. Last year Logan had a girlfriend, only for a couple months, but every time the phone rang Josh would relentlessly tease him that it was her calling to play kissy face while making loud smoochy kissing sounds into the phone. Rob put an end to that particular teasing after Logan slugged Josh in the stomach and Josh locked him into a headlock then knuckled his head until he cried.

As they chatter away during the meal, the sun sets and the street lights flicker on. Silence settles in and the adults talk quietly, enjoying the easy breeze while they finish their meal. Ballsac finishes first and impatiently tosses pebbles at the other boys as they try to fit in bites between battling him off.

Carol notices the boys are finished and tells them that it's time to go home. Shuffling away from the adults, they huddle together in the darkness then Logan asks, "Are you guys gonna be around to play football tomorrow?"

"I may have to watch my sister till my mom gets home, so maybe later," Ballsac offers.

"I can play after lunch. My mom always tells me to *get the hell out* of the house by noon anyway," Stoney confesses with a laugh as they break up.

"All right I'll call you 'bout eleven," Logan yells at their retreating backs.

This night will be one of the last this summer that Logan feels the completely innocent emotions that only belongs to a thirteen year old.

Two

Carol has cooked a big breakfast; pancakes; eggs and fried potatoes smothered in onions. Shoveling the potatoes greedily onto his plate, Logan rushes to get his share before his dad gets in the kitchen.

"You know your dad's going to tell you that's too much," Carol cautions him.

Of course Rob hears her from the bathroom and yells, "Tell that kid to stop being such a hog!"

"I warned ya," she says raising her eyebrows and pressing her lips together into a thin line.

Logan jams potatoes in his mouth and chews ninety miles an hour keeping one eye out for his dad's shadow in the hall. Rob loves fried potatoes more than he loves cars; don't hold the pepper and onions.

Carol observes him gobbling away, "If you don't slow down, you'll choke yourself."

Logan flinches when Rob's work boots clunk against the kitchen tile when he tosses them by the door. With a quick grin Rob adds in a sour tone, "If he doesn't slow down, *I'll* choke him."

He leans against the counter next to Carol, sipping his orange juice and watching Logan mow through his potatoes. With a shake of his head and a small snort of laughter, he notes, "He's even starting to sound like a pig."

Pausing to swallow, for once, between bites Logan mumbles, "C'mon dad. Don't blow a gasket."

"You'd better watch your smart mouth. Your grandpa will skin your hide if he hears you back talking like that," Carol warns.

Rob frowns lightly at Logan and claps his shoulder, "You know better than that buddy."

Logan chews in silence as Rob scoop potatoes onto his plate and grumbles, "Throw another potato on the fire next time."

"There's not enough potato's in the state of Idaho for the two of you."

"It's *not* me. *He's* bound to eat us out of house and home," Rob laughs out loud.

"I'll tell Ginger we need a thirty pound bag when we're shopping today."

"Do they even come in thirty pounds? If he keeps eatin at this rate, I'll have to double up on the over time to pay for it all," Rob states.

"He's so skinny. Where does he put it all?" Carol pokes Logan's ribs with her index finger.

"He's growing like a friggin weed and he runs none stop, that's where it goes. He could eat ten pounds of potatoes in the morning and still burn it off before noon."

Logan pushes his plate away, chugs his milk and complains, "You guys always talk about me like I'm not here."

"Yeah? Well you're lucky we think about you at all," Rob teases through a mouth full of potato.

"Say it don't spray it," Logan chortles, pointing at Rob's mouth.

"That's enough already. You're driving me batty," Carol sits her plate beside Rob's.

"I'm done mom. Can I go now?" Logan asks, already knowing the answer as he slides his chair back.

"Where are you going? What are you doing? And who are you going with?" she asks in her usual fashion.

Logan isn't the kind of boy that keeps many important secrets from his parents, but as a matter of pride he answers, "I don't know. I was just gonna ride my bike around."

"Well all right, just call me if you're going to stay anywhere for a while. Call me in an hour, OK?"

As the screen door slams behind Logan, Rob turns in his chair and yells, "Stay away from the construction on Yorkshire!" Then he asks Carol, "Do you think he heard me? There's a lot of work trucks up there and those damn guys drive with their heads up their asses half the time."

Separate from the house, the garage is filled with tools. Logan takes his dad's safety glasses from the bench grinder then duct tapes his BB gun across the handle bars. He runs his bike across the grass, balancing on one pedal as he pushes off the grass with the other foot. When his bike rattles over the small dirt mound at the end of the drive he throws his leg over the seat and shoots onto the side walk.

Stoney's house is just around the corner. Logan takes a shortcut through the yard behind Stoney's house but his neighbor is hanging out the laundry and she yells brusquely, "You're killing our grass, Logan."

Caught again, he jumps of his bike and pushes it while apologizing sheepishly, "Sorry, I'll go around next time."

Stoney is waiting in his front yard. He reprimands Logan, "I *told* you to stop goin through their yard. You're lucky the fat man wasn't home. He told my dad the next time we cross his yard he's going to spray us with the hose."

"I know, I know. Are you ready?"

"Sure," Stoney's BB gun hangs over his shoulder by a string.

"Is Ballsac coming?" Logan asks.

"Nope, but Johnny and Brad are gonna be on our team."

"Cool," Logan pushes off.

When they reach the end of the block Logan pushes Stoney's handle-grip to get his attention, "Let's go around the school so my dad doesn't see."

Even though his dad already warned him to stay away, the construction of new homes along Yorkshire is their destination.

Piles of wood, partially framed houses and holes waiting to be filled with concrete make perfect hiding spots during a BB gun war.

As they drop under the bridge where Yorkshire crosses Skunk Creek to wait for Logan's dad to drive by, Logan whispers urgently, "Hurry up, it won't be long. He drives by here on his way to work," mild anxiety crackles his voice.

After they stow their bikes in the tunnel, they crouch behind a stack of old railroad ties being used for the new guard rail. Josh's Chieftain turns onto Yorkshire and they duck their heads as it rumbles past then Logan stands, "My dad's taking Josh's car. I bet it wouldn't start again and they had to jump it."

As Stoney pushes his bike up the bank to the road he asks, "How's Josh getting to work?"

"He'll have to ride my dad's bike. I bet he's mad."

"Yeah, he thinks he's such a big shot now."

When they reach Yorkshire they stop their bikes in the street in front of a corner house. Stoney looks for the other boys and says, "I told them we'd meet 'em right here."

A sharp pain in his thigh tells him they just found the others, "Ow, what the..." Realizing that he'd just been shot he drops his bike and yells, "Run! Time. Time out!"

As they scatter into the half standing house, Stoney is shot in the back two more times. Hiding behind the plywood wall of what will soon be a garage, he lifts his shirt to check out the damage, "Man. That hurts!"

His back has two deep red bruises forming already. Logan yells indignantly across the street, "Hey! You're only supposed to use one pump!"

Logan spots their other team members. Johnny is running helter-skelter between the two-by-fours of the house next door, but Brad follows more cautiously further behind. Before he crosses the dirt between the two houses Johnny drops to his knees and holds up his hand to let Logan know he's on his way. When Brad huffs up they both charge across the gap between the houses. BB's from across the street whiz past, kicking up little puffs around their feet and clunking into the beams around their heads.

On his knees next to Logan, Johnny points across the street, "They're in that house there."

Stoney pulls up his shirt to show Johnny and Brad his injuries saying incredulously, "They almost broke the skin. Why are they shooting above the waist?"

Johnny rubs his cheek where a BB permanently resides under the skin, thinking about the day they made that rule, "There's six of them now. Two new kids moved in."

"Did they tell them the rules and to only use one pump?" Stoney asks as Logan fires a shot at a kid he doesn't know that's running between the houses across the street.

"Yeah, I told 'em. Before we started at the corner."

Logan notices Johnny's safety glasses and hurriedly slips his own on while saying with relief, "Man, I almost forgot about these."

A volley of BB's bounce off the wall and Logan watches as the other team splits, two boys running across the street into the house on their left and two on their right.

"Man I wish Ballsac were here. It'd be more even," Stoney notes wryly.

The house on their right is a two story and the construction is further along than the one they are hiding in. The other two boys run up the stairs and start firing down on Logan's team. The wall to the front and left provide good cover, but they are completely defenseless on their right and the BB's hit home. Logan's team aggressively returns fire on the second story window. They hear the other boys laughing as the BB's bounce harmlessly around them. One of them pokes his head out of the window and shouts, "You're never gonna beat the Johnson Spoilers."

"Johnson Spoilers? We gotta get those guys," Logan exclaims. He grits his teeth in determination as he jumps to his feet. "Follow me."

Logan's team runs across the dirt into the house on the right and slide under the stairs for cover. Stoney has taken another hit to the calf. He rubs his leg and cringes in pain, "They must be using three pumps or something."

Johnny yells up the stairs, "One pump man, one pump!"

One of the boys laughs and yells down, "You're only saying that 'cause you're getting your butt kicked!"

Johnny looks at Logan questioningly while pumping three more pumps into his gun. Logan nods and they all follow suit.

"On three we're going up there," Logan whispers. Counting so fast that the words all slur together, "*one-two-three*," he leads the charge up the stairs and shouts when he reaches the top, "You're toast!"

They run into the room where they last saw the enemy team, then peek out the window. The other boys are out on the first floor roof and shoot back into the window then drop to the ground. Before Logan's team can fire off a shot they're retreating across the street. Firing uselessly at their fleeing backs Stoney laughs with respect, "Man those guys are crazy."

All six boys on the other team are gathered across the street behind the house. After firing another volley, they run into the bushes jump on their bikes and ride off. One of the boys rubs the loss in when he yells back, "See ya later losers."

Logan's team unhappily watches them leave while Johnny gives them the finger. Defeated, they start down the stairs. Johnny pounds the wall to listen to the rumbling echo through the empty house. Brad joins in and the thundering is so loud that Logan is sure it can be heard by anyone nearby.

Truck brakes squeak out front and Logan notes uneasily, "Those construction guys are coming to run us off now. We'd better get out of here."

Johnny asks, "What are you gonna do now?"

"I guess go back to my house and swim," Logan offers.

"Thanks but I can't. My ear is infected. I have to stay outta the pool. I'll see ya later. C'mon Brad," Johnny loops his gun over his shoulder as he walks away.

On the way to Logan's they stop at the bridge to shoot cans; setting the empty cans along the completed section of the guardrail.

"Man that was a bummer, we got creamed," Logan says flatly, aiming at the only unopened pop can they found.

"Tell me about it, my back's killin me," Stoney twists around to look at his wounds.

"Call Billy and make sure he knows the rules. Maybe you can get the new guys phone numbers and tell them too."

Logan shoots the can and pop sprays in circles as it spins around on the pavement.

"That is cool. I wish we had more of those," Stoney says wistfully as he watches the can spew.

They spend the next couple hours drilling holes in the cans until the gaps are so big that most of their BB's just fly through, leaving the cans sitting on the rail mocking them.

As they slowly pedal their bikes toward Logan's house he asks, "Did you hear that kid call their team the Johnson Spoilers?"

"Yeah, I did, what a dork,' Stoney snorts as he focuses on balancing with no hands.

Logan dodges Stoney's wandering bike, "No kidding. You stopping at home to eat?"

"Yeah, my mom is probably cooking. I'll call Ballsac and see if he wants to come over after lunch," Stoney leans his bike towards his house.

"Well hurry up. I gotta deliver my route this afternoon."

Logan has had a paper route for six months. He wanted to get it last year but they don't hire kids until they're thirteen now. His brother got his first route when he was eleven, but they changed the rules since then. Some lunatic abducted a paperboy and they never found his body. About a week after his disappearance someone found his head floating in the canal, just his frigging head. When they caught the creep he was sent over to San Quentin in California, where no one ever escapes. Logan's heard his dad tell Larry that he wishes he could get just ten minutes alone with the guy, just Rob and his ball peen hammer.

That story doesn't bother Logan though. He has plans. His bike is a hand-me-down from his brother; a scratched up Schwinn it's wheels were already bent when he got it; so he's saving half of his money each week for a new Rollfast paperboy bike. He uses his other money for 'running around cash', as Uncle Larry calls it. Almost every Saturday there is a different show at the matinee and most of the kids from school hang out at the quad afterward. He also likes to get a chocolate bar each day on the way home from delivering his route. They're only five cents at the Circle K and the guy behind the counter is usually pretty cool and lets him hang out in the back where he reads the comics and sneaks RC Cola from the fountain machine.

When he gets home he finds his mom left a note saying that she's shopping with Ginger and won't be back till four, so Logan makes himself a burger from last night's leftovers. While he's eating, he watches Wallace and Ladmo. Last month he'd sent a postcard entry for the Ladmo bag drawing but they never call out the winner until the end of the show, so he hopes Stoney will take his time. After turning up the television he settles on the cement floor in front of the couch and sings Clementine along with Huckleberry Hound then happily mutters in a slow drawl, "*Oh yeah.*" Deputy Dog and Quick Draw McGraw are his favorite cartoons and they are running back to back.

The show ends but Stoney hasn't shown up yet so Logan rolls his bike into the garage to work on it. The front wheel is missing three spokes and the back is missing five. His dad bought him new spokes at the Try Me Bike shop and told him to get it fixed by the end of the week. Rob always makes Logan work on the family cars with him and Logan has to maintain his own bike. Rob says this will help him learn to be independent. He doesn't have much time and has to work fast but only gets the front wheel repaired before it is time to do his route.

On his way to his route he stops at Stoney's house. Stoney answers the door, "Sorry my mom made me clean up my room first. I'm almost done."

"Well I can't wait. I'm supposed to be done with my route by three-thirty," Logan says glumly.

"I'll meet you at the football field at four then. Those guys said they'd be there about then."

Today is insert day and Logan has to fold the coupon booklets into each paper before loading his bike. Pedaling hard, he notes that the other paper boys are already loading their bikes. Jake, another paperboy, keeps stealing some of his papers and the last time it happened Logan swore he would confront him. Logan quickly counts his stack before the others leave and lets out a small sigh of relief when he finds the count is correct, 'cause Jake is already fifteen and a lot bigger than Logan.

One of the other boys tips over as he rides up the hill to his route spilling papers across the road. Logan watches the other paperboy's ride away, struggling with their loaded bikes, sighs and wishes Stoney could have helped him today. They could have gotten done faster and would have had time to stop at the Circle K before the game.

Three

It is four-ten when Logan gets to the playground and the other boys are already playing football. When Stoney sees him ride by outside the fence he yells, "Hurry up we need you."

Logan notices there are extra players and counts as he runs to the huddle. Stoney's team has the usual six players but the other team has eight.

"Where did those other guys come from?" Logan asks.

"It's those guys we saw this morning. They live by Billy and joined his team."

Ballsac is the quarterback and calls the play. Logan and Stoney line up as pass receivers but two boys cover each of them and they can't get open. The other team tags Ballsac down behind the line. They run the ball on the next play, but lose ground again. On third down Ballsac tries to pass to Stoney, but he's totally covered again and the pass is incomplete, so they have to punt.

With the benefit of the extra players, Billy's team easily moves down the field in six plays and scores a touchdown. Stoney is the fastest runner, and on the kick off makes it halfway down the field before one of the new kids tackles him. His mouth filled with grass, Stoney pushes the bigger boy off growling in irritation, "No tackling. We're playing two hand touch."

As they get up the other boy hooks Stoney's heel and flips his leg hard enough to cause him to fall back down. With a derisive laugh, the new boy high fives his team as he heads into the huddle.

Stoney's team doesn't make any ground on their offensive plays and Logan punts again. When they line up on defense Logan calls to Stoney, "This isn't fair. They need to sit out two players so we have an even chance."

The other team throws a pass and moves the ball way down field. One of the new kids, the bigger one, runs the ball on the next play and charges with his head down, right into Logan's chest. Logan tumbles to his back and the other boy intentionally rams his shoulder into his stomach. After the success of the play, the other team calls it again and the big boy bowls Logan over and lazily trots in for a touchdown.

Holding his chest and trying to catch his breath Logan waves Stoney over complaining, "Those new guys are playing tackle rules."

Stoney runs to Billy and grumbles, "You *know* we play two hand touch, stop tackling and head butting. You have too many players too. Can't you switch out two players on each down?"

Stoney's team has been the slightly better team for a while and Billy is tickled pink with his newly found success and responds, "We'll stop playin tackle but we're not sitting anybody."

In the huddle Stoney tells his team Billy's compromise. As he watches the other team getting ready to kick the ball Logan notes, "They've got three players bigger than anyone on our team."

Billy's team kicks the ball short in an on side kick and then recovers the ball. Logan objects, "That's not allowed in touch. That's a tackle rule. It should be our ball."

Billy tosses Logan the ball as he says lightly, "All right. We were just trying it. You can have it on the fifty yard line."

The new kid—the one that bowled Logan over two times— punches the ball out of Logan's hand with his fist and yells, "No friggin way. You don't know the rules." Surprised, Logan watches him chase after it as it tumbles end over end. He catches it then lays it on the line of scrimmage with a tough look at Logan then waves the others into the huddle. His team watches for a second then reluctantly follows his lead.

Ballsac kicks the ball at their huddle insisting, "C'mon Billy, you know we don't play that way."

Billy looks at him nervously while the new kid picks up the ball and puts it back on the scrimmage line.

The new kid stands with the ball between his feet and looks down at Ballsac with a harsh determined expression, "That's how we played back home." He's about half a head taller.

With the exception of the two new boys this group has been playing football all summer and hasn't had a single fight. They've had a few shoving matches when someone has gotten a little too rough but all the boys have gotten along well.

Ballsac looks uncertainly at Billy over the bigger kids shoulder and declares, "We don't want to play that way."

Billy shrugs his shoulder uncomfortably. With a sudden step the big kid shoves Ballsac roughly, "Go home then. We don't need you anyways."

Ballsac shoves him back, "*You* go home. We don't even know you."

The new boy trips Ballsac to his back then jumps on his stomach. They wrestle for control but the bigger boy gets the upper hand fast and rabbit punches Ballsac's face six times before the other boys can drag him off.

Wiping his bleeding nose and the tears in his eyes Ballsac bawls, "You're dead man!"

The bigger boy punches him in the ear again then demands with an ugly grin, "What are you gonna do about it?"

Ballsac runs at the bigger boy, tackles him around the waist and drags him to the ground. The bigger boy rolls on top of Ballsac while punching him in the face. Angry that his friend is getting hurt, Logan grabs the boy by the neck, choking him as he drags him off.

The boy is a lot bigger but Logan is used to wrestling Josh and squeezes hard, pulling on his neck until the boy's smaller brother punches Logan in the neck. Surprised, Logan lets go and the bigger boy pushes him to the ground then punches him in the face several times. Stoney shoves the smaller brother and they grapple to the ground. Seeing Logan on his back Ballsac jumps up and kicks the bigger kid in the kidney then grabs around his neck and punches him in the face.

Billy and the other boys jump in, pushing and tugging the fighting boys until everybody is standing apart huffing and glaring at each other.

The new big kid breaks the silence, "Let's get outta here." Pushing Logan one last time as he passes, his brother follows him across the fields.

Ballsac wipes his nose with his forearm, examines the blood distastefully and asks Billy, "Who are those jerks?"

"That's Lloyd Johnson and his brother Ben. The big one calls himself LJ. They live down the street from my house," Billy answers.

"Don't bring them to our football games anymore," Ballsac demands angrily.

"Cool, I won't. Sorry man," Billy promises as they walk away.

Logan slips his shirt over his head then uses it to rub the blood off of his face. Stoney looks at the bloody mess and says wryly, "Your mom's gonna kill you."

Searching the shirt for a clean spot to wipe his nose Logan admits, "I know. I'll throw it away before I get home. Maybe she won't miss it."

They stop at the fountain to clean the blood off of their faces. Logan rinses out his shirt and when he feels it's clean enough he says, "It doesn't look that bad now. I'll just stick it in the bottom of the laundry bag."

Unlike yesterday's exciting race, they coast silently down landslide hill with Logan riding in the front. As they gain speed

Logan's dad drives up behind them and honks his horn until they look back, then he waves them onto the sidewalk. Logan turns his head away so his dad can't see the drying tears when he drives by. When they ride into his side yard he wipes his eyes with his shirt, drops his bike and zooms into his bathroom leaving the other boys waiting outside.

Logan shuts the door quietly, locking it behind. He's never been in a serious fight and he's never had his face punched, really punched hard before and is still struggling to hold back the tears. After splashing his face with cold water he examines his nose and the bruises on his face. There's not going to be a way to hide this from his dad or uncle. He rinses his shirt until there isn't any visible blood, rings it out in the tub then takes all the laundry out of the basket and drops it into the bottom. As he throws the towels on top of it he attempts a smile in the mirror and his grim appearance makes it turn into a real grin. He whispers softly, "You're in so much trouble."

His mom knocks on the bathroom and asks curiously, "What are you doing in there? Your friends are out back waiting."

"I'll be right out," he answers trying to sound plucky while another grin covers his face in the mirror. Moving close to get a good look he rubs his puffing eye and thinks quickly. A plan to hide the fight from his dad begins to evolve in his head. He hopes to swim until long after dark when his dad will probably be reading or watching TV, maybe he won't find out until tomorrow.

He cracks the door then listens for his mom. She's in her bedroom, so he runs out the back door slamming it on the way. His dad shouts from the garage, "I told you about that Logan."

"Sorry dad," he yells before dropping to the deck next to Stoney and Ballsac and dipping his feet in the pool. He splashes his eyes then slides into the pool and ducks his head under the water, scrubbing his face. Then holding his eyes just at the water surface he watches the slight ripples in the water as he backs around the pool in circles. The other boys wash the dirt off their legs with the garden hose then sit on the poolside watching him.

All of them are brooding over the fight and why it happened. They know the boys from school and get along well with all of them.

Stoney breaks the silence, "That new guy, LJ started it."

Digging at the water in his ear with his little finger Logan nods, "He did. He's a jerk off."

Ballsac frowns earnestly, "If he weren't so much bigger I would'a beat him." *It's a matter of pride with boys; they generally know they should win every fight and when they lose, there is usually a good reason and it's never their own fault.*

"I don't know, he's pretty tough," Logan says skeptically, raising his eyebrows in doubt.

"He's not that tough," Ballsac remembers the bright taste of blood and shoots a stream of water between his front teeth.

"I don't think he's that tough either, just a douche-bag. Ballsac could kill him if he weren't so big," Stoney wants his friend to know he supports him.

"Next time, I'm gonna kill him," Ballsac announces trying to sound aggressive.

Logan's dad walks from the garage and the boys silently wait for him to enter the house. When the door shuts Stoney climbs onto the deck and runs into the shed. Carrying out a wooden step ladder he leans it against the side of the shed. The bottom step is broken and he has to jump over it to reach the second step and grab the gutter along the roof edge. He climbs onto the shed roof, crouches at the far end away from the pool and yells, "Cannonball!" The roof is short and he only gets in four steps before he jumps as high as he can, straight at Logan. Wrapping his arms around his legs he flies from the shed roof into the pool as Logan dives away.

Boys are resilient and it is impossible to hold them down for long. Like all boys, they get angry quickly and bounce back just as fast. All of them will keep thinking about what happened, later when they are alone, and have time to imagine what might have happened, if only things were different.

Logan splashes Stoney, "You almost landed on me!"

Stoney splashes him back and declares, "You were eliminated by the bomb of destruction."

All three of them join in the splashing war, but Ballsac has a trick way of throwing his arm into the water and making the water fly so hard it stings the other's faces.

With his eyes burning so bad that he can't keep them open any longer Logan covers them in the crook of his arm and surrenders, "I give. I give." To escape, he rolls onto the deck, jumps over the rail and climbs the ladder onto the shed. He jumps high off the shed in a figure four; his splash reaches all the way to the patio of the house.

Shaking his head in disbelief as he takes his place on the shed, Ballsac asks, "How do you do that?" His splashes don't ever come near the patio.

They track the furthest distance the water travels with each jump but no one can come near Logan's figure four jumps. Each of them has four jumps before Logan's mom sticks her head out the arcadia door and warns him in a loud whisper, "Your *dad's* gonna beat you Logan."

Out of breath from running in and out of the pool, the boys laugh together and Logan replies gratefully, "Thanks mom." He doesn't know that Rob and Carol have seen every jump out the back window.

While watching the boys run back and forth to the shed, Carol had told Rob about Logan rushing into the bathroom when he got home and asked him if he knew what was going on with the boys. He told her that he had heard them whispering about a fight, but the boys were trying to keep it a secret. She winced and ducked, putting her hand to her head when Logan flew off the shed and almost clear over the pool; Rob waved his hand like a traffic cop and yiped, "Woah, it's time to shut 'em down."

"The only reason you won is…," Ballsac pauses while thinking for a second, "is home field advantage. You probably even practice when we're not here."

After dumping out an old piston that is being used for an ashtray, Stoney rinses it off with the hose spewing water from the swamp cooler. Then in typical Stoney fashion he places it ceremoniously on the decking, "We award you the official battle trophy. You are the Cannonball King." Then he claps his hands grandly, encouraging Ballsac to join in as he pretends to hold a microphone and asks Logan, "What do you have to say to your fans? Mr. CK?"

Logan pushes Stoney's hand out of his face self consciously, "You're a dork." But as always, he laughs at Stoney's gag on the inside.

The back door opens and Ginger shouts, "Hey Logan. Rusty and Lizzy are here. They want to swim too."

Rusty and Lizzy live across the street. Rusty is on their football team, but he usually has too many chores to do and doesn't often hang out with the boys. He's only twelve and the smallest boy that plays, but always gives it his best.

Lizzy is Rusty's sixteen year older sister. She's been in love with Josh since…, forever. She never misses his basketball games and over the last year, in the way of true love, they have slowly become closer. She always wants to be around Josh and comes over whenever she thinks he's home. Josh should be home any minute and Logan thinks she probably made Rusty come along with her to disguise her intentions.

Spreading her towel on a lawn chair next to the pool Lizzy steps out of her flip flops while Rusty runs up the stairs bounding off the rail into the pool with a cowboy yell. Lizzy squeals as she dodges the water then scowls at Rusty as she drags her lawn chair out of reach of the splashes. Wearing her best cut off jeans and a cheer leader t-shirt over her swimsuit, she wants to look her best when Josh gets home. She tosses her curly blond hair over her shoulder and crosses her legs then lies on the lawn chair watching the boys welcome Rusty with a dunk fest until he calls uncle. With a testy shake of her head, she closes her eyes and dreams about Josh, hoping he'll get home soon.

While the boys walk in circles to start the whirlpool, Rusty notices Logan's eye and winces with sympathy, "Ooh, your eye is messed up man."

Feeling the sore spots with his finger tips Logan asks, "What's wrong with it."

"It's all blue underneath, like a shiner, right there," Rusty points at the growing lump below his eye.

Stoney grabs Logan's head pretending to be a doctor as he examines his eye and confirms, "Mr. Cannonball King, let me tell you. That'll be a black eye for sure."

"My dad's gonna kill me," Logan groans in dismay with a glance at the house.

"Tell them you did it in the pool," Ballsac suggests.

"You want to swim don't you? I have to tell them about the fight," Logan frowns shaking his head gloomily.

"I wouldn't tell *my* dad," Ballsac declares as Rob and Larry exit the back door.

The boys stop talking instantly when they hear the clunking sound of Rob knocking the grill with a hammer and dumping in a bag of charcoal. They watch as he grumbles under his breath, "We need more charcoal." While Rob searches the garage for charcoal Larry digs at the coals then squirts lighter fluid onto the coals and lights the fire.

Josh's pulls the Chieftain into the drive and parks in front of the garage, honking the horn playfully at Rob. As Josh climbs out he announces, "It works great now dad, thanks."

Rob replies, "Sure," then tosses an empty charcoal bag into the trash, "Can you run to the store and get some charcoal and lighter fluid?"

Even though his car is not in the best shape Josh loves it and uses every reason he can think of to drive. He answers happily, "Of course, can I change my clothes first?"

"All right, ask your mom if she needs anything else too."

As Josh runs in the house Lizzy calls out timidly, "Hey Josh."

"Hey Lizzy. What's going on?" Josh hadn't noticed her before and changes directions to walk past her.

"My brother wanted to go swimming and my mom said I have to watch him," she lies, crossing her legs demurely and smiling prettily.

Trying to be indiscreet, he checks out her legs as he passes by but his smile beams infatuation, "He can swim over here anytime he wants."

His attention makes her feel alive and a cloud-nine smile uncontrollably covers her face. She watches his muscular shoulders remembering the basketball games she's watched him play. He's not the tallest player on the court but he's always the fastest. At the finals last year he had dunked over the top of the other team's center and she screamed until she was hoarse. As he takes off his shoes she smiles coyly, making him blush unconsciously before he goes in the house.

Rusty splashes water at Lizzy and vehemently denies her white lie, "You liar. Mom didn't say that."

"Stop it Rusty. She did too. You just weren't listening," Lizzy earnestly whispers while she dries her legs off with her towel.

"She likes your brother lots. She won't stop talking about him at home. It's sickening," Rusty tells Logan, as if he didn't know.

Logan knows that Josh likes Lizzy's attention but he's also well aware that if his brother found out that he has said anything about it he'll suffer one way or another, so he keeps his mouth shut.

Uncle Larry is pushing the charcoal around with an old screwdriver, trying to bring life to the flames, when Josh comes out the back door and asks Lizzy, "You want to go the store with me?"

Smiling with enthusiasm she tries to sound relaxed, "Sure, that would be fun."

As she follows Josh to the car Rusty makes a kissing sound and she gives him the finger without turning her head.

Seeing the exchange Uncle Larry shakes his head and snickers wonderingly, "Brothers and sisters."

Rusty swims to the side of the pool furthest away from the men, motions the other boys over and whispers, "I called Billy after the game today."

"What did he say?" Ballsac asks.

"He told me those guys that you got in a fight with are really tough and like to fight a lot."

"Is he going to bring them to the games anymore?" Stoney hopes to never see them again.

"He said he wouldn't. LJ is fifteen years old and got held back a couple times. Guess what?" He pauses as if it is do-or-die information, "He's only going into eighth grade next year."

"Eighth grade? He'll probably be in my class," Ballsac moans.

"Ben, that's his little brother, is in the eighth grade too."

"I bet *he'll* be in my class then," Logan ponders.

"Or the other way round," Rusty twirls his index finger.

The boys absorb the bad news for a second then Logan asks, "What else did he say?"

"Billy said their step dad is a jail bird. He just got out of prison and they moved here from Tucson."

"My cousin lives in Tucson," Stoney says.

"So what? Is he a jailbird too?" Ballsac asks teasingly.

"No. We went there in June. There was nothing to do and it was really hot," Stoney explains then splashes Ballsac when he covers his ears. Ballsac dives under the water, grabs Stoney's feet and tosses him head over heals.

Logan's grandparents live just down the street and his grandfather stops by almost every day when he takes his exercise walks. His grandmother has bad knees and usually stays home, but she still calls Carol every day to gossip about Grandpa. Seeing everyone out back as he passes on the sidewalk his grandfather waves then ambles into the back yard and sits next to Larry and Rob at the grill.

While the other boys wrestle, Rusty watches the men then tells Logan, "Your grandpa's really old."

"I know he was in World War One."

"Did he kill anybody?"

"I don't know, ask *him*," Logan answers indifferently.

The Chieftain clunks to a stop in the drive and Josh turns off the headlights as they get out. He drops the shopping bag by the grill then holds Lizzy's hand as they stroll into the darkness behind the garage talking quietly. They've been good friends for years and discretely dated each other since the beginning of the last school year but they've been openly affectionate all summer.

Larry observes, "That's a pretty girl. You'd better watch that boy."

Rob points his finger at Larry suggesting strongly, "He's *fine*. Just leave him alone tonight OK?"

"I'll do my best," Larry half promises with a wink as he rips open the charcoal bag.

It's not long before the chicken is done and everyone gathers in line at the picnic table. Logan hovers behind his brother hoping to hide his bruises, but Carol is dishing out the food, overfilling everybody's plate. When he reaches the front of the line he turns his face away and tries to excuse her, "I'll get it mom. Go ahead and get yours."

Pulling him closer by his shirt she says curtly, "Just come here. I got it."

Larry's sitting next to his dad at the end of the picnic table and asks with an intentionally exaggerated tone, "What happened to your eye boy?"

Pretending that he didn't hear him Logan turns his back and starts to the swimming pool deck where the other boys are already eating, but Larry won't give up, "Hey Logan, come here for a sec."

As he approaches, Rob asks him, "What happened?"

"I hit my face playing football," Logan whispers remorsefully.

Larry butts in with a poor John Wayne imitation, "*That's* a shiner. It looks like you got in a fight."

Rob raises his eyebrows at Larry, as if to say, *enough already*, and makes a chopping motion as he asks, "Are you sure you didn't get in a fight?"

With a shake of his head Logan takes a bite of his corn bread then looks away.

"You look just like Joe Frasier after a match," Larry is obviously pleased with his own joke and holds his fists in front of his face.

"Can't I just eat dad?" Logan asks nodding at Larry with a he-won't-leave-me-be look.

"OK. We'll talk later," Rob pats him on the back.

While he eats, Logan tells the other boys dejectedly, "My dad knows I had a fight." He isn't sure what his dad will do and doesn't want to find out tonight.

All the boys deny telling anyone about the fight but this isn't the kind of thing that is easy to hide in a close family. Rusty has already told Lizzy; before the night is over Lizzy has told both Josh and Josh's mom; she told Ginger and so forth; until everybody knows exactly what happened.

After dinner the adults drink a beer while the boys maintain their distance, keeping to the darker side of the pool. When it cools down, Carol brings out a store bought apple pie. Quickly forgetting their injuries, the boys run over for a slice. As she cuts the pie, Stoney tells everyone about how Logan won the cannonball competition; Logan punches him in the kidney and whispers in his ear, "They're not supposed to know we jump off the shed, *upidstay*." Stoney utters a soft, "Oops," as he slinks away. Logan is hiding last in line again and Carol gives him an extra scoop of ice cream then rubs his cheek saying with a soft smile, "Here's a prize for being the Cannonball King." Thanking her with his eyes Logan runs over to the other boys.

Four

During breakfast Carol tries to sound indifferent when she asks Josh, "How did things go with Lizzy last night?"

Josh set his glass down, pretending to be cool, "She asked me to go to the dance at OLDV." Our Lady of Deer Valley has dances once a month.

"I didn't think they were Catholic."

"They aren't, she just goes to the dances," he explains, gratified for the subject change.

"I see. You like her?" Carol asks directly. Lizzy's mom is in the parent teacher association with Carol and she knows that Lizzy is one of the top students. Last year basketball distracted Josh from his schoolwork; he could use a positive influence this year.

"She's cool," Josh keeps his voice even.

Logan, surprised to see Josh up so early in the day asks, "Why're you up so early?"

Josh is working two summer jobs, part-time with his dad at the shop and part-time at the grocery store. Many nights this summer he has worked from ten to twelve stocking the store shelves and normally sleeps in until the family breakfast is over. The morning noises always wake him up but he usually rolls over and covers his ears with his pillows. The same bumps woke him today but he kept thinking about his time with Lizzy last night,

They kissed and held onto each other for a long time; the memory of her soft curls brushing his forehead and tender skin under his fingers aroused him, and he can't clear his mind. Tossing and turning, squeezing his eyes shut, he had listened to his mom making breakfast then finally just gave up, got out of bed and combed his hair with a cheery grin in the mirror.

"I'm going to work with dad this morning." He hadn't planned on working. He had planned on hanging out with Lizzy all day, but he couldn't think of anything else to say. Most of Fossil High students go to the movie theater quad at least one day a week—Josh's entire basketball team can usually be found there after practice—and he was hoping to take her to a movie then get a shake at the Rusty Spoon.

Finished with breakfast Rob leans back and tells Josh, "You'd better hurry if you want to ride with me."

"I'll meet you down there in a little bit. I only want to work till noon. We're going to do some stuff later," Josh mentally changes his plan to call Lizzy until sometime in the afternoon.

"We're behind at the shop. I could use you till three or four," Rob hints with a wink.

Josh wants to keep the cat in the bag so he says agreeably, "That's cool. I could use the money anyways."

"The Chieftain needs tires. You would make enough money to put new ones on the front. I already ordered 'em and they'll be in tomorrow."

Josh had initially planned to use any extra money to take Lizzy for a burger and shake after the dance but now he'll have to cut in to his savings to treat her. Grunting his assent he spreads jelly on his toast.

Tossing his napkin on the table Rob rises, walks to the door and leans on the handle before he leaves, "Bring the car down tomorrow afternoon and you can learn how to run the new tire machine."

After Rob walks out the door Josh lets out a big disappointed whooshing sigh. Carol asks, "What's the matter?"

"Nothing. I wanted to do some stuff this afternoon."

Logan rinses his plate in the sink as he announces, "I'm going to Stoney's now."

"No fighting. Stay away from those kids and be back for lunch today," Carol orders.

"Dad said he'd buy me lunch if I met him at Zoney's," Logan loves fish and chips and Zoney's has the best.

"Well Ginger and I are going to the shopping center this afternoon so if you come home..., stay out of stuff."

The last time she went to the shopping center Logan had his friends over, and between Stoney and Ballsac three bags of chips disappeared. "I know Mom," Logan indirectly promises as he slams out the door.

Cutting through Stoney's neighbor's yard he stops at the side of the house and checks to see if anyone is outside before he speeds across their lawn. He and Stoney are going over to the high school to race bicycles. The sidewalks at the school are wide enough for three bikes side by side with plenty of room for passing. Built on a hill, the west end of the school is several hundred feet lower than the east and the sidewalk's have short flats and long downhill sloping sections that provide a fast racing track. The public pool is next to the school and a group of kids that are always ready to race hang out at the snack bar.

When Stoney pulls his bike out of the garage he looks at Logan, "Your eye is fugly." He's heard his dad say this and thought he'd try it out.

"What's that?"

Stoney whispers his explanation, "Friggin ugly."

Logan laughs heartily and asks, "You mean f...?"

Slapping his hand over Logan's mouth, Stoney whispers urgently, "*Shut up*; my dad's home. Yeah that's what it means."

Pushing his hand away Logan apologizes with a crooked grin, "Sorry man. That's funny. Let's go."

The racing kids aren't at the snack bar when they get to the pool so they watch through the chain link fence as the swim team finishes their laps. Logan dreams out loud, "If I didn't have a paper route I'd get on the swim team."

"You couldn't play football in high school then. Football practice starts in the middle of the summer at the same time as swim team."

"I want to play basketball like Josh anyway. You can't play both, and Josh is gonna help me out," Logan explains.

The swim team is filing out and the boys squeeze inside the pool gate as the last swimmer exits. Noticing them sitting at the pool edge a life guard asks, "Aren't you Josh's little brother? You swimming today?"

Logan nods and Stoney starts to get up to go pay at the gate.

She winks in confidence and puts her hand on Logan's shoulder, "That's all right you don't need to pay, but just this once."

There's usually a big crowd of their school friends at the pool but since Logan has a pool at home he and Stoney don't go that often. The diving boards are the coolest part of the public pool so the boys dive in and swim across to the deep end. Flipping and cannonballing, they keep an eye out for the arrival of the kids that race bikes.

Logan is climbing out of the pool when Lizzy walks up with another girl that he recognizes but can't remember her name. Lizzy mimic's his whooping laugh with a silly giggle and says, "I knew it was you. What are you doing here?"

"What's it look like?" Logan answers.

"Don't be so smart," she pretends to be injured." She follows him to the high dive and asks, "Is your brother here?"

"Nope, he's at work," Logan starts up the ladder.

She watches him run and jump off the board as far as he can. The boys are competing to see who can land the farthest distance from the board.

As he swims to the side Stoney moves a towel to mark his distance. "That was even farther man," Stoney bumps into the girls and shoves his way around them as he runs to the board.

Logan pulls himself out of the pool with the gutter and the lifeguard calls down to him, "Please use the ladder young man." Nodding to the lifeguard, he watches Stoney run off the board and is marking the landing spot when Lizzy says affectionately, "I knew it was you. I could hear your Woody Woodpecker laugh all the way out front."

Blatantly imitating Woody, Logan runs around Lizzy to the diving board. Running the full length of the board he spins in a circle before hitting the water. She is waiting for him at the ladder and asks, "When will Josh get home from work?"

"My dad said he has to work till four," Logan takes his place to mark Stoney's next jump.

She makes a wry face to her friend then watches Stoney fly off the board before asking, "Are you guys having a barbecue tonight?"

"Maybe. My uncle said he was coming over again last night."

Moving the towel for the last time he yells to Stoney, "I give up. You win. Let's go race now."

"Tell your brother I'll see him later. C'mon Karen," Lizzy knows he probably won't relay her message to Josh.

"Sure, see ya," Logan agrees as he and Stoney head to the snack bar.

"See ya later Woody," she yells at his back. Karen reproduces Logan's whooping giggles in perfect animation and he looks back at her curiously. Both girls have the same haircut and matching suits except for a slight difference in the shade of red. When they see him looking they titter and imitate his laughter in harmony. He shakes his head with amazement at Stoney and asks, "What's that girls name?"

"Karen," Stoney answers as he looks into the snack bar over the fence.

Four boys are sitting in the snack bar when they walk through the open gate. After ordering a taffy Stoney sits at the picnic table across from them and rips the wrapper off of his candy. After tearing it in half he gives a piece to Logan then asks one of the boys indifferently, "Are you guys racing today?" He knows they are but in typical boy fashion, he wants to be James Dean cool.

Lester, the leader of the bike racers, watches him eat his candy for a moment then answers proudly, "We race every day. You wanna race with us?"

"Maybe... Yeah, when we're done swimming," Stoney answers absently while watching another boy flip off the high dive. He doesn't want them to assume they came to the pool with racing in mind.

Lester exits the pool with his race gang following and is getting his hand stamped at the gate when he calls to Stoney, "Hey, Stoney! We're out here hanging out."

Stoney and Logan make their rounds at the pool, saying hi to all of their friends then take another round at the diving boards. On his last dive Logan spots Lizzy and Karen at the snack bar and intentionally blasts his Woody laugh, getting their attention as he dives. He waits for Stoney at the ladder and tells him, "Let's go now." They don't see the other boys by the bike racks so they ride through the school gate and search for them on the football field.

The racers are resting in the shade of a tree when they see the boys riding through the field. They get on their bikes quickly, ride over and Lester takes charge, "Follow me."

After showing them the starting line he leads the boys around the track pointing it out as he goes. When they get back to the starting line he tells them the rules in a warning tone, "Three laps, and if you take any cuts you loose automatic."

Stoney lines up against two of the boys and Logan swings his arm to start the race. The boys race down the straight then turn a corner around a building out of view of Logan. He knows the remaining two boys from school but they are in the heat of battle so he keeps his distance. When they come back in view Stoney is in second with the boy in last right behind. The final third of the race is uphill and Stoney is passed in the last few feet, coming in third.

He rides up to Logan gripping his mouth in a tight disappointed line, shakes his head and huffs, "Man that was hard."

Logan takes his place with Lester and the other racer and swings his pedal to the top of the range to get a fast start. Stoney waves his arm and they take off but Logan's foot slips off the pedal. Not only does he crack his shin on the pedal but he is way behind at the first corner. He silently curses and gives chase, pedaling so hard his tire skids when he rounds the corners. The other boys are bigger than him and pull away even further until the uphill where Logan makes up ground fast and passes one boy, coming in second behind Lester. Lester has a light bike and is the king of bike racing around here, but Logan is *pretty* sure he can beat him; he just needs the right opening.

They spend the next few hours racing each other; resting under the tree by the football field and laying out different courses. They're beginning to wear out when they race a course that is almost entirely up hill and Logan barely beats Lester. Tired and hungry they go back to the pool to cool off. Stoney buys two more taffy bar's and they have another diving contest before they head home for lunch.

When they reach Stoney's house they see it is already two-thirty in the afternoon. Logan rubs his stomach noting with surprise, "No wonder I'm so hungry."

Stoney searches hopefully through his fridge and asks, "Do you want to eat here?"

"Dang it! No, I was supposed to eat lunch with my dad, but he probably ate already. I should go home and eat the leftovers so they know I had something for lunch."

As Logan goes out the front door Stoney calls out, "Hang on a sec." Logan waits until Stoney comes out of the hall and tosses a shirt at him, "Here's your shirt."

Logan holds it up by the sleeves, "This isn't mine it's Ballsac's."

"Oh. Can you drop it off on your way home?"

"OK. See ya," after wrapping it around his handlebar Logan rides towards Ballsac's house taking the long way around the block. When he finds Ballsac isn't home, he hangs it on their empty clothesline with a giggle of anticipation as he thinks about Ballsac's reaction when he finds it hanging there all alone.

A ticking sound from his bike makes Logan stop to see if he picked up a sticker. He stoops on one knee and lifts the back tire off the ground, spinning it as he inspects the tread. Squealing car tires on the next street draw his attention and he watches as a truck skids sideways to a stop at the corner sign. He shades his eyes with his hand and squints against the sun to see who it is. The tires squeal against the hot pavement as it turns in his direction and quickly accelerates towards him. He stands up as it roars past and thinks he sees LJ driving with his brother Ben on the passenger side and Lizzy holding onto the dash in the middle. A haze of black smoke follows the truck as it passes his street and heads toward Creek Road. It slides to a stop at the sign, grey smoke coming from all four tires. Then with a clank and another big puff of smoke it crosses the t-intersection and the curb into the field; the tires chunking up the loose dirt as it disappears towards the river.

Turning back to his bike Logan coughs as the smell of gasoline fume lingers. After removing a rock stuck in the tread he jumps on his bike and follows the truck. When he reaches his street he crosses it and looks down the creek dirt road as far as he can but only a thin cloud of dust is settling over the road. He listens for the sound of the truck then pedals towards home thinking about Lizzy and speculating reasons why she would be riding with LJ. They must be going to the river. LJ's only fifteen and can't have his driver's license yet. Driving like that, he'll probably get a ticket and maybe even arrested. With a grin to himself at the thought, Logan drops his bike against the house and goes in to eat his leftover chicken, quickly forgetting about the truck as he sings along with Huckleberry.

Five

LJ presses the gas pedal to the floor and laughs irrationally as the truck drifts across the loose river sand. Her face scrunched in fear, Lizzy screams, "Slow down!" Sand flies in little puffs behind the back tires as the tired engine coughs black streams of smoke through the river bottom. When they cross a deep set of old tire tracks the rear end bounces nearly two feet off the ground and Lizzy's head jams into the ceiling. With one hand holding her stiffening neck and the other pressed against the ceiling she screams forcefully, "LJ Slow down!"

LJ's back compresses into the seat cushion as he pries both feet on the brake pedal. It sinks nearly to the floor before the wheels lock up and the truck skids sideways to a splashing stop with the front tires sitting in several inches of water. Lizzy has tumbled into the dash and banged her head into the rear view mirror bending its face straight down at the dash. Dropping out of the truck, LJ bellows gales of laughter and stomps splashes of water over his head then shouts, "*Holy shit* that was close!"

Ben sloshes around the front of the truck mimicking LJ by kicking water into the air then high fives his brother grandly, "That was super cool!"

LJ slaps the hood with both hands and tilts his head at Lizzy who is still sitting in the middle seat with her hands to her neck. "C'mon Lizzy get out."

"You *said* you would drive me *home*," she confronts him in a discouraged voice.

"We will. We just wanna hang out here for a while," LJ swooshes his arm in maître d' fashion towards the river.

"When?" she demands bluntly, her tone making it clear that she is totally unhappy with the unexpected situation.

"*After* we go swimming and have some fun," LJ announces, taking off his shirt and tossing it on the hood.

She watches LJ and Ben climb over the rocks to the bend in the river where the water runs deepest. A rope dangles from the thin branch of a tree that leans in agony over the pool, one thick root wrapping around a granite boulder its last lifeline. A board tied at the bottom of the rope skips across the river, lazily trailing a rough v in the surface of the water. LJ dives in and swims to the rope while Ben wades across to the tree then drops a stick into the river and watches it drift away. After clawing up the steep bank under the tree LJ locks his thighs around the rope then pushes off the big root. He waves stupidly at Lizzy as he swings over the water shouting, "*All right!*" The rope is long, creating a long slow arcing swing back to the tree; he kicks off the trunk and back flips off the rope at the highest point of the swing. Ben watches in admiration. When his brothers head bobs up he praises him, "That's bitchin, I wish I could do that."

"You can. It's not that hard," gripping the board in both hands over his head he swings the rope over to Ben with a grunt.

Ben climbs onto a high limb and drops with a girlish squeal. When he nears the high point of the swing his stomach flip-flops making him involuntarily scream "*Oh shit!*" then slings off of the rope and flops on his back with a crack. Floating on his back and groaning, he kicks to the bank, rolls to his stomach and sprawls in the shallow water feigning death.

LJ snickers meanly and mimics Ben's girlish squeal, "*That's bitchin. Do it again.*"

"No way man that kills," Ben closes his eyes waiting for the stinging pain to subside.

Lizzy is watching their antics, hoping they will stop being so ridiculously stupid and take her home like they promised. She had just left the pool and was walking in the shade of the trees at the front of the high school when they passed her with a toot of the trucks horn, Ben's head and shoulders sticking out the passenger window like a dog enjoying the scents of the hot summer air. They turned into the parking lot then sat at the gate in the idling truck waiting for her to walk up; it looked like they were having a lot of fun so she thought.., *"It wouldn't hurt to have some fun on the way home"*, plus, she wouldn't have to walk so far in the heat. The second she slid in the seat between them LJ tore across the parking lot. At the sound of the tires peeling out she laughed briefly, then caught the smell of alcohol and sucked her breath in, a sickening tightening in her stomach instantly taking hold. She'd never ridden with a drunk driver before and watched LJ's silliness with sudden concern. She had just pointed out her street and asked if he'd stop speeding before they got to her house when she saw Logan shading his eyes as he watched them pass. But LJ just ignored her as if she hadn't said a word.

Catching an old tree root with both hands, LJ swings out of the water then lifts his brother to his feet, *"I* got something that'll take care a' that." LJ pushes Ben toward the truck, tripping him cruelly several times along the way and dunking his head in the shallows to show off for Lizzy. After a particularly long dunking he lets Ben up, but then backs away and tackles him by the waist, wrapping his head in a tight headlock while smiling flirtingly at Lizzy.

But Ben's tolerance is reaching the end of his rope. When his head has been underwater for a little too long Ben slugs him in the kidney and shoves him away with an annoyed shout, "Can't you just *quit?*"

LJ kicks water in Ben's face and pushes him towards the truck, "Don't be such a cry baby."

Trying to disguise her fear Lizzy's expression is a mix somewhere between anger and disdain as she watches them approach through the dusty windshield.

She flinches, barely able to stifle a scream in her tightening throat when LJ punches the hood with a bang as he passes in front of her. Noting her concerned expression he fakes a crooked smile, as if it could somehow cheer her up. Their eyes meet uncomfortably as he leans over to reach under the driver's seat and dig around. She quickly looks away, and listens to the rough scraping and rustling sounds of the disturbance of whatever unfortunate item has found its way under the seat. He mumbles, "There it is." as he pulls out a brown paper sack. With a grand magician's swish he reaches in the bag and slides out a bottle of whiskey, shows her the label then rests the bottle on her thigh. He leans it against her side, their noses almost touching as he raises his eyebrows in a strange encouraging fashion. He fills the sack with air then pops it at her. Unable to stop herself this time, a dry scream rattles out before she cuts it off by clamping her own hand over her mouth. Suddenly a flash of ideas run through her mind as she imagines herself jumping out the passenger door and running away, however, except for a slight tremble, she doesn't even move at all, frozen stiff, unable to escape his sour breath. With a surprised look he pulls his face away from hers and she can't help but notice how much the movement makes him look like a turtle retreating into its shell. He shakes his head at Ben and crushes the bag before dropping it into the truck bed, then swinging the bottle of mescal over his head like a crazed cowboy he announces, "This'll kill anything."

Ben sits in the water with his back against the front wheel watching the tiny streams created as it flows through the trucks wheel. He blocks the flow with his foot to create a little river of sand between his legs as LJ takes a glugging gulp.

LJ opens his arms wide, leans back and howls into the sky then hands the bottle to Ben and prescribes in a bossing tone, "Take a *big* drink and you won't feel no more pain."

Ben pretends to drink a big slug but he only takes a small sip. He grimaces as the burn fills his throat and chest. "That tastes like shit," he hands the bottle back with a flourish.

Standing outside the truck LJ runs his elbows through the window and leans against the open driver door and holds the bottle out to Lizzy, trying to look friendly but failing miserably, "Want some?"

"No!" Lizzy cries emphatically.

"Why not?"

"I'm *not* even supposed to be here," she declares crossing her arms tighter.

"Nobody knows. It's no big deal. Take a drink," he urges as pleasantly as a used car salesman with a parking lot of rusted junk pitching to an eager sixteen year old.

"No. I need to go home and my neck hurts," she pouts.

"Ben liked it and he don't have no more pain. You should try it." Slipping around the door with a knowing glance down at Ben he scoots across the seat next to her and holds the bottle up to her face, "Here smell it."

She sniffs at the bottle, turns her face away and coughs, "That smells really gross."

After another swig LJ lies poorly with an impetuous smile twitching at the corners of his mouth, "Well it tastes better than it smells."

"What is it?"

"It's mescal, the best stuff in Mexico. My dad drinks it all the time."

Ben is watching them through the driver's window and tells Lizzy, "It's not all that bad."

LJ hands Ben the bottle and watches him reluctantly take another sip as he says, "See, just like I told you." After taking another gulp LJ roughly clasps her fingers around the bottle.

"It smells sickening," Lizzy pulls away, leaning toward the passenger seat on her elbow.

"Hold your nose then. C'mon before it's all gone," LJ coaxes, his impatience obvious.

Suddenly he catches her head tightly in the crook of his arm and shoves the bottle firmly against her lips. She grabs the bottle with both hands, but he pushes harder tipping her head back against the seat. She submits to his painfully rough grip and takes an unwelcome drink.

LJ laughs coarsely at her reddening face, "It's good huh."

Her eyes water as she pushes his hands away and replies in a strengthless whisper, "It's *not* good."

Half empty when LJ opened it, he raises the bottle to eye level and shakes the remaining liquid. As it settles he raises one eyebrow and says expertly, "There is only one finger left so we gotta share."

Ben holds his hand out but LJ rejects him, "Huh uh. *I'm* gonna hold it."

Leaning over he lifts it to Bens mouth and lets him drink a small amount while quietly commanding, "*Don't* be a bogart."

After taking another drink LJ examines the contents. "There's only two drinks left."

LJ wraps his arm around Lizzy's shoulder and asks sweetly as a filthy wolf, "You like it now. Right?"

His fiery breath burns through her nostrils but she sees no escape and nods hesitantly, "Not really."

"Well you tried it once and it didn't hurt ya so take one more."

"OK. But let me hold it this time?" she asks timidly.

LJ watches closely as she takes a small sip then squeezes her eyes shut and holds the bottle towards him. Covering her fingers tightly with his, he pushes the bottle into her hand and orders, "Take a *real* drink."

Squinching her eyes closed she takes a bigger drink then throws the bottle on the dash and spits the whiskey out the passenger window. LJ chases the clattering bottle across the metal dash yelling, "Watch it!" and catches it just before it falls to the floorboard.

With a sour scowl at Lizzy he chugs the remaining liquor then jumps out of the truck, his legs buckling under him. He crawls around the door, wraps his arms around Ben's knees and wrestles him to the ground. With a satisfied grunt he pushes off of Ben's chest in mock victory and skips back to the river. Hooting in exhilaration, he dives in then climbs the rope and swings on the board with his legs dangling in the water.

Ben and Lizzy watch him from the truck, neither of them moving. Spinning from the rope in a lazy circle LJ calls out, "Get in. It's nice."

Ben takes a few steps towards the water but stops when she whispers in a quiet scared voice, "Hey Ben. I don't want to swim anymore."

He walks back to the door looking at her as if feeling a tiny trace of compassion. He's used to his brother's ignorant dominance and knows what she's going through. He asks dumbly, "You sure?"

"I swam at the pool already and I'm hungry and tired," she pleads with an inviting tilt of her head, trying her best to sound and appear convincing.

Ben watches LJ stand on the board and try to climb up the rope. When LJ falls into the water and swims to the near shore Ben yells expectantly, "Hey dad's comin home soon."

LJ throws a rock at the truck, watches it bounces off the grill and yells back, "He's *not* our dad. His *name* is Carl and I don't give a shit. I hate him."

"That doesn't matter for nothing. If he sees the truck gone he'll kill us both."

LJ picks up another rock; skips at the truck then throws it at the window; it bounces off with a loud crack; right in front of Lizzy face. She looks at the dusty little mark it left and smiles nervously at Ben, "Please, I *gotta* go Ben."

Ben walks around the truck to run his finger tips over the scuff mark in the glass. "If you break something he'll know we took the truck for sure." He glances through the passenger window at Lizzy then at his feet as if thinking hard. After a minute he looks back at her fearful yet hopeful expression and sympathetically adds, "You know that butthead aint gonna be gone all day."

"All right all ready! I heard before!" LJ hop-skips back then angrily slams the door and starts the truck with a hiccup. Pumping the pedal he grins madly as the engine revs high than laughs as dark smoke billows into the cab through the driver's window. Tossing his head back he howls again and screams, "Let's ride," then drops the transmission into reverse before the engine slows; he tugs on the steering wheel as the engine rattles but the truck refuses to move. He frowns and pumps the gas pedal then the wheels start to rotate. The truck bed hurdles upwards as the tires spin over the rocks; moving backwards in a slow half circle after he misses the brake pedal; finally stopping with the back tires covered up to the axle in the river. Banging the shifter with his forearm, he floors the gas and water flies over the cab dropping muddy splotches on the front window. Ben holds his arm out the passenger window and catches the splattering drops until the truck lurches forward with a groan, skittering across the rocks to the dirt road. LJ flips on the wipers, grins through the muddy window and spins the wheel back and forth, fish-tailing the truck on the loose gravel. They reach eighty miles an hour on the narrow curves before he pumps the brakes; his eyes grow large in panic for a brief second when he doesn't think he can get it to stop for the dead-end. He turns on the pavement and adjusts the rear view mirror as he shouts proudly, "What'd you think of that?"

Lizzy grips her seat tighter, wishing she'd just kept on dealing with the heat and grits her teeth. Ben pounds the dash yelling out, "Bitchin, that was stone cold bitchin!"

When they whizz right past Lizzy's street she screams, "Hey that was my street."

LJ glances backwards, "OK. I'll turn around up here."

The truck almost tips onto two wheels when he spins the steering wheel too far, yanking it off of the pavement onto the dirt. He jams the brakes and spins the wheel faster causing the truck to slide sideways to a stop. Laughing hysterically LJ pounds on the steering wheel as the dust swirls in the windows. Coughing, Lizzy is preparing to shove Ben out of the way and jump out when a car honks then turns in front of them and stops.

LJ can't believe it. His step dad jumps out of the car and pounds the hood with his fist as he runs to the truck's driver door. He grabs LJ by the throat demanding, "What do you think you're doing with my truck?" But the tight grip on LJ's larynx stops him from answering clearly and only a moaning croak leaks out.

LJ and Ben's *loving* stepdad, Carl Baxter, used to having things his way or somebody pays, is about to blow a gasket. He's three-sheets-to-the-wind and his favorite whipping-posts are directly in his sights. The typical afternoon bender, he'd spent the morning holding down a barstool in the Shark Tail tavern. He'd still be there if the bartender hadn't noticed his inebriated condition and thrown him out on his duff while listening to Carl's angry protests and threats that he was going to burn the place down. He was in a bitter mood before he saw the boys and it's ratcheted several notches higher now.

Grabbing the empty bottle off the dash Baxter waves it accusingly in LJ's face, "What the hell is this?" He opens the driver door, searches the floor then forcefully slaps LJ's face with his forearm, bouncing LJ's head off the back window. He grunts lividly, "Are you drinking my whiskey?"

Trembling, LJ shakes his head and Carl looks questioningly at Ben. But Ben can't move or speak either; he's too scared to think.

"All right you little piss-ant. You're gonna regret the day you were born." He slams the door and shakes his fist in front LJ's nose, "Follow me."

They silently follow as he drives the few blocks to their house. Stopping in front of the house he motions for LJ to park the truck under the attached car port. They sit in the truck frozen with fear, flinching when he slams his car door and stomps up the driveway. Yanking open the driver's door he asks rhetorically, "You sittin' there all day? Hell no! Get in the damn house."

LJ gets out of the drivers side and his dad slaps the back of his head then shoves him towards the door, "Git! Git in there!"

Ben and Lizzy are on the other side of the truck slowly shuffling toward the tailgate. She's tempted to run but is frozen by doubt and fear. Baxter pounds on the sides of the truck while herding them in the house. When she stops outside the door, he shoves her neck with an evil grunt, "You too, you sleazy little tramp."

LJ and Ben huddle together between the kitchen counter and table waiting for his well understood attack while Lizzy edges around to the other side of the counter next to the kitchen sink, unsure what is going to happen. He locks the door as he unhooks his belt buckle then yanks it out of his pants as he crosses the room. Ben crouches behind LJ, hoping to avoid the worst of it. Baxter lashes at LJ's head. LJ blocks with his forearm then both boys try to cover their backs by cowering under the counters overhang while he swings his arm in swift circles yelling horribly, "You think you can help yourself to my shit."

With his lashes and knuckles focused on LJ, Ben crawls under the kitchen table and slides a chair between him and his step-dad. Hearing the harsh lashes slapping across LJ's back mixed with the boys cries, Lizzy screams out in terror. Cringing with each slashing stroke, she coils into a ball behind the counter trying to become invisible.

Bawling in pain, LJ kicks at his step-dad's legs; only angering him that much more and Carl punches LJ on top of his head with an animalistic grunt. With the rare chance for escape open to him, Ben runs to the back door. The squeak of the back door hinge draws Baxter's attention and he chases Ben several steps onto the patio before realizing that he'll never catch him. When he returns he sees LJ disappearing down the hall. Lumbering across the room in a flopping run he enters the hallway and slips, his legs fly out in front of him and he falls on his back with a woof. LJ locks and slams the bedroom door shut then throws the wadded bed sheets in front of it. With shaking hands he quickly opens the screen-less window and dives headfirst through onto the ground. Baxter struggles with the door for a second before stumbling back through the house and watching the boys run down the alley. He used to be a fast runner, and fantasies of chasing them down and dragging them back screaming and whining pass through his tiny trapped mind, then an appalling but satisfying mental picture of him beating them until they beg for mercy. He kicks the door shut and thinks, *"They'd be hurting units if only I hadn't busted my leg up that last time."* With a glance out the back window he cast his bitter mind back to that night when he'd left the Silver Buckle Saloon with that ugly whore, and the asshole lawyer stepped off the curb in front of his car. He'd tried to miss the idiot but his car's brakes and *maybe* his own reactions, weren't that good. The lawyer's body thudded off the car and because Carl's reactions were so poor he had only turned far enough to slam into a telephone pole. His knee crunched into the dash leaving a dent the size of his fist and him unable to perform hard physical labor any longer.

  After kicking a chair against the counter he rights the table on its legs then leans his elbows on the kitchen counter blinking and rubbing his blurred eyes to clear the drunken stupor. He spots the top of Lizzy's head and smiles a disgustingly horrible leer. His fiendish ogling eyes are the last to ever see beautiful Lizzy Camber alive.

Six

Ginger and Carol are in the house cooking dinner, meat loaf, green beans and fried potatoes with onions and peppers. The boys are hungry and *had* been hanging out in the kitchen watching them cook but Josh kept sneaking potatoes out of the skillet whenever Ginger's back was turned so she ordered them out of the house, "Get out of my hair and go outside before I have a conniption".

Although he'd heard her say it a thousand times before he asked honestly, "What's a conniption?" She flung a pot holder at him and chased him giggling out the front door.

Uncle Larry's Corvette is 'acting like a Ford again' and he asked Rob to look at it. The hood is up and he is revving the engine while Rob pokes around under the hood. From across the yard Logan watches his dad and tells Stoney, "He *never* asks for my dad's help. He always takes it to the dealer but they messed it up this time."

Josh is lying on his back by the front wheel trying to help when Rob admits, "I can't see a thing. Josh, get me a flashlight." The sun is getting ready to set and Logan is eager for the cool of the evening. Josh comes out of the house with Ginger scolding him, "I told you to stay out."

"Your pants on fire?" Larry asks Josh when he jumps out of her reach.

"Not yet, but they will be if he doesn't stay outside," Ginger points her finger warningly at Josh.

Rob adjusts the carburetor with his screwdriver and revs the engine then lets it smooth into an idle. He messes around with it for fifteen minutes before he is satisfied. After shutting the engine off he asks Larry, "What do you think?"

"It still doesn't seem right."

"Drive it around the block and check it out."

Larry waves Josh into the passenger seat then backs onto the street; revving it like a big kid he twitches his eyebrows at Rob; then drops the clutch, smoke flies from the tires as they speed off. Rob and Logan sit side by side on the curb listening to Larry hot rod around the neighborhood. They haven't heard the sound of the engine for several minutes when Logan asks, "Where did they go?"

Rob cups his ears and turns his head, "I can hear them. They'll be right back." Just then the lights of the Corvette appear at the end of the block. After gunning it down the street Larry skids to a stop in front of Rob, Josh rolls his window down smiling.

Larry leans over and squints one eye at Rob, "It's pretty close. How 'bout I bring it to the shop tomorrow and you finish it then?"

"Sounds good. You parkin' it? Or do you want to keep scaring my neighbors away? Ouch!" Rob exclaims, his knees popping as he stands.

Larry backs into the drive while trying to lure Rob into a race, "I was hoping you'd get out your car so I could show you what it's all about."

Ginger opens the door, "Hey you big kids, dinner's ready."

"It'll have to be later," Rob grins at Larry.

Josh expected Lizzy to come over for dinner and has been watching her house all night. Seeing his constant glances across the street Rob asks, "Why don't you just go over there?"

As his family files in the front door Josh runs across the street and knocks on Lizzy's front door. He had seen her parent's car drive away a few minutes ago and wonders if she went to the store with them. After knocking again he waits a few minutes then runs over to her bedroom window and taps on the glass. When she doesn't answer he walks dejectedly home. Carol sees his disappointment and asks, "Not home?" Shaking his head crossly he stabs a slab of meatloaf and drops it on his plate.

Stoney and Logan eat fast then go out back to play while everyone else visits around the dinner table. Larry is trying to goad Rob into a drag race after dinner when the doorbell rings. It's Rusty. He asks Josh, "You seen my sister tonight?"

"No. She was supposed to come over for dinner."

"I know. She told my mom that this morning but she hasn't come home yet."

Carol walks up behind Josh, sets her hands on his shoulder and asks Rusty, "Where did she go?"

"She went to the pool this morning and isn't home," he explains, a strained absorbed expression on his face.

His worry obvious to Carol, she opens the screen door and looks across at Lizzy's house, "Are your parents home?"

"Not now. They went over to Lori's house to see if Lizzy is there."

"Well have them call us when you hear from them. OK?"

"OK," Rusty looks down the street, a worried furrow wrinkling his forehead.

Carol pats Rusty's shoulder assuredly, "She'll turn up. She probably just forgot to call."

Rusty rides his bike down the street, calling Lizzy's name every few houses. She watches him disappear as she contemplates where Lizzy may be then turns to go back into the house and collides with Josh on his way out the door with his car keys. She asks, "Where are you going?"

He jumps around her and skips to the side yard as he yells back, "To help them look for her."

"Where at?"

"I don't know yet. I'm just gonna drive around and stop at houses where I know the girls and see if she's there," he taps his keys on the roof of his car as he explains.

As the Chieftain rumbles away the same direction Rusty went, Rob wraps his arms around her waist to comfort her, "They'll be home in a minute and we'll find out what's going on."

An hour later, Josh arrives home and sees a police car sitting in front of Lizzy's. Carol is waiting for him at the front door and whisks to his car, "Did you hear anything?"

"No. What are the police doing over there?"

"They just got home and the police came with them. We haven't talked to anyone yet."

Josh starts across the lawn towards Lizzy's house but hesitates when Carol calls out, "You should wait until they want to talk to us. We can't just butt into their business."

Josh reluctantly follows his mom in the house and finds Larry and Ginger sitting in the living room talking with his dad. Rob asks, "What did you find?"

"I asked all the girls on the block but they haven't seen her since the pool this morning."

Rob leans forward and cocks his head at Carol as if to say, *that's unusual*. Carol claps her hands together as she remembers out loud, "Logan went to the pool this morning I'll ask him if he saw her."

She slides around Rob to the back door and calls Logan. They're playing flashlight tag and it takes a minute for him to give up his hiding spot willingly. He flashes the light in her face as he approaches, "What mom?"

Blocking the light beam with her hand she says, "Stop pointing that in my eyes. You went to the public pool today didn't you?"

"Yes, me and Stoney went," he replies absently, watching Stoney run after Ballsac.

"Did you see Lizzy at the pool?"

"For a minute."

"Was she there when you left?"

"Probably, I don't know. She was asking about Josh *again*," Logan's voice has a tone of slight disapproval as he flashes his light around searching for the other boys.

"It's almost time to come in and the boys need to go home in a minute."

Logan shouts, "OK," then apologizes sheepishly when she covers her ears, "Oops, sorry mom." Then he runs into the dark shouting, "You're still it."

Carol slides the door shut while repeating what he'd said. An hour passes before a knock finally comes at the door. As expected, it's Lizzy's mom Christy Camber, but she has the police standing behind. Carol invites them in.

They crowd into the living room and the tears streak down the tracks in her face as Mrs. Camber cries in a stifled voice, "We can't find Lizzy. She hasn't come home."

The policeman holds her trembling elbow while saying consolingly, "We'll find her." Then addressing Logan's family he asks, "We were wondering if you've seen her today?"

Josh offers, "She was here at dinner last night."

Carol adds, "She was at the pool this morning. Logan saw her."

The policeman eyes light up and he opens his mouth in a big questionable expression of oh? and asks Carol, "Is Logan here?"

Carol calls Logan into the house and the boy's crowd into the middle of the room. Logan drops onto the couch and nervously looks at the policeman, "What's going on?"

Seeing his panicky reaction Carol quickly explains, "Lizzy didn't come home tonight and they want to ask you about when you saw her at the pool."

"You saw her at the pool today?" the policeman directs his questions to Logan.

"Yeah, she was there this morning."

"How long were you there?"

Looking at Stoney for confirmation Logan scratches his head and replies, "Till like one or two." Stoney nods.

"She was still there at two?"

"I think so."

Looking at Stoney the policeman asks, "Did you see her at two?"

"I saw her at the snack bar with Karen a little bit before we left," Stoney taps his fingers in the air.

Carol interrupts excitedly, "Karen who? What's her last name?"

"I don't know."

Josh interrupts, "That's Karen Eaton, her best friend. She's been over here before. They always hang out."

As if trying to recall what Lizzy told her, Mrs. Camber acknowledges, "She did say she was meeting her friends."

Carol asks Josh, "Did you talk to her tonight?"

"No. She wasn't home."

Mrs. Camber shakes her fists vigorously, "We called Karen first but she said Lizzy went home at lunch time."

Logan suddenly remembers seeing her in the car sitting between LJ and Ben and says pensively, "Oh yeah. I saw her on my way home from Ballsac's."

Holding his hand up for silence the policeman frowns as he asks, "Who?"

"My friend, Robert. I went to his house to give him his shirt and saw her on my way home."

"What was she doing?"

"She was riding in a truck with the new kid LJ."

Mrs. Camber asks eagerly, "Where? Where were they going?"

"I think they were going to the river. They went down Creek Road that way."

"Did you see her after that?" Mrs. Camber asks not waiting for the policeman.

Shaking his head, Logan looks at Mrs. Camber then at Rob, "No."

"Can anyone tell me where this LJ lives?" the policeman asks.

Everyone looks at Logan but he shrugs his shoulder, "I don't know. They're new kids."

Stoney interrupts uneasily, "Billy knows. They live by him."

"Can you take us to Billy's house?" Mrs. Camber asks, sounding more helplessly desperate with each the breath.

The policeman asks, "Do you know his phone number?"

Stoney scratches Billy's number on the policeman's pad while Carol does her best to console Mrs. Camber with firm hugs.

Sliding his pen in his shirt pocket the policeman asks, "Did any of you see her or this boy LJ at any other time?"

Everyone looks expectantly at the boys again but they shake their heads.

Taking hold of Mrs. Camber's quivering hand he leads her to the door and nods with a thin smile, "Thanks for your help."

Carol hugs Mrs. Camber one last time and they all stand outside the front door and watch the policeman lead her home.

Seven

Officer Dixon radios in his progress as he drives to LJ's house. An old truck is in the drive and light flickers out the front curtains onto the weeds and dead lawn. Shining his light through the dirty truck windows he notes the empty bottle of whisky on the dash then knocks on the carport door. He can hear the television but there isn't an answer. He raps the door with his flashlight, waits, then walks around to the other door and knocks again. He's flashing his light on the house windows when the door cracks open. A disheveled shirtless man looking like he just woke up, peeks out apprehensively at the officer.

"Sorry to bother you so late. Are you the father of LJ and Ben?"

"Their step dad. What did they do now?" he opens the door further, his eyes narrowing into tiny dark slits.

"I'm not sure they did anything. I would like to ask them a few questions if you don't mind. Are they here?"

"No," he answers bluntly.

Dixon flashes his light across the man's face as he asks, "You say you're not the boy's father. What is your name?"

He grumbles under his breath, "I don't know what you want my name for," then answers with a jolt, as if he'd been jabbed with a pencil, "Carl Baxter."

Writing his name on a pad Dixon asks, "Where are LJ and Ben now?"

"They went with their mom to their grandma's," he answers sullenly.

"Can you tell me where her home is?"

"In Flagstaff. Don't know her address," he states plainly as if that explains everything.

"Maybe you have her phone number?" Dixon asks patiently.

"It's probably here somewhere," he leaves the door open and looks around the room with a disgruntled sigh. He searches under newspapers and a stack of magazines next to the phone while glancing at the policeman repeatedly out of the corner of his eye. Bending over with a muffled grunt he lifts a handful of magazines from under the table; it slips from his hand tipping over the remaining stack and the officer hears him mumble, "This is a bunch of shit." He pulls a small notebook out of the pile and walks back to the door flipping through the pages. Holding the notebook towards the officer he points at the last entry, "Here. It's right there at the bottom of the page."

When he sees the policeman is finished writing the number he pushes the door almost shut and peeks out, "Is that it?"

"Almost. Is this your truck?" Dixon pushes the door open further with his light then flashes his beam on the truck.

"Yes," Baxter edgily shuffles his feet.

"I see the plates are out of date. Have you been driving it?"

"*No*," his voice changes to bold defiance.

"Do you know if LJ has been driving it?"

"It won't even start, the battery is dead," Baxter nervously touches his eyebrow.

With a glance at his sheets the officer says, "Logan Palmer said he saw your sons LJ and Ben driving it today. Are you sure?"

"He didn't see nothing. Who's Logan?" Baxtor demands.

Realizing his mistake the office redirects, "I wouldn't worry about that. Did the boys drive the truck today?"

"They couldn't. They've been in Flagstaff all day."

This stops Officer Dixon in his tracks. With a questioning frown he hesitates, then flashes his light on the truck and back to Baxter's face.

"Call their mom and ask her if you want." Limping to the phone, Baxter clutches it in one hand then carries it towards the door; but the cord tangles, shortening it drastically and he drops the phone when it reaches the cord's end. Cursing angrily he unravels the mess with grunts of frustration, "Those damn kids." When it appears the knots are about to defeat him he yanks the phone and a few feet of cord pull free from under the leg of the couch. He pushes the phone at the officer and half orders him, "Call her yourself."

The officer moves back a half step and patiently urges Baxter, "Why don't *you* call and then I'll talk to her."

Baxter glares at the officer with obvious disdain then dials and barks into the phone, "Let me talk to Mary." With the phone to his ear he waits. Avoiding Dixon's eyes he inspects the officer's uniform, unknowingly creating a dull sandpaper scrubbing sound as he scratches at the hair on his chest. Suddenly he bursts out, "There's a cop here. He needs to know you guys went to Flag' yesterday." As Baxter holds the phone out for the officer he hears her talking and puts the phone back to his ear, his voice growing louder with impatience, he says in a forced paced rhythm, "Listen, there's a cop here *right now*. He wants to ask you some stuff."

Baxter holds the phone out to Dixon with a smug flat smile.

Dixon takes the phone, "Mrs. Baxter?"

"I'm investigating a missing girl," nodding into the phone he continues, "Mr. Baxter here says you took your sons to Flagstaff yesterday."

After listening for a few seconds he asks again, "Are you sure you left yesterday morning?" another pause, "OK. That's it." Then shaking his head, "No thank you, you don't need to call us."

He hands the phone to Baxter while saying quizzically, "Well, hmmm. Sorry for the inconvenience." He flashes his light and searches Baxter's self satisfied face again, "Thanks for your time."

While turning around in Baxter's driveway he looks for signs of the truck being driven recently. He notes that it's covered with dust and probably hasn't been washed in a year and thinks to himself, "It probably *doesn't* run," he backs out of the drive and checks his watch. It's getting too late to disturb Logan's parents so he makes a note to call them in the morning.

Eight

The phone rings, waking the household. Lizzy is still missing and her parents need everyone's help. Rob and Carol tell the boys to stay home while they search. Josh watches them leave then waits for their car to turn the corner and tells Logan, "I'm going to go help." Logan knows his parents might call so he stays behind and watches the traffic come and go at Lizzy's. He pictures her hair when LJ's truck whipped by and wonders where she could have gone. Letting out a bored sigh he turns on the television and watches the morning cartoons while he waits by the phone. He's beginning to wonder when his parents will be home when he hears sirens whooping nearby; he spins around on the couch and watches everyone run out of Lizzy's and speed off. He rolls his bike out of the garage to follow them then stops and weighs the trouble he might get into. His parents will be mad if he's not home for their call so he grudgingly twists his handle-grips as he kicks the stand. There isn't anything to watch on television and he can't think of anything else to do so he waits on the couch inattentively reading his dad's car magazines. When he finally hears the familiar sound of his parent's car he runs to the door and is surprised by a procession of cars parking along the street. Everyone in the city seems to be going to Lizzy's. Logan runs to his parent's car. Both of them are crying, desperately hanging on each other.

Bewildered, he follows them into his house asking several times, "What's wrong mom."

Shaking her head in horror and disbelief she runs into her bedroom slamming the door as she dives on the bed. Rob leads Logan into the kitchen and sits at the dinner table next to him then stutters through clenched teeth, "We found Lizzy. But she, she, something bad happened to her." Putting his hand on Logan's shoulder he continues with his eyes closed and his face clinched in sorrow, "She's gone now."

"What do you mean?" Logan reaches out and shakes Rob's shoulder, "Dad? What do you mean? Dead?"

"Yes. That's what I mean," he replies opening his eyes and watching Logan's reaction carefully.

"What happened to her? Did they crash the truck…, or drown?"

"No, something else happened. I can't tell you what. But it was something horrible and unthinkable."

"What…is it *really* bad?" Logan asks as he absorbs the news.

"Well buddy, it's something we don't want to talk about. I'd like it if you didn't ask a lot of questions about what happened. Is that OK?"

Confused, Logan offers doubtfully, "I'll try dad."

Thinking out loud Rob says, "You'll hear the adults talking about it but it would best if you try not to listen. Whenever you hear anyone talking about it, just go play or something. OK?"

Lost in thought, Logan nods and stares out the front window as Josh enters Lizzy's house. He's never experienced the death of someone so close and the foreign emotions of sudden loss tugging at his heart bring hard tears into his eyes. He is standing alone at the front window numbly watching cars parking along the street when Larry and Ginger drive up in his Corvette. They sit in their car talking for a few minutes before they see Logan. When she notices him Ginger waves to him gently. With a cross expression she whispers rapidly to Larry, pointing her finger at him as they walk to the house. Through the window Logan hears her say, "Just keep your mouth shut for once", but she is reserved when Logan opens the door. They sit at the kitchen table whispering and waiting for Rob to come out of the bedroom.

Two hours pass and Logan does his best to ignore them and maintain control of his emotions. He doesn't know what to do with himself so he invites Stoney to go swimming then searches the garage for the inner tubes his dad said he would bring home from work; finally finding them in the trunk of Rob's car. He is filling them with air when Stoney arrives.

Stoney watches him work while sitting on his bike just outside the garage, "What do you think happened to her?"

"My dad is making it a big secret. He thinks I'm too little to tell," Logan replies somewhat flustered.

"Do you think it was something gruesome?"

"It must have been or he'd a told me."

Silently they watch the tubes fill as the generator rattles away and their imaginations run wildly in every conceivable direction. Logan is half tempted to ask Josh anyway but he's not sure that he really wants to know. He'd rather remember Lizzy the way she was when he last saw her at the pool, happy, beautiful, and playful.

Rob brought home five regular car inner tubes and one big truck tube. When he sees how big the truck tube is Logan says, "This one is mine." After it fills he rolls it to the pool; he's five feet one and it's taller than his head. Stoney tosses two of the smaller tubes in the pool then runs back into the garage for the others while Logan rolls the truck tube up the stairs then tips it in. Stoney runs up the stairs and drops the others in the pool.

The tubes cover the majority of the surface of the pool and Stoney notes, "There's no room to swim." Logan jumps onto the truck tube but the hole in the center is so big that he slides through the center. To keep it from tipping he has to sit in the truck tube like a tire swing, by flipping one side over his head. Stoney drops off the platform backwards onto a smaller one, his legs sticking up in the air. They're arguing over the big tube when Ballsac unexpectedly dives on the tube bouncing both of them off.

When he realizes who tipped him over Logan splashes him, "Hey!"

Ballsac takes possession of the big tube, wrapping his legs around it and preparing to fend them off. They try to tip him over but only succeed in flipping the tube, leaving him hanging on like a monkey by his arms and legs.

"You're toast," Stoney gives up trying to dump him and climbs out of the pool onto the shed.

Ballsac splashes him, "You're Texas Toast."

Stoney jumps at the big tube from the shed shouting, "Bombs away!" But bounces off the tube and flies backwards out of the pool with his arms rotating wildly. He lands flat on his back and rolls to his side holding his back. Logan slides over the pool side and kneels next to him, "Are you OK man?"

Moaning in pain, Stoney waits for Ballsac to climb over then jumps up, "Gotcha." Both boys watch in surprise as he runs up the stairs and dives onto the tube.

Logan is about to give chase when Rob calls from the back door, "Logan come in the house for a sec." The boys run to the door but he stops them, "Just Logan. He'll be out in a minute."

Looking at his dad questioningly Logan follows him to the living room and is surprised to see the policeman that had come over last night sitting on the couch. Rob says, "This is officer Dixon. He wants to talk to you about what you saw yesterday."

Ginger sits on the recliner and Larry is behind her leaning on the head rest. Rob stands next to Larry so Logan sits on the floor across the coffee table from the officer. Rob tells Logan, "Just tell him what you saw again."

"When I saw Lizzy?" Logan asks sliding his hands on his thighs.

"That's right," Dixon nods.

"She was at the pool and in the truck with LJ and Ben on my way home," he answers briefly. Everyone is watching him expectantly and he feels nervousness taking hold.

With a brief glance at Rob, Dixon asks, "Where was the truck going when you saw it?"

"It went past our street and down Creek Road."

"Which way did it go on Creek Road?"

"Towards the river."

Leaning forward with his elbows on his knee's Dixon asks, "How sure are you it was Lizzy?"

"Pretty sure I guess," Logan shrugs.

"Are you absolutely sure or are you just guessing?"

Logan raises his eyebrows as he looks down at his palms, "I don't know what you mean. I *thought* it was her."

Rob interrupts, "Buddy this is really, really important you need to be positive it was her."

Dixon adds, "That's right. What were you doing when you saw them?"

"Working on my bike on the sidewalk."

"Was the truck going fast or slow?"

"It was going real fast. Like cars on the highway."

"Can you *show* me what you were doing when you saw the truck?"

Logan looks at his dad questioningly, "I don't know."

Rob encourages him supportively, "Take a second and try to remember what you were doing."

Logan kneels on one knee and holds his hands out like he's spinning a tire, "I was working on my bike like this."

"Pretend this table is your bike and show us what you did when the truck drove by," Dixon pats his palm on the table.

Scooting over to the table Logan leans on one knee then stands up and pretends to watch something pass. His face flushes pink with embarrassment as he says, "Like that."

"Did you see Lizzy's face?" Dixon asks observing him closely.

"Sorta it was going pretty fast. I saw her hair for sure."

"How about LJ and Ben. Did you see their faces?"

"I think so. It looked like them."

"Did you know that LJ and Ben were in Flagstaff all day yesterday?" Dixon asks Logan with a tilt of his head.

Looking at Rob in confusion, Logan stutters, "No. Dad…, I thought…"

Dixon watches him as if waiting for an answer. With a glance at Rob then back at Logan he asks, "Would you recognize the truck if you saw it again?"

"I don't know," Logan apprehensively looks down at his hands as he rubs his palms together.

"Do you know if it was a Ford or a Chevy?" Rob asks.

"No. I think it was green."

Closing his notepad Dixon asks Rob, "Would you mind taking a ride with me by their house?"

"No. Let's go Logan," Rob ushers Logan out the door after Dixon. He leads Logan to the front passenger seat then sits in the back seat behind him and pats his back saying caringly, "Just do your best buddy."

During the drive to LJ's house Logan points out where he was standing when the truck passed by and the direction it was going. Dixon stops, gets out and stands at the curb taking notes, then seemingly satisfied with Logan's explanation he gets back in with a final glance toward Creek Road. They park across the street from LJ's house so Logan can have a good view of the truck.

Logan rolls his window down while seeming to speculate, "Maybe. That could be it."

Rob leans over the back seat and their eyes meet, "You need to be sure buddy."

Logan gets out, crosses the street and stands at the end of the drive shading his eyes. He's feeling confident that it's the same truck when he notices the curtains move and sees Baxter dark face peeking out at him with a curious scowl. Feeling an awkward tremor of fear he runs to the driver's window of the police car and admits, "I can't one hundred percent tell. I think that one's blue. It's so dirty."

"It *is* blue," Dixon waves at him to get in the car. Pulling away slowly he asks with a downward turn of his lips, "What do you think? Was that the truck?"

Turning around to look at Rob Logan answers sadly, "I don't know, absolutely for sure. It might be."

Dixon parks at the curb in front of Logan's house; turns off the engine; exits the car and stands with his arms on the roof waiting for them to get out. Rob opens the door for Logan while asking, "Do you want to talk to Logan any more?"

Dixon shakes his head ruefully, "No, I guess that's it."

Patting Logan on the back with respect Rob tells him, "You can go out back with your friends now."

With an uncertain glance at Dixon Logan asks, "Is everything OK dad?"

"You did your best buddy. Everything's good. Go ahead."

Logan shuffles slowly towards the side yard and stops when he is about to round the corner. His dad and Dixon are intently whispering across the car roof. Dixon shakes his head a couple times then waves to Logan before he gets in and drives off. Logan watches Rob's face as he crosses the lawn, looking for any sign of an emotion, but he only whistles tunelessly until the door slams behind.

Carol is standing next to the pool and Ballsac and Stoney are floating in the inner tubes when Logan walks up. She is asking them, "You want ham or turkey?"

Stoney sees Logan and announces, "Hey, he's back."

Logan walks to Carol and she puts her arms around his shoulders searching his eyes carefully, "Are you all right buddy?"

Logan can't figure out it if his parents are mad or not. He isn't even sure if he's in trouble. "Yeah. Are you making lunch now?" he asks, uncomfortably looking away.

"I'm making sandwiches," she says hoping he would have told her what happened while they were with the officer. "Do you want chips?"

"Of course," Logan notices a drained feeling overtaking him as he sits on the pool stairs.

After Carol enters the house Stoney asks, "We thought you were arrested. Where did you go in the police car?"

Logan tells them then Stoney says in a wishful tone, "It's cool, riding in a police car."

Shaking his head Logan rubs his twitching cheek and mumbles sheepishly, "It's not that cool. I didn't really like it."

Ballsac throws a tube out of the pool and tries unsuccessfully to break the somber mood, "Let's make a whirlpool." With their sandwiches on the laps, they float on the tubes in slow circles talking quietly; trying to guess what might have happened to Lizzy and why the police were questioning Logan.

Rob is taking the trash to the garage when he sees Logan wrapping his paper bags around the handle bars of his bike. The other boys aren't around so he asks, "Where'd your friends go?"

"I have to do my route so they went home," Logan looks up briefly.

"I thought they usually went with you?" Rob wonders, frowning slightly.

Tightening the straps with a grunt Logan replies, "Sometimes, but they didn't want to today."

"Put your bags up. Josh can drive you."

It's a warm afternoon and Logan doesn't feel very energetic; he wasn't looking forward to pedaling his bike with a full load of papers, "Thanks dad!" After rolling his bike into the garage he follows Rob into the house. He looks around but can't find Josh and asks Carol, "Where's Josh?"

"He's over at Lizzy's right now."

When Logan steps into the street he spots a police car in front of Lizzy's. He doesn't want to go over while the police are there. He was starting his route early and it will be a few minutes before his papers are dropped off so he turns around and waits for Josh in the front yard. Trying to be discreet so he doesn't bother his parents, he sits on the curb for a few minutes then climbs the old ash tree. The low hanging limbs make it easy to scale and it has been his fort since he was four. Taking his familiar spot in the middle of the tree he watches Lizzy's house. There are a lot of people standing in the shade of their tree and under the patio. He thinks, *I wouldn't want to be in the house either; it must be really hot and crowded in there.*

He hasn't seen this many cars on his street since the wedding the Cummings had in May. Counting out loud, he finds nineteen cars that he doesn't recognize and thinks, *That's almost as many cars as on the used car lot by the store.* Rob opens the door and calls through the screen, "Logan?"

"Yeah dad?"

"I thought you were delivering your route?"

"I'm waiting on Josh."

"Go get him. He doesn't even know you're waiting," Rob insists shutting the door.

The police car still sits in the drive and Logan doesn't want to talk to Dixon again. Logan looks for any sign of Josh. If he were in the front yard he could call him over, but he isn't. Climbing down the tree slowly he starts to go in the house to call Lizzy's and ask for Josh then hesitates. Fluttering his lips together and unconsciously making a quiet horse whinny, he thinks his dad may not like that. He mutters out loud, "Oh man," then starts over to Lizzy's, his tennis shoes dragging across the grass. He looks in the windows of the police car as he passes, tracing the letters on the door with his finger tips and making lines in the dust. He doesn't recognize anyone in the front yard so he rings the bell. Rusty opens the door not saying anything, his eyes red as if he had been swimming all day. Logan says cautiously, "Hi Rusty, I'm looking for Josh."

Rusty opens the door to let him in. The living room is filled with people Logan doesn't know so he passes through into the kitchen. Lizzy's mom and dad are sitting at the table with Dixon. When they see him, Dixon offers a small smile and asks, "Hi Logan. Did you want to talk to me?"

"No thank you. I'm looking for Josh. My brother," he answers trying to be as polite as possible.

Logan's eyes momentarily meet Lizzy's dad's frantic eyes as he flips his thumb over his shoulder, "I just saw him out back."

"Thanks," Logan squeezes between his chair and the counter to get to the back door. Dixon smiles at him again as he opens the screen door. Logan hears him say quietly, "It's too bad Logan…" before he sees Josh talking to some other boys. Gratified that he didn't have to talk to Dixon he runs over to Josh and interrupts, "Dad said you have to help me deliver my papers."

Contemplating for a second Josh's face twists in hurt and he rubs his eyes with his fist, "Are you sure? Why?"

"I don't know. He just wants you to drive me."

Josh sighs reluctantly then tells his friends, "I'll be back later."

During the drive to the paper station Logan turns on the radio and clicks through the buttons but Josh punches it off saying weakly, "Leave it off. OK?"

Nodding, Logan rolls the window down and watches his brother drive. He keeps wiping tears from his chin and tapping his fingers impatiently on the wheel then sighing deeply and shaking his head. When they arrive at the station a truck driver is stacking bundles of paper while the other paper boys wait. With a glance at Jake, Logan tells the driver, "My bundles are short all the time. Can you leave me an extra paper?"

The driver closes his tailgate and leans on it saying, "If you're short papers you need to call and let me know. I always leave an extra paper for each of you." He jumps in the cab, backs his truck around and leans out the windows, "Don't steal papers from each other. You understand? I have to pay for those."

Josh turns his flashers on and plays absentmindedly with his steering wheel while he waits. As he breaks his bundles Logan counts the papers and stacks them in the Chieftain's back seat. He notes his bundles contain one extra paper but he knows he's often short and says with surprise, "I do have an extra."

Blankly looking out the driver's window Josh croaks, "Hurry up will ya? I want to get back to Lizzy's."

"This is the last one," Logan rushes, popping the tie on a bundle.

"Well hurry up," Josh whimpers softly

Balancing a stack of papers on his handlebars Jake pushes his loaded bike over to Josh's window, smoke from his cigarette trailing behind and asks, "Hi Josh. Do you know what happened to Lizzy?"

Nodding, Josh turns his head away, hiding his thoughts and emotions.

Jake waits for an answer then asks impatiently, "Well, what?"

"She died," Josh keeps his head turned away from Jake and raises his left elbow to the steering wheel.

"How?" Jake persists.

Spinning his head around Josh snaps abruptly, "It's none of your business. Get lost!"

Jake gives Josh a startled look then pushes his bike off the curb and pedals away with a single questioning glance back. Logan watches the exchange then closes the door softly, "I'm ready."

After he starts the car Josh sits mutely, watching Jake ride away then drops it into gear and asks, "Where do we start?"

"Over on Brill." Logan can tell that Josh doesn't want to talk so he directs him to his stops by pointing the directions. As he expected, he has one paper left after his last stop and tells Josh, "That's it. We're done."

Josh parks at Lizzy's and walks into her house without saying anything. Upset further by Josh's disconnected demeanor Logan throws his scraps from his route in the trash then puts the extra paper on the kitchen table for his dad. He can hear his mom and dad talking fervently through their bedroom door. He doesn't want to disturb them so he rides his bike to Stoney's and they spend the remainder of the afternoon tossing the football in his back yard.

That night is the quietest dinner they have had all summer. Even Logan doesn't have anything to say and goes to bed early to read his old comics until he falls asleep.

Nine

Dark storm clouds have raced up and down the mountains all morning. As they have waited for the afternoon and the mourning of the funeral a low fog has drifted through the town, dulling the neighborhood sounds and creating a strange isolated silence that only allows brief glimpses of the grey sky. The thick cool mist in the air makes Logan uncomfortable and he can't loosen the tight gripping sensation in his chest, almost as if a cold band of ice envelopes his entire body. More dismal than he's ever been the unusually cold weather disheartens him. He shudders and trembles as they follow the slow procession through the wet streets. Logan's gaze is unfocused and straight ahead; the wipers intermittently clearing the tiny droplets from the windshield. He blinks each time the wipers cross his vision; for a brief second the blur worsens when they smudge the window. The glass slowly clears, looking clean and new then the unfocused world behind disappears as the tiny drops reappear.

His brother's head tilts back against the seat next to him, staring blankly out the side window, keeping his thoughts to himself while his mom does her best to keep her face free from streaks of dark makeup. His dad drives, clenching his jaw and grinding his teeth, the only one in the car with a task to distract him from the dreadful affair.

A motorcycle streaks by the window; Logan watches the flashing blue light as the rider directs their car into the cemetery. His dad gets out of the car and opens the door for his mom. She hands him her umbrella before checking her makeup in the mirror one last time. While Rob flips the umbrella open he motions Logan out of the car.

Logan watches over the roof as his parents follow the trail of mourners to the grave site, his brother trudging a few steps behind them. He waits until the ceremony starts then stands alone behind the mass of people listening to the sermon. Feeling evermore disconnected and of out of place he stands off by himself, but notices another lone man leaning on a tree across the grave yard lane and thinks that it must be acceptable to keep to yourself at a funeral. Through the most difficult parts of the weeping speeches he hears things that he doesn't completely understand and concentrates on the first point made. Her name was Elizabeth. Lizzy was what she allowed her closest friends to call her. He rubs the tears from his eyes with his sleeve reflecting on the meaning of that. He has a lot of friends, but had never realized how close he is to Lizzy and Rusty. Doing his best to stop the shuddering that keeps wracking his shoulders he watches her family struggle while their friends console them. He wishes he could do something, *anything*, to help but can't think of what that would be.

His parents lead Lizzy's family to their car while Josh follows behind like a zombie. He hasn't said a word to anyone all day and seems dazed and lost to Logan, like a weary ghost of himself. As his parents get in the car Logan hugs Josh and he releases a small wheezing sound under the pressure but doesn't speak, keeping his swollen eyes turned to the ground.

The drizzle had momentarily slowed but it has gotten colder and the dark clouds have moved in fast and low. As they drive to Lizzy's the rain increases and the already slow moving cars slog through the puddles, the wipers flying as the sheets of rain bounce off the windshield. Logan searches his family's faces for a shred of hopefulness but can't find a hint. He submits to the misery and listens to the water splashing from the wheels of cars passing by in the next lane.

As they wait at a stop light he watches the cracked tires of the old car next to them. Covered to the hub caps with water, a small cascading waterfall flows down the tire surface as it rolls backward. His dad eases off the brake in anticipation of the light changing, moving their car forward. The other driver's window is partially down and Logan recognizes the man's face. It is the man that was glaring at him through the curtains at LJ's house.

Rubbing the fog off the window Logan turns in his seat for a better look. As the car begins to turn right the man glances at Logan and their eyes meet. The car stops abruptly as the man punches the brakes and peers through the rain at Logan. Logan scrubs the dew from his breath off the glass then rolls his window down to get a better view.

"Hey! Roll that up," Rob orders, entering his thoughts. Slightly startled, Logan heart skips a beat before he cranks the window closed.

Rob bends forward and lowers his head to look at Logan in the rear view mirror, "What are you doing? Can't you see it's raining?"

"I'm sorry. I saw someone..."

Rob interrupts softly, "Well don't roll the window down in the rain buddy."

Turning all the way round in his seat Logan looks through the back window to find the car. He thinks he spots the brake lights blinking on and off but the rain is thicker than an ocean fog.

Cars already fill Logan's drive so Rob parks at the curb next to Lizzy's house. They sit silently in the car watching the milling crowd at Lizzy's house, gathering themselves for the rough emotions to come. Feet covered in mud, everyone is bunched under the patio to escape the downpour.

As Rob walks around the car to open the door for Carol, she turns and looks at Josh with concern, "Are you all right? You haven't said a thing all day."

Rob opens the door. Josh gets out and starts to answer but only a soft murmur escapes. He clears his throat then croaks tearfully, "Tonight, I was supposed to take Lizzy to the dance tonight."

She rushes around the car and wraps Josh in her arms while Rob waits for Logan to get out. Logan is watching the clumps of mud melt down the driveway and hasn't moved so Rob sticks his head in and asks, "You coming?"

"In a minute."

Logan sits in the car and watches his parents and brother slop through the muddy water then take off their shoes and enter the house. He searches the crowd for his friends but they are mostly adults or strangers, except for Rusty, no one his age is there. Taking off his tie he leans into the seat and listens to the rains comforting tap-tap-tapping on the roof.

A car approaches with it's headlights on, throwing a big spray on the side windows as it passes. Logan catches a glimpse of the driver through the flying water and frowns thinking, *that's LJ's dad again.* He watches the car drive away but dew inside the back window and the taillights glare obscure the driver's face. It stops at the corner and backs into a drive, returning slowly as if looking for a parking spot. Sticking his head out the window, Logan shields his eyes from the falling rain. As the car nears, the driver's window rolls down. Logan sucks his head in and ducks slightly, but he still gets a clear view of the man stretching his neck to see Lizzy's house. Positive it is LJ's dad, he pokes his head out the window again. The car stops in front of Lizzy's drive. The reverse lights turn on and the car backs up a few feet. Logan sees the man's head bobbing around to get a better view of Lizzy's house. The reverse lights turn off and the car sits there for a minute. With a light clunk the brake lights flicker off and it idles forward again; little puffs of fumes hovering behind all the way to the corner where it turns around in the street. Crouched in the middle seat, Logan watches it idle closer giving him a full view of the man's face, strengthening his belief that it is LJ's dad. The hood drops briefly when the driver taps the brakes as it passes Lizzy's house then it passes Logan and turns the corner disappearing behind the houses.

Logan wonders in bewilderment. *If he was at the funeral he would want to go to Lizzy's house. Wouldn't he? Maybe he didn't want to get wet in the rain? Is that really LJ and Ben's dad? They're new in town.* Logan's sure they don't even know Lizzy's parents. *Besides that, who goes to a funeral without shaving either? His hair was totally messed up too. You don't go to a funeral like that.* With these thoughts rebounding in his head he runs home, dodging puddles and the chunks of mud that were dropped by passing cars.

He brushes the water off his dress clothes as he hangs them up then calls Stoney. He answers Stoney's questions about the funeral then asks him for Billy's number. Stoney gives him the number without asking what he wants it for. Billy was in his class last year but Logan doesn't know him that well. He debates himself briefly then dials. Billy answers the phone, "Hello?"

"Billy? This is Logan."

"Hey. How'd you get my number?"

"Stoney," he is unsure how Billy will feel about his next question.

"Didn't you go to Lizzy's funeral?"

"I just got home from it. You know LJ?"

"Uh huh."

"How long have they lived there?"

"You mean, by me?"

"Yeah. When did they move in?" Logan asks.

"I think their dad has been there since early in the summer. LJ and Ben just moved in a couple weeks ago."

"When we had the BB gun war with them?"

"A couple days before that. Why do you care?" Billy asks.

Thinking quick Logan says, "I just don't want them at our football games any more."

"That's cool. I won't tell them when we play. But I already asked them to play BB gun war."

Logan doesn't say anything though. He's busy thinking about LJ's dad. Suddenly he abruptly says, "I gotta go. I'll talk to you later Billy."

After hanging up the phone softly he tries to put his thoughts in order. *They just moved here. They don't even know Lizzy's family. He went to the funeral all by himself? What was he doing driving by like that so slow and sneaky, like he was snooping around or something?*

Ten

Sunday papers are much bigger than the weekday's and Logan is glad when his dad tells Josh to help him deliver again. He is still stressed from yesterday's funeral and can't get the memory of LJ's dad peering at him through the rain off his mind. The vision of his beady eyes and bulging forehead pressed against the misty window glass kept Logan from sleeping this morning.

With a bag of rubber bands on his lap, Logan is waiting on the bumper of the Chieftain when Josh stumbles sleepily into the driver's seat. During the drive to the paper station Josh mumbles that Rob wants them to hurry so they can go to church with Lizzy's family. This weeks papers is even thicker then most Sundays and Logan has to stuff them with comics and several coupon inserts then wrap the paper with a rubber band, it seems to take forever. Josh sits in the driver seat, resting his head on the steering wheel and sleeping lightly while Logan works.

Logan has seventy-five papers to deliver. He stacks them across the back seat then wads the wrappers into a ball and shoots a basket in the trash drum before he gets in. Last night's rain has left the sidewalks wet and the yards soaked leaving Logan no choice but to walk the paper all the way to each doorstep. Hurrying to please Josh, he takes two or three papers at a time, drops one on a porch then cuts across the yards plodding through the puddles to the next stop. His soaked shoes keep sticking in the mud and several times he has to pry the sticky goo off with a stick.

He's delivered half the papers when he tells Josh, "Turn off the car, I need to rest for a minute."

Josh coasts to the curb and distractedly watches Logan remove his wet shoes and socks. He checks his watch, puffs his cheeks and blows softly then notes, "It's already after eight. They probably went to church already."

With his foot on the seat and leaning against his knee Logan rubs his wrinkled toes, "Sorry man."

They sit for a minute watching a dog sniff its way down the street. Logan says, "That stupid dog tried to bite me the other day."

"How'd you get away from it?" Josh asks only half interested.

"Threw a paper at it and yelled till it ran off."

Josh turns sideways in his seat and studies Logan before he asks, "Did you really see Lizzy with some kids?"

"*I* think so. Why?" Logan's tone is mildly defiant.

Ignoring his question Josh's attention is sparked, "Where?"

"I already told mom and dad and the police about it."

"Look, just tell me what you saw or I'll punch you in the head," Josh impatiently points his finger in Logan's face.

"I *was* telling you," Logan defensively shifts against the passenger door.

Rolling his eyes in annoyance Josh tries to calm his angry tone, "Go ahead then," then listens intently while Logan talks.

When Logan finishes he asks, "They were going really fast huh?"

"Yeah and their truck skidded all over in the dirt," Logan wiggles his hand like a snake.

"After you're done delivering your route, let's go down to the river and check it out," Josh jingles his keys in the ignition.

Logan wrings his socks out the window and asks, "You don't want to go to church anymore?"

"If there's time after the river."

Logan hurries through his deliveries and the muddy puddles soon sop up his pant legs to the knees until they're so heavy that he can't run anymore. Josh hands him his last five papers then follows the curving sidewalk, listening to the radio as Logan picks his way through the muck. As he trots to the car after his last paper sits safely on the door mat, Logan slips and cracks his tail bone on the cement. He's bent over nursing it when Josh unsympathetically orders, "You're not hurt. Get in."

Sitting sideways on the seat Logan pushes his feet against the floorboard and stretches out his legs with a grimace, "That hurts."

Lost in thought Josh ignores him while he drives to Creek Road. When they stop at the intersection where the dirt road begins he looks around and asks, "Is this where you saw the truck?"

"Yeah, right there. It was fishtailing all over and going that way," Logan points down the road toward the river.

Josh parks and searches the dirt in front of the car until he finds a faint track in the mud then asks, "Is this the tire track?"

"I can't tell. I was way up there," Logan points to where he was standing when the truck passed him.

"You're *not* helping. Get out and look at it," Josh demands reproachfully with his hands on his hips.

There are several tracks running through the mud but only one track that looks like the tires were spinning and sliding around. Logan digs at it with his toe, "That's probably it right there."

Walking along the track Josh looks towards the river and whispers thoughtfully, "I bet they went to the crooked tree."

Logan stands staring at the track recalling what he saw, when Josh slams his door then yells out his window, "Get in, you zombie."

They drive the dirt road to the river, but its running high from the rain runoff and they can't drive any further. The brush filled water rushes past fast, large boulders clunk noisily together as they watch from the bank. Josh points over the water, "It's too dangerous, we can't go over there right now but there's a cool spot to swim over by that sand mound. A lot of people hang out around here."

"I heard about it before."

Josh walks along the riverside to get a better view of the swimming hole then turns around and walks back slowly, kicking a stick along in the dirt and watching Logan skipping rocks over the tumbling surface. He crouches on his heels along the bank, rocks back and forth to his toes and speculates quietly, "I wonder what happened down here?"

Lost in his own world Logan doesn't hear and exclaims, "Man did you see that? It almost hit the other side."

"That's cool," Josh is staring into the distance and rolls a rock into the water past his foot with a bowling motion.

Logan throws a flat rock and is counting the skips when Josh turns him by the shoulders and asks, "Do you know where those guys live?"

"LJ and Ben? Yeah the police took me and dad there."

"Can you show me?"

"It's just over by Billy's. You know where it is," Logan answers throwing another rock.

"Just show me. Get in the car you retard," Josh says irritably, hitting Logan in the head with a pebble.

Rubbing his head as he slides in Logan asks, "What'd you do that for?"

"For a while," Josh cranks the Chieftain to life. "Where's Billy's house?"

Logan punches him in the arm, "Go back to the pavement and I'll show you."

As they pass the sidewalk where Logan was standing when he saw Lizzy riding in the truck he points it out again. Josh parks then gets out and stands where Logan was. After looking up and down the road he leans on the passenger door to look in Logan's eyes, "If you stood here and I drove past a couple times, could you tell me if that was how fast they were going?"

"I'll try."

"Let's try this. I'll drive by four times and you tell me which one matches their speed."

Logan feels ridiculous and conspicuous as he stands in front of the house watching his brother approach at the twenty-five mile per hour posted limit. As the Chieftain passes he shakes his head and points his thumb up yelling in the window, "Lots faster".

Josh's second pass is at forty but Logan shakes his head again, "Faster".

Josh turns the car around in the drive a few houses down then stops next to Logan and asks, "Faster than that?"

Nodding in agreement Logan's voice thins with tension, "Yeah, the truck was flying."

Nervous that he may get a ticket, Josh floors his car from the corner and reaches sixty-five before he passes Logan then stabs his brakes. Logan is waving his arm when he returns and jumps in the car pointing at the house, "The lady came out front when you went by." Josh sees her suspiciously looking out the window and waves as he slowly pulls away.

With an anxious check of his rear view Josh asks, "Was it really that fast?"

"Uh huh, about like that."

"That's pretty fast," Josh notes incredulously. "Could you see their faces really good?"

"I had a fight with LJ and his brother. That's the only time I've seen them close but I've seen Lizzy lots. You know her hair… Nobody else has nice hair like that. It looked like her hair to me."

Josh takes a deep breath as the memory of Lizzy's curls flash through his mind then asks, "Is that the fight you had last week?"

"Yeah. LJ started it with Ballsac, then..., I don't know, we all started fighting," Logan twists his mouth in a pucker as he recalls the sting of the punches.

"Which way to their house?"

Logan directs him but Josh parks down the street, two houses away. Josh gets out of the car and Logan jumps out to follow, "What are you doing?"

"I'm gonna check it out. You can stay in the car if you want."

Logan has to trot to keep pace with him. They cross the dead weeds and grass, stopping next to the truck. Josh circles the truck once as he looks in the windows then asks, "Is that it?"

"It looks the same to me, but it's not the right color. I think the one LJ was driving was green."

"Was it as dirty as this?"

"Uh huh."

"How could you tell what color it was?" Josh asks matter-of-factly as he opens the passenger door. He searches under the seat and runs his hand along the crack where the seat back and bottom meet. The glove box won't open so he bangs it with his fist and it falls to the floor, spilling its contents out the door. He shuffles through the papers until he finds the name of the owner, "Carl Baxter," he says the name aloud to memorize it. He drops the papers on the floor then closes the door and walks around the front. Bending over slightly he looks at the streaks in the dust then runs his fingers across the hood comparing the difference to the streaks his hand made.

Logan watches with a confused frown, "What are you doing?"

"I told you I'm checking it out."

Rounding the hood on the driver's side he notices the empty bottle of mescal on the dash and opens the door. He slides into the driver's seat reads the label and smells it. Wrinkling his nose he tips it and tastes the few drips that fall into his hand. After tossing it to the floor he holds the steering wheel and looks on the dash for anything obvious. Not quite satisfied with his search he slips out and looks under the seat again. He shuts the door quietly, wipes his hands on his pants and knocks on the carport door; knocks again and then walks to the living room door and rings the bell. Logan stands at the back of the truck hoping there isn't an answer.

After three attempts Josh says, "No one's home."

"I'm glad."

Josh grabs Logan's wrist, "Follow me." They trot into the back yard where he checks the back door. It's unlocked and opens. Poking his head in he calls out, "Hello?"

Logan grabs his arm apprehensively, "What are you doing? Let's get out of here."

Josh shakes him off as he enters the house, leaving the door open behind. Logan hisses frantically at his back, "Get out of there!"

"I'm *just* looking," he responds, holding his hand up in a stop sign and leaving Logan alone at the door.

The family room has a small metal table with three metal chairs with bent legs that look like they couldn't support a house cat, stuck under its dirty top. The kitchen counter is covered with a dozen or more empty beer cans and dirty dishes stacked haphazardly next to an old toaster. The sink is filled with upside down beer cans. The fridge is smudged with black finger prints and a picture of a half naked girl. The entire room stinks with the rank smell of stale beer. Disgusted by the stench he looks in the living room. It has two worn out couches and two small home made tables covered with car and girly magazines.

As he heads into the hall Logan whispers loudly, "Where are you going?"

Josh points down the hall and Logan thinks, *"If we get caught we'll both go to jail and dad will kill us"* as his head frantically swivels around looking for anyone that might be observing him. His heart is racing and he stands ready to flee into the desert behind the house at the first sign of a car.

The first door down the hall is a bathroom. The toilet looks like it's never been cleaned and black moldy goo covers the ceiling and walls around the tub. Next to the toilet another stack of girly magazines are soaking in a puddle of dirty water. A magazine is plastered face down to the side of the tub and floor, the rotting pages hanging in the standing pool. The filthy sink is covered with the remains of hair and toothpaste and a forgotten toothbrush lies in the bottom, toothpaste covering the browning bristles. Behind the faucet, beer cans line the wall and another toothbrush stands in the pop top hole of a partially crushed beer can.

The next door is a front bedroom. Two small dingy box springs sit next to each other on the floor. Boy's clothes are scattered around the room as if they had been poorly aimed in the general direction of the two cardboard boxes under the window. A flattened football and a lonely baseball held in an old mitt lay together in a corner.

The corner bedroom at the front of the house has a car engine sitting under the window on a wooden crate and boxes of car parts stacked against the wall. A pond of black oil surrounds the engine and the boxes are dark and warped with stains of the oil they have absorbed. A vacuum cleaner is in pieces, the parts scattered across the floor in front of a small opened tool chest. Holes jabbed through the wall surround the light switch, obviously made by the screwdriver that is still implanted in the wall.

The master bedroom has a larger mattress sitting on the floor and a home made shelf with cardboard shoe-boxes cut to size for drawers. Rolled into a tight knot, the pillows and blankets hang off the bed onto the floor. Torn off the hinges, the closet door is crutched against the closet wall behind a pile of clothes.

Logan calls out desperately, "Josh c'mon. I don't like this."

Josh spins in a slow circle, looking through each door one more time before he turns away from the lonely disaster shaking his head. Logan has entered the house to get him and they bump into each other as Josh comes out of the hall. Logan urges him, "Let's go *now*." They leave through the back door and Josh steps over a pile of bicycle parts with an appalled expression, "They are a bunch of filthy pigs."

As they walk back to the car Logan asks, "What did you see?"

"Nothing. No wonder they don't lock their door. They don't have anything but a bunch of garbage."

"What were you looking for?"

"Anything."

"What did you find out?" Logan presses.

"I found out that they don't live like humans," he answers broodingly. He cringes as he imagines Lizzy's terror at being stuck in that foul disgusting hole.

Logan interrupts his thoughts, "Why were you smelling that booze bottle?"

"I don't know. It just seemed weird. The lid was off but it still had some in it."

Logan gets in the car, his face twisted in confusion, "So what?"

"Well dad said the police told him that LJ's dad's truck was broke down and hasn't been driven in a long time. Why would there be an open bottle with whisky left in it. You know how fast stuff evaporates around here."

"Maybe it doesn't evaporate as fast as water."

"It does. I'm sure of it. Maybe even faster," Josh nods his head confidently.

They drive past the house and the half opened curtain reminds Logan of the grizzly man's face he saw peeking at him; an uncontrollable jitter twitches at his shoulders.

"Hey, you know what happened yesterday?"

"Of course I know what happened," Josh shakes his head ruefully.

"Not the funeral," Logan reproachful tone gets Josh's attention, "I saw LJ's dad at Lizzy's funeral."

"His name is Baxter. Carl Baxter. How do you know it was him? Have you ever seen him before?"

Logan tells him how he saw his dark face at the house window and how he drove past Lizzy's several times yesterday. When he's done Logan wrinkles his forehead in question, betraying how mystified he feels, "You know what else? I think I saw him at the funeral too. There was a man standing under a tree all by himself. I think it was him."

"That doesn't make sense Logan. You've only seen him that one time. You're probably wrong."

"I'm not. I promise. I'll come back and look at him to make sure."

"I don't think you should do that without me, dad wouldn't like it," Josh adopts Rob's fatherly voice.

"He won't know. I'll just tell you."

Josh parks in front of the garage door and takes note that Rob's car is already home. He shuts off the car and holds Logan's eyes with a long concerned stare then says, "OK. But stay away from those kids. They're animals."

He opens the door; puts one foot on the ground; then slaps the seat to get Logan's attention, "Just don't tell dad. And shut up about all of this, they're already home from church."

"Cool," Logan eyes are wide in deliberation.

They don't realize it at that moment, but this agreement is the cement that binds and leads them together down a very harrowing path.

Eleven

The next morning Stoney tries to line up a football game but can't find enough kids to make a single team. Logan is supposed to be at the field at eleven so he calls to give him the bad news before he leaves his house. They hadn't planned anything else so Stoney goes to Logan's to swim. They haven't been in the pool since last week and the storm filled it with dirt and leaves. Logan is netting leaves out of the pool when Stoney arrives.

Stoney hangs his towel over the fence and grunts at the grungy pool, "Oh man! That will take all day to clean."

"Yeah, but we don't have anything else to do," Logan agrees glumly.

Stoney retrieves the inner tubes with a broomstick and stacks them in the grass, "Why can't anybody go to the park?"

"My dad said the other parents at church were going to ground their kids until they figured out who did that to Lizzy."

"That's probably it. My dad said I can only leave the yard if I'm with somebody."

"They can't be grounded all summer, can they? Schools still a few weeks away," Logan wonders aloud as he empties the skimmer bag.

"The fair starts this Wednesday, I'm going to that no matter what," Stoney says defiantly. The Fossil County Fair runs for two weeks as summer winds down each year.

"Let's go together like we did last year. They'll probably let us go then. My dad always says there's safety in numbers."

"That's cool. I'll ask my dad today," Stoney commits, hoping that his dad will allow it.

Logan has already skimmed the leaves from the top of the pool but the bottom is still blanketed in patterns of brown and green. With a bored sigh he begins to scoop slowly along the bottom, stirring up the dirt and leaves and making the water murky.

Stoney connects the vacuum to the handle and pushes it over the dirt but the basket fills up right away and the vacuum uselessly pushes the leaves across the bottom. He lifts it out of the pool and plucks the leaves from the plugged hose forlornly, "That was a bad idea."

Logan tells Stoney how he and Josh went down to the river then over to LJ's to look at the truck but skips the part where they searched the house.

Stoney furrows his brow questioningly, "What was Josh looking for?"

"He was checking out my story. He believes me now," Logan gives a satisfied thumb's up.

"I believed you before."

"Thanks. My mom and dad *and* the police don't believe me, so Josh didn't either."

Logan drops the net and shakes his arms, "This is taking forever. My arms are about to fall off." He slides into the pool then scoops the leaves while dragging the net across the bottom as he walks in circles. The net fills faster than before but his feet stir up the dirt so he can't see the bottom.

Stoney drags the trash can to the side of the pool and spins it in a circle, "That's gross you can't even see your feet."

As Logan walks around scooping the leaves into the trash can he tells Stoney about seeing LJ's dad at the funeral then says with concern, "That's the only thing that Josh isn't sure of. I need to go to LJ's and make sure that it was the same man. Then he'll believe me all the way."

The trash can is overflowing with leaves by the time they've dragged the bottom of the pool. Logan cleans the pool's filter and pushes the vacuum through the dirt that is settling back to the bottom. The vacuum leaves a clean blue line as it sucks the dirt off the pool bottom so he starts to write his name in the dirt but as he finishes the L he decides to write Lizzy for some reason. Stoney's curious voice intrudes his reflections, "Why did you spell that?"

"I can't stop thinking about what happened to her. Josh said it was brutal," Logan answers in a small strangled voice.

The filter clogs again as he underlines her name and the vacuum refuses to lift the muck, stirring up a thick cloud of dirt. Like a mysterious fog eerily floating over a gravestone, the cloud drifts together and settles over her name as if directed by an unseen hand. He stands frozen as the image slowly grows fainter; then drops the pole and rubs the goose bumps on his arm, his mouth open in awe, "That's too creepy." He quickly climbs out of the pool and Stoney helps him back-wash the filter; by the time they reluctantly return to the vacuum they are happy to see the ghostly image of her name has completely faded.

Stoney arms aren't that tired so he takes over the vacuum and Logan gets them a drink from the house. While Stoney works he sits on the edge of the pool stirring his lemonade and reflects out loud, "My brother really likes Lizzy, I think he wanted to marry her someday." Unsure what to say Stoney concentrates on his work pretending to be unaware of Logan's' sadness. When the pool is as clean as they can get it by hand, Logan back washes the filter again and leaves the pump running. As they hang the pool equipment in the shed he says hopefully, "By the time I'm done with my route it should be clean enough to swim in."

The two of them finish his paper route early and stop at the Circle K for a candy bar on the way home. Logan is reading his favorite comic book, The Wyoming Kid. A western, the hero's black shirt makes him appear extremely strong with broad shoulders and an unusually thin waist. It covers his chest in a wide V shape that's lined with buttons. Logan thinks it's the coolest shirt he's ever seen. He's likes it so much that he once even tagged along with his mom and aunt on a shopping trip to find one like it, but to his disappointment didn't find anything that closely resembled it.

Stoney sips his RC Cola noisily through a thin straw then interrupts his reading, "When are you going over to LJ's?"

"What?"

"When are you going to check out LJ's dad?"

"I guess today," Logan organizes the comics on the shelf then flips through the Superman's before he reluctantly asks, "You ready?"

People are lined up at the counter and the clerk is busy bagging milk and doughnuts but he takes the time to wave bye to Logan as they leave.

While pulling his bike from the metal rack Logan says, "He's pretty nice to let us sneak the RC." They follow a short cut along the dirt path that leads by the electric plant and across the fields until they reach Skunk Creek. He stops at the bridge to see if the new guard rail is done.

Out of breath from pedaling through the loose dirt and gravel Stoney asks, "Are you gonna knock on the door?"

"LJ's door?"

"Yeah."

"No way. My brother said they live like animals and to keep away from them."

"What are you gonna do then?"

"I don't know. Maybe just sit on the corner until he gets home or something," Logan answers as he climbs onto the guard rail that runs over the edge of the creek. Balancing on one foot he hangs his arms out over the twenty foot drop and bounces on his toes. Suddenly Stoney grabs Logan's ankle and shakes, but Logan clutches Stoney's hair for balance. He jumps down onto the asphalt and pushes Stoney then declares in astonishment, "You almost made me fall!"

Stoney trips him in return then runs over to his bike and coasts down the hill into the creek and slides sideways to a stop at the bottom to see if Logan is following. Logan throws a stick down at him and yells, "You're toast." Stoney ducks the well aimed shot and races up the wash, giggling and laughing out loud when he sees Logan chasing. After a couple hundred yards Stoney is too winded to keep going and Logan crashes his bike into him. They tip over, lying on their backs in the sand laughing and catching their breath. Stoney gets up first, brushes his pants off, then pushes his bike to the dirt bank and waits for Logan as he watches a covey of quails trailing away. When Logan sees Stoney isn't looking, he throws a handful of pebbles at his back then pushes his bike up the hill while listening to Stoney's whining. It's another mile or so to LJ's street but the dirt is loose so they push their bikes and watch the houses through the waves of heat rising from the desert.

Stoney waves his hand in front of his eyes, "I wonder if that's what a delusion looks like."

With an infectious grin Logan asks, "You mean an illusion?"

"You know what I mean big shot. It looks like the houses are melting."

Logan shades his eyes with his hand, "It does. That's cool."

As they cross a dirt trail Stoney says, "You know what. This cow path leads over there behind LJ's house. We could spy on them from the desert and they couldn't see us."

Weighing the idea against hanging out on the street corner like a vagrant Logan acknowledges, "That's a good plan."

They ride their bikes on the path where it follows a meandering wash behind the houses. When they have a good view of the rear of LJ's house, they coast into the gravel wash and watch from the bank. Standing on an outcrop of rocks Logan's view is better than Stoney's who has to tip toe in the dirt to see. They're about an eighth mile away from the alley where the garbage man wakes all the neighborhood dogs twice a week.

Stoney asks in a whisper, "When do you think they'll be home?"

"My dad gets home about five or six. His dad probably does to."

"What time do you think it is?"

"Don't know. It was five-fifteen when we left the store."

A horny toad runs across the rocks by Logan's feet and he yells, "Horny toad, get it!" He chases but it zooms across the sandy wash, kicking up a mini cloud of dust before it slips under a boulder. Dropping to his knees Stoney digs in the sand under the rock while Logan tries to chase it out with a stick. Holding one ear to the sand Stoney closes one eye and peeks under the rock, "It's flattened out between the sand and rock."

Logan tosses his stick aside, "Let me see." He ducks his head under the rock and sand flips into his eye and mouth from Stoney's shoe. Coughing and rubbing his eye he announces, "We'll never get it out now." Spitting sand as he climbs up the bank he suddenly ducks and drags Stoney down by the shoulder, "Watch out!"

"What did you see?"

"They're   outside,   out   there   in   the   back   yard."

"Who?"

"LJ and Ben."

They crawl to the top and watch LJ and Ben carrying boxes across the alley. As they stack them a woman exits the back door with another box in her arms. She sets it on top of the other boxes and talks to the boys with her hands on her hips. They can hear her serious voice but the words are tantalizingly lost.

"Who is that?" Stoney asks.

"Probably their mom. I've never seen her before."

LJ runs in the house and comes out with another box. As he runs across the alley he trips and the contents spill across the dirt. Stoney laughs, "What a doofus."

Their mom dusts off LJ's pants then opens the box she brought out while he rounds up the scattered remains. Holding something in her hand she shakes her arm like you would shake a paint can then throws it into the desert away from the house. When she does it a second time Logan frowns, "What is she throwin'?"

"I can't tell. Follow me."

Like army men they crawl backwards into the wash, then crouching, they run, following the twisting wash to a point where it gets closer to the houses. With only a hundred yards between them and the houses they watch quietly as LJ shakes a can, throws it and yells gleefully as it spews liquid across the rocks.

In assembly line fashion, their mom shakes the cans then hands them to the boys to throw. Whenever a can skitters over the dirt and doesn't break open, LJ stomps it. His pants are quickly soaked from the spraying liquid.

Logan shakes Stoney's shoulder and whispers, "Why are they wasting that stuff?"

"Beats me," Stoney shrugs.

With four boxes to go through, it takes them a while to finish and when they walk back to the house Ben is holding his shoulder and rotating his arm in big circles as if it hurts from throwing. His mom puts her arm around the boys, hugging them tight against her sides while they walk across the alley into the house.

As they run back to their bikes Stoney huffs, "Let's ride past and see what they were throwin'."

They push their bikes through the sand to their closest vantage point. When they reach the top of the bank and see the coast is clear, they jump on and pedal hard through the low brush. When they reach the cans littering the desert they slow down enough to read the labels then speed away until they're several houses past LJ's. Skidding to a stop behind a shed in a back yard Stoney breathes heavily and waits for Logan to catch up.

"Did you see what it was?" Stoney asks after he catches his breath.

"It was Fossil beer."

Coughing, Stoney asks, "Why did they buy it then just throw it away?"

"My brother said they live like animals. Maybe that's what he meant," Logan replies quizzically.

"Animals don't buy beer stupid."

"I know. I didn't mean…" Logan's voice trickles off as he thinks about what he'd said.

"Let's go to your house," Stoney smiles at his discomfort.

As they ride towards landslide hill Logan observes, "That was a lot of beer."

"My dad says beer is really bad for you."

"Mine too. He says you can only drink a little or it can kill you."

As they cross the road a car speeds towards them but it isn't slowing. They hurry to the curb and watch it pass. Logan sees the man behind the wheel and whispers urgently, "C'mon, that's LJ's dad."

They chase the car the short distance to the corner. It slows for a stop sign then turns right towards LJ's street so they cut across a dirt field to gain ground. They reach the pavement on the other side first and watch it brake at the next stop sign. They are pedaling fast towards the stopped car when the passenger window rolls down. Logan coasts to a stop three houses away. The man is looking through the open window at him. Logan checks behind for Stoney who is already stopped a few feet back.

Stoney asks uneasily, "What's he doin'?"

Watching the man intently, Logan doesn't answer. He's waving at the boys trying to get them to ride over to the car.

Stoney knows the answer but asks anyway, "Are you goin' over there?"

"No friggin way," Logan's voice has a nervous edge. He turns his bike off of the pavement to get ready for flight.

The car turns in their direction so Logan rides into the middle of the field over the roughest rocks where a car can't drive then stops, looking back at the car and Stoney who is still struggling over the rocks. The man watches them through the passenger window. After Stoney reaches the rocks, the car backs into the dirt then turns around facing LJ's street. With his arm sitting on the driver's door the man idles down the street; looking over at the boys expectantly, then speeds up as he passes out of sight behind a fence. Logan drops his bike, runs back to the sidewalk and watches the car drive down the street then park in LJ's driveway. When he sees the man's head appear over the car roof he recalls the other times he has seen him and the connections he has been weighing become concrete.

He runs back across the rocks to his bike yelling at Stoney, "I knew it was him." Stoney is already pushing his bike over the rocks and yells back, "Lets get out of here!"

Logan grabs his bike and stumbles through the rocks until he reaches a path. He jumps on his bike, racing after Stoney. When they reach Landslide hill both boys are out of breath and coast down, gathering speed all the way. Although it is a blind corner they don't slow down to look for cars at the bottom and streak past the stop sign across the street. They take the shortcut through the houses onto Stoney's street then jump over the sidewalk through the yards onto Logan's street. They don't slow until they slide to a stop next to the pool in the back yard. They both fall to the ground on their backs, their sides heaving. A few minutes pass before Logan recovers and is able to sit up with his back against the pool and his arms wrapped around his knees.

Stoney leans back on his hands saying earnestly, "You *gotta* tell your dad now."

Pressing his pulsing side to lessen the sharp pain Logan replies, "I can't. He would *kill* me. Plus I told Josh I wouldn't."

Gagging as if about to toss his cookies Stoney implores, "You have to man. That was crazy. He was after us or something."

"I know, but my dad would be really mad at me."

"Why?"

Going against his judgment Logan tells him how he and Josh went inside LJ's house then adds, "We weren't stealin'. Josh was just checkin it out. You can't tell anyone."

After thinking for a minute and allowing the painful cramp in his side to subside further Stoney agrees, "You'd get in a whole lot of trouble if your dad knew about that."

Logan stands with his back flat against the pool then looks down at Stoney, "See I told you. I just have to tell Josh now. He'll know what to do."

He doesn't want his parents to see him so he takes the long way around the yard to Josh's bedroom window then knocks on the window frame, keeping watch for his parents at the same time. Josh opens the curtains and mouths, "What?"

"Come out here," Logan whispers while beckoning frantically with his hand.

Carol follows Josh out to the boys and asks Logan," Where have you been all afternoon?"

"Oh, we did my route and went down to the creek."

"Didn't your dad say you need to tell us where you're going?" she's obviously upset, her hands on her hips.

"No. He just said to have someone help me deliver the papers and don't leave the house unless I'm with somebody."

She glances at Stoney then repeats his words slowly as if she doesn't believe him, "As long as you're with somebody..." with a doubtful shake of her head she turns to go back in the house, "Just make sure you're never alone when you leave this house. Meet Stoney halfway."

"I will," Logan promises.

Josh leads them behind the garage where they can't be seen from the house then asks, "What's up?"

"I saw LJ's dad today. It *was* the same man, just like I said."

"Did you see him too?" Josh asks Stoney.

"Yeah, he followed us."

"What? What do you mean? How far did he follow you?"

Logan explains by saying, "He didn't chase us. He just followed a little ways and tried get us to go over by his car."

"Like to talk or something? Why would he do that?"

"I don't know. We chased him on our bikes and he must've seen us, because he stopped at the sign and watched us for a minute."

"You didn't tell dad did you?"

"You said not to," Logan answers defensively.

Josh sits on a stack of old wheels and absorbs the events, tying the information together while Logan and Stoney wait. When he doesn't say anything after a minute Stoney is unable to contain himself, "You know what else we saw them doing? LJ and Ben were smashing beer cans in the alley while their mom watched."

Nodding, Logan adds with a crooked grin, "Yeah, full cans. More beer than dad bought for our party on the Fourth of July."

Josh tilts his head forward, lowering his eyebrows in puzzlement as he asks, "Smashing beer cans? Why were they doing that?"

The boys look at each other shrugging.

"You guys look like the three stooges. I want you to show him to me soon. I'll tell you when. All right?" Josh asks as he checks around the side of the garage for his mother.

"What are you gonna do?" Stoney asks.

"I'll tell you later. Do you know where LJ and his brother hang out?"

With a shake of his head and quick glance at Stoney, Logan answers, "I've only seem 'em a couple times."

"Well if you see them around, come get me. I want to talk to them."

"What are you gonna ask them?" Stoney asks.

"Stop asking so many questions Moe," Josh pushes Stoney. As he gets up to walk in the house he reiterates, "If you see them, *don't* talk to them. Just tell me where they are."

Stoney waits until Josh is almost in the house and says as if it was a fact, "He's gonna get in trouble."

"For what?"

"I don't know. Sneaking around in other people's business is trouble." He shoves Logan with his forearm as he retorts indignantly, "You know what I mean!"

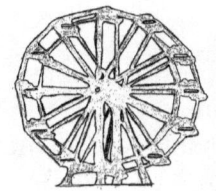

Twelve

Logan awakes to the wonderful smell of frying onions and pokes his head out his bedroom door, "Are you cooking potatoes?"

"No, I'm making meatloaf for your dad's lunch," Carol answers from the kitchen.

"Oh *man*, that smells so good, Logan claps his hands together in dismay.

Rob walks by Logan's bedroom, pushing the door open as he passes and orders, "You keep your mitts off my food."

Carol is slicing the meatloaf when Logan notices the empty kitchen table and asks, "What's for breakfast?"

"Cereal, toast and a banana," Rob answers tossing him a banana.

"Man!" Logan whines, dropping it to the table. "I wanted fried potatoes."

"You can't eat that for every meal, your veins will turn to glue," Carol remembers the heart attack her dad had last summer. *We're lucky he's still with us.*

"I know. It just smells so good."

The phone rings and Josh runs in to answer it then hands the phone to Logan disappointedly, "It's Stoney."

Logan listens for a second then asks, "Can Stoney come over for breakfast?"

Carol answers, "As long as he likes Cheerios."

Logan hangs up the phone and runs out the door shouting, "I'm meeting him at the end of our street."

Carol watches him ride his bike up the street and back with Stoney. When they come through the kitchen door she asks, "Rob, did you tell him to finish cleaning the pool?"

"Oh yeah. It looks a lot better this morning. He did fine, I'll take care of the rest after breakfast," Rob replies.

Sitting side by side, Logan pours the cereal while Stoney peels the bananas.

Carol slices strawberry into their bowls as she asks, "What are you planning today?"

"Ballsac's taking his cousin to the public pool and we're meeting him down there," Stoney answers.

"Why do have to call him that disgusting name?" Carol wrinkles her nose.

Stoney laughs nervously and Logan kicks his leg under the table, "Robert's cousin is here for the week so he wants to hang out."

Rob rinses his bowl in the sink and takes his lunch out of the fridge and Stoney says, "Hey my dad said we could go to the fair any day this week. He got free tickets from his work."

"Oh yeah. Can I go to the fair this week?" Logan asks Rob.

"Only if Josh goes with you."

Josh sets his glass on the table and wipes the milk from his mouth with his wrist, "Do you have a ticket for me?"

"My dad brought home a stack of twenty tickets."

"When do you want to go?" Josh asks, happy to have something to do that may take his reeling mind off of Lizzy for a while.

"Tomorrow night?" Logan asks.

Stoney nods, "That sounds good."

Josh taps the table emphatically with his index finger, "All right, I'll be here at six to pick you up. Make sure you're here."

Logan is surprised that it was so easy to get his dad to agree. He had overheard Carol telling Rob that she thought it would best if he didn't go anywhere until school started. She was even considering having him quit his paper route. He fought a long time to get it and although it's hard work, he doesn't want to give up the money. He kept his grades up even with the route, and feels he earned the right to have it. With an inner sigh of relief he watches his mom put the meatloaf in the fridge.

Thirteen

Logan and Stoney are locking their bikes in the rack when they hear Ballsac calling them from the pool. He's standing on the high dive waving his arms and when he is sure they are watching he flips off the end, waving comically as he flies head over heals. Stoney laughs at his antics and runs to the entrance slamming the seventy cents for their entry on the counter. They run across the rough concrete deck toward the diving boards. As they near Stoney yells at Ballsac, "Where's your towel at?"

Ballsac points behind the diving boards. They take their shoes and shirts off then pile their stuff on his. He climbs out of the pool holding his stomach then waits at the ladder for another boy. A bigger boy with a bundle of red hair follows him as he walks bent over, holding his stomach with both hands saying painfully, "Ow, ow, ow." When he reaches the towels he leans on his knees and introduces the new boy with a thin voice, "This is my cousin Will."

Logan sets his hand on Ballsac's back and asks, "What happened to you?"

"I tried to do a flip and a half off the high dive but only did one and a quarter and landed on my face."

Logan looks at his bright red stomach and chest and notices his pale face then says compassionately, "You should sit down for a second. You don't look so good."

Ballsac spreads his towel over the concrete and lies on his back shading his eyes with his forearm. Logan hears him muttering to himself and watches him shifting uncomfortably on the towel, "You want me to get a lifeguard?"

"No. Just leave me alone for a minute."

The boys stand in a small concerned circle around Ballsac's towel. His eyes are closed and he's holding back the tears, hoping he isn't really hurt bad. After a minute he sits up and rubs his forehead. "I'll be OK in a while. You guys go swim."

Logan wants to make sure Ballsac's going to be all right so he crouches next to him and urges the other boys, "I'll hang out with him while you guys swim."

Will climbs onto the low diving board; bounces up and down on the end then does a perfect back flip. Stoney exclaims in wonder, "Wow, how'd he do that?"

As Will climbs out of the pool Ballsac tells Stoney, "He's in gymnastics. That's all he ever does. He was teaching me to dive when I belly flopped."

The high dive is twelve feet above the water; when Will notices Stoney watching him he passes by the low dive for the high board to show off. Without hesitation he walks to the edge of the board, turns around and performs a backwards one and a half flip. Most of the boys don't flip off the high dive at all. Experiencing one bad landing or just *seeing* someone crash land is all it takes to deter a sensible boy. Stoney is impressed. He stands next to the low board and watches Will climb up and do a double flip.

"Can you show me how to do that?" Stoney asks while Will pulls himself out of the pool.

"Probably not that dive. But I can show you a different one."

"I can already flip," Stoney says proudly.

"Show me."

"I can only do it on the low dive," Stoney admits as he goes up the ladder. Backing to the end of the board he bends down then runs off the end, kicking his feet over his head ungainly. His arms and legs poke out at four different angles but he completes a full rotation and lands on his feet. Will smiles to himself but promises not to laugh.

"That's not too bad. It's easier if you go slower and bounce off the board then throw your arms forward and tuck your knees into your chest and grab them like this," Will demonstrates on the deck.

"Show me again."

In perfect form Will flips off the board and Stoney whistles in admiration, "That looks so cool. I can do it."

Stoney walks out to the end of the board and attempts to bounce neatly on the end like he saw Will do but doesn't throw his arms forward hard enough into his tuck. When he realizes he's going to land on his back he kicks his legs out and his back hits the water with a resounding splat. He climbs out of the pool with a grimacing look and stands next to Ballsac arching his back.

Ballsac smiles weakly at him, "It's not that easy huh?"

Stoney, feeling humbled, shakes his head and sits cross legged on his folded towel.

Putting on a clinic, Will executes competition level dives as the boys sit timidly watching. Logan has been studying his form and thinks, *"That doesn't look that hard. You just have to do it right."* He asks Will, "Can you show me what you showed Stoney?" then listens intently to the instructions and practices on the deck before he gets on the low dive.

As he climbs the ladder Ballsac yells out ruthlessly, "Another victim."

Will has a slight twinge of a smile when Logan looks down at him for support and says, "I hope this works."

Logan takes his time and practices his jump without diving off of the board. Stoney shouts, "He's gonna crash too, and we'll *all* be sitting her like, see no evil, hear nor evil and speak no evil."

"Shut up Stoney," Logan barks edgily.

A little smaller and more coordinated than the other boys Logan's flip is more successful, in that he doesn't land flat on his back. Thrilled with his modest success, he proudly runs back to the board and Stoney teases jealously, "Ooh you must have escaped from the circus!"

Logan ignores him and his second attempt is more passable. His confidence rises and his third attempt is better yet. He sits on his towel and tells Stoney, "You can do it. You just hurried too much," then urges him, "Try it again."

Not easily discouraged, Stoney arches his back tentatively, "It's not hurting so much anymore." He's doesn't take as much time as Logan did when he practices his jump; but he still does a better flip than his last one and is all smiles when he sits down shaking his hands like he'd just touched something hot, and says, "That was scary."

Logan and Stoney take turns off the board, and after few more tips from Will they aren't quite so close to experiencing excruciating pain with each attempt. Ballsac has gotten over the pain and has joined them but he is no longer willing to take the risks they are.

Several girls have been watching the boys from behind the lifeguard tower. When Stoney swims to the side one of the girls asks him, "Isn't that Josh's brother?"

He points at Logan, "Yup, that's Logan."

She approaches Logan timidly, "How is Josh?"

"He's fine."

"Where is he at, like right now?"

"He's at work till later," Logan answers, glancing at Stoney questioningly.

Noticing his confused expression Stoney tells him, "This is Karen, Lizzy's friend."

"Oh yeah, I remember you," Logan looks at her hair as he realizes how much the loose curls reminds him of Lizzy's.

She smiles and sits next to him on her towel. While they watch Will and Ballsac dive Logan keeps glancing at her hair. After a few minutes he notices her flushed cheeks and thinks, *she looks embarrassed*. She smiles again at his attention and asks quietly, "What's Josh been doing?"

"Just working, I guess."

"Is he going to the next dance?"

"Maybe," Logan replies then adds, "But we're going to the fair this week."

"Is Josh going too? When?" She asks quickly.

"Tomorrow night. He's drivin' me and Stoney. Yeah, he'll be there."

Karen lightly taps Logan on the wrist and whispers in his ear, "Tell Josh I said hi and that I'll be there too. OK?" After he nods, she rolls to her feet, adjusts her suit and smiles happily at him before she runs over to her friends.

Neither boy says anything but Stoney raises one eyebrow at Logan then announces, "I'm hungry."

The snack bar is run by twin sisters; one of them was in Stoney's class last year and she talks incessantly to him whenever she's around. When Stoney reaches the front of the line she says smoothly, "Hi Stoney."

Logan has sat on a picnic table and when Stoney turns around to see if he heard; Logan raises his eyebrow in return to settle the score. Stoney shakes his head, sticks his tongue at Logan and tosses a quarter on the counter, "Payday."

She puts two candy bars on the counter and explains with a flirting smile, "Today's special is two for a quarter." He checks the price on the menu behind her then turns away with an embarrassed half grin, "Thanks."

After tossing one of the bars to Logan he attempts a weak explanation, "She gave me two."

Logan knowing grin doesn't mask his satisfaction in Stoney's discomfort, "Aren't they fifteen cents apiece?"

Stoney nods, "Two for a quarter today, I guess" Smiling inwardly he opens his candy bar and glances back at the girl when she waves. Logan sees the subtle exchange and bumps into Stoney with his shoulder.

It reminds Logan of when Lizzy used to call on Josh. He can picture her deep blue eyes attentively watching Josh while he mowed the lawn. She used to be crazy at the basketball games. Every time Josh dribbled down the court she would scream insanely, "Go Josh! Go!" The peanuts stick in his tightening throat; his throat spasms and he lets out a short cough.

Stoney claps him on the back and a peanut shoots from his mouth, bouncing off his palm, "You OK?"

Wiping the moisture from his eyes Logan half fakes a grimace before replying, "Thanks. I was choking on a peanut."

They exit the snack bar and Logan spins to shoot his wrapper in the trash when he sees Karen again. He gives her a wave as they head back to the boards.

A group of girls younger than Logan are lined up on the edge of the pool watching Will flaunt his skills. Will has a big smile of satisfaction and is obviously aware of their attention. Stoney looks on with a sense of honest envy as the girls ooh and ah when Will double flips off the high dive. Stoney knows he can't compete with Will so he gets silly when he leaps off the high dive, spinning around sideways and kicking his legs. He unconsciously wanted the girls attention but their laughter makes him feel stupid; fortunately Ballsac helps relieve his pride by getting in the spirit, yelling, "Bonzai," as he streaks through the air kicking and waving his arms. Logan runs off right after him and splashes the lifeguard with his cannonball, earning a reprimand.

The girls are giggling at their antics when Will copies Ballsac, earning Stoney's greatest respect. The boys line up at the high dive ladder and Ballsac says loudly enough for the girls to hear, "I thought we were diving with James Dean for a minute." Of course Will thumps him in the kidney as he climbs the ladder.

Logan is judging the right jumping angle to soak the lifeguard when he hears yelling from the snack bar. Two boys are fighting outside the fence. They fall over the bike rack their arms flailing, and end up wrestling on the ground rolling over until one captures the advantage and holds the other down, punching his face. A lifeguard jumps the fence and pulls him off and gets kicked in the leg for his effort. The winner and another boy run down the sidewalk with the lifeguard chasing them. They jump the chain link fence into the high school baseball field then run around the other side of the pool, leaving the lifeguard in the dust. They have stopped running and are waving insolently to the lifeguard when Logan recognizes they are LJ and Ben.

Logan calls down to Stoney, "That's LJ!" then dives in and swims to the ladder, but Stoney is already on the board putting on an act. Logan doesn't want anyone to overhear so he waits at the pool side and urgently whispers, "Let's go get my brother."

Dunking his head to slick his hair against his head Stoney looks up at Logan, "Let's get him in a while. I'm having fun."

Logan follows him back to the diving board line and watches LJ and Ben throwing rocks at the football scoreboard. When Stoney is next in line to climb the ladder, he whispers, "Look they're getting away."

Stoney glances over at LJ then begs, "C'mon, just a couple more."

LJ and Ben break a glass bottle on the scoreboard then run behind the school building while Stoney jumps off the board and swims to the side. Logan slaps his thigh when they disappear and says disappointedly, "They're gone."

"Hang on. This will be my last one," Stoney runs to the line again.

Logan rolls his t-shirt on over his head; gathers their towels then stands at the gate by the snack bar waiting, however when Stoney climbs out of the pool, he runs back in line shouting, "One more. There's no one in line."

Exasperated Logan sighs and leans on the chain link and mutters, "Hurry up man!"

After he dives, waving his arms like a monkey, Stoney runs after Logan. The lifeguard yells in his mega-phone, "Walk please."

Walking in the herky-jerky motion of an Olympic walk racer Stoney follows Logan to the bike rack. Logan has already unlocked the bikes and is sitting on the rack putting on his shoes when Stoney exclaims, "That was fun man. Will is a *great* diver!"

"He is, but we have to hurry."

Stoney is still putting his shoes on when Logan gets on his bike and impatiently starts away. Stoney shouts, "Wait up."

"I've been waiting for awhile. Hurry up."

Stoney pushes his bike for a second then jumps on and follows Logan but can't keep up because he has such a big head start. He finally catches him after several blocks when Logan is waiting to cross a busy street.

Logan asks him angrily, "Why didn't you go when I asked you too?"

"I don't know. I was having fun. I'm sorry," Stoney admits regretfully.

It's still another mile and half to Logan's dad shop when a car honks behind them. Logan's uncle Larry swings his Corvette around the boys, who are riding down the middle of the street. Logan stops at his window, "Hi."

"You shouldn't be in the street. Where are you going in such a big rush?" Larry asks looking up at him.

"Dad's shop."

"It's pretty hot to be going so all fired fast, "Larry observes.

Logan nods and says, "Uh huh," giving Stoney a 'be quiet or your dead' look.

"I stopped you 'cause your dad told me to keep an eye out for you. Make sure you're stayin' out of trouble. So are ya?" he asks playfully.

"We're just hangin out. We're not doing anything wrong," Logan can't keep the defensive tone out of his voice.

Slapping his hand on the roof top Larry laughs lightly to reassure him, "Don't worry I'll tell your dad the coast is clear." He turns the radio up and smiles then shouts, "I'll see ya tonight," as he speeds away.

They've dried off and heated up from the fast pace, so they ride along slower. Stoney says, "No offense but your uncle's kinda nosy."

"He's just doing what my dad wants. My dad probably won't fix his car if he doesn't," Logan chuckles at the vengeful thought.

Suddenly a volley of oranges plops around them in the street. An extra ripe one splatters noisily on Stoney's back, tipping him over. He drags his bike under a tree. Logan follows and hides behind the tree trunk trying to find their assailants. Stoney sees feet and legs crouched behind a car on the other side of the street and yells, "I see you behind the car."

LJ stands and throws several more oranges—Ben's head and shoulders appear as he sets a box of oranges on the trunk and joins in. Defenseless, Logan and Stoney back further under the trees searching for an escape route then dash into the next yard, pushing their bikes under another tree. Seeing their prey about to escape, LJ and Ben run closer and cross the street, using a truck to hide their advance. Seizing the chance, Logan and Stoney rush down the sidewalk until Logan feels they are a safe distance then stop to look back. LJ throws a rock but it rolls past their feet harmlessly.

Stoney feels the sticky mess on his back and exclaims angrily, "Dang it! Let's go get your brother."

Logan watches LJ kick his brother in the rear then pick up his box of oranges and thinks, "*I wish I was stronger right now.*"

The ride to the shop has several steep hills that they have to climb and they're out of breath when they lean their bikes against the wall behind the building. Stoney takes his shirt off and rinses it in the bathroom while Logan finds Josh. He's bolting the new tires on the Chieftain. Logan taps him in the back and whispers urgently, "Out back. Follow me."

Josh looks around then follows Logan behind the garage.

Logan asks, "Where's dad?"

"He's out front changing some brakes. Why?"

"I just saw LJ. I know where he is right now. Can you get out of work?"

"Yeah, I'm done for today. I've just gotta mount these tires and I can leave."

Logan thinks for a second then says, "We'll meet you at home in a few minutes. OK?"

"This will take me ten minutes to finish 'cause I have to put the tools away and wash up. I'll be there in fifteen minutes or less."

Josh hurries through his work and speeds home, arriving in less than ten minutes. Logan and Stoney are greedily drinking ice water in the kitchen when he tosses his lunch bag on the counter and immediately asks, "You ready?"

They pile into the Chieftain and Logan directs him to the street where they received their pelting, but they drive around the block several times without finding the offenders. Logan doesn't want to give up and guesses, "I bet I know where they are. They were at the school earlier."

"The high school?" Josh asks turning the car around.

"Uh huh. By the pool."

Josh does a California roll at the next stop sign and although Logan wants him to hurry he cautions, "Don't get a ticket."

Checking his mirrors Josh replies carelessly, "They don't write tickets for that around here." He circles the swimming pool parking lot two times while looking across the football field then drives to the other side of the school into the teacher's parking lot. He stretches his neck over the steering wheel as he searches between the school buildings then turns onto the street towards the pool again and says, "Let's park at the pool and walk through the school."

As they pass the front of the school a lemon bounces off the driver's window. Josh slides the car to a stop and gets out. A hollow thump resounds as another lemon skids across the trunk lid leaving a trail of gunk. When another flies over the roof of the car he tracks it and points, "There they are." Leaving his car in the road with the driver's door open he runs across the school grass between the buildings.

Logan is right behind and sees LJ and Ben running past the cafeteria and shouts, "Over there!"

Josh turns around then yells, "Follow me," and runs back to his car. He spins it around in a tight circle then slides into the school parking lot with the tires screeching over the pavement. They search between the buildings as he heads toward the football field. The gate is shut so Josh jumps out and looks through the chain link. He spots LJ and Ben running across the football field toward the school's back fence, "Which one is LJ?"

Logan points, "The big one with the black hair."

"I think we can drive on the canal road behind the pool and catch 'em." The Chieftain's new tires squeal as Josh shoots sideways back onto the street from the school parking lot. He barely slows as he approaches the pool entrance. A gate blocks the canal road entrance, so Josh drives through the pool parking lot and jumps the curb; driving across the small grassy park past the picnic tables and onto the dirt road. Logan pushes his palms against the metal dash and watches Josh's hands jerk when the tires thump over the curb. As Josh spins the wheel hand over hand, Logan searches his brother's angry face and notes the tight skin over his clenched jaw. Logan feels like they are flying down the narrow canal road and uneasily watches the speedometer hovering at fifty-five. He watches the water rushing by outside his door then back at Stoney. Stoney's feet are braced against the back of the seat and his hands are gripping the bottom of the seat cushion as if his life depends on it; his body is in a tight knot and his face his clenched in worry. Out of the corner of his eye Logan sees the cloud of dust rising behind the car and yells apprehensively, "Slow down. That waters ten feet deep!"

The canal follows the curving fences of the baseball diamonds around the back of the school. They spot LJ and Ben running across the outfield, then watch as they begin to climb over the chain-link fence onto the canal road. Josh floors the accelerator. The Chieftain responds and rocks ding off the undercarriage as it slides sideways around the bend. Josh struggles with the wheel as the tires skid on the verge of the bank. LJ points at the looming car then dives into the murky canal and starts swimming across. Logan sees LJ waving at Ben and hopes that Ben's too scared to get in. As his brother reaches the other side Ben tries to wade in but the bank is steep and he falls, flopping on his face and starts swimming to the other side.

Ben is climbing the opposite bank when Josh slides the car to a stop and the trailing cloud of dust chases them over the water. All three boys jump out of the car but it's too late. On the other side of the canal LJ pulls Ben into a big mud puddle and they both slip and fall forward to their knees. They crawl through the muck leaving a trail like wounded frogs, quickly reach the other side then scramble over a fence into an old orange grove.

Josh slams his fist on his hood, "Damn it. I almost had them."

"I told you they're wacko," Logan remarks as Josh turns the car around and heads towards the pool.

Stoney asks warily, "You're not going to zoom down the road again. Are you?"

Josh checks Stoney's pale face in the rear view mirror and lifts his foot off the gas, "No. Sorry, I didn't mean to scare you."

"I wasn't scared. I just don't want to crash in the canal," Stoney uses the bravest voice he can muster.

Logan turns around in his seat and confirms, "I was scared. Bad."

"I was a little scared too when we were sliding on the edge. The back tires almost went off the edge," Josh admits as the car bumps into the parking lot.

Logan punches Josh in the arm, "The back tire over here was hangin' over the side."

"Well, we didn't fall in, so it's cool. Don't tell anybody about that. Dad would take my car away if he knew I was driving

like that," Josh says, then thoughtfully continues, "You know...,
he'd take it away if he knew we were on the canal road."

Logan points at Stoney, "He's the one that always says
stuff."

Josh meets Stoney's eyes in the mirror. Stoney stammers,
"Don't worry. My dad would ground me all summer and I'd never
be able to come over again. I'm not sayin nothin'."

They drive by Logan's paper station and he spots his papers
sitting on the curb, "I almost forgot about my route."

"You'll get grounded if the route master tells dad you're
late."

"I know. Can you drive me today?"

"OK. But you have to give me gas money this time," Josh
raps his fuel gage with his knuckles.

The papers are small—without inserts for once—and with
Stoney's help they deliver the papers in less than an hour. Logan
asks if he'll stop at the store to get his customary candy bar, so
Josh parks and waits in the car. When Logan picks up the latest
Matt Savage comic and opens the cover Stoney cautions him,
"You know, Josh is waiting."

"This is the new one. I just want to see what happens in the
beginning."

Stoney pours RC into a cup and looks out the window as he
sips it, "He's getting ready to come in."

Logan quickly drops the comic into the rack and jumps to
the window. Josh is still sitting there poking at the buttons on his
radio.

"Gotcha," Stoney laughs and runs around the counter to
avoid the retribution but Logan is staring out the window, standing
on his toes to see over the cigarette rack. Stoney asks, "What are
you looking at?"

"LJ's dad is out there," Logan cries, alarm covering his
face.

"You'd better not be kidding me," Stoney warns as he runs
to the window.

Parked right next to Josh, Baxter tosses his cigarette butt on the ground and looks nastily over at Josh before he gets out. Hitching his pants by a broken belt loop, he crushes the butt and spits over the hood of his car. His sweat stained t-shirt is partially tucked into the front of his jeans but rides high in the back exposing his Fruit of the Looms. One leg of his pants is tucked inside his cowboy boot and the other leg covers the top and drags behind the heel. The store window rattles when he slams the car door, startling Logan.

Logan drops to his knees behind the magazine rack dragging Stoney down with him and exclaiming, "Hide!"

"Where?"

With his fingers to his lips, Logan ducks as the door squeaks open. The clerk asks, "What's up Carl?"

"Not much. The wife got into the beer again," Baxter replies unpleasantly.

The clerk responds simply as if he's heard it before, "Yeah?"

The boys hear his boots clunk into the back of the store past the frozen food to the beer freezer. Logan is trembling but stands up anyway to risk a look. Baxter's back is to them, so Logan crouches and pulls Stoney by the shirt out the front door.

As the door swings shut the clerk calls out, "See ya later Logan." But Logan silently keeps his head down and drags Stoney around the passenger side of Josh's car. The car is running and Josh watches in amusement as they pass the hood. When they climb onto the floor behind the back seat he spins around, "What are you doing?"

"Turn around before he sees you!" Logan demands.

"What are you…," Josh begins but Logan whispers loudly, "Turn around now!"

Josh looks out the front window and Logan says, "He's in the store."

"Who?"

"LJ's dad! He's buying beer."

Josh watches the staggering man set a case of beer on the counter then walk to the door and look out as he talks to the clerk. He opens the door and walks to the end of the building, looking around the corner. When he passes the ice machine he draws his arm back and spins in a half circle then punches the machine's door. He glares at Josh before he walks past the hood to the other side of the building and disappears.

Logan asks quietly, "What's he doing?"

"Cussing like a mad man and punchin' stuff. He went behind the store. Shut up before he gets back."

"He's outside already?" Logan asks fearfully.

"*Shut up*! Here he comes."

Baxter stomps past the Chieftain and slaps the hood, giving Josh a fierce look through the windshield on his way back into the store. Josh's eyes narrow in boiling rage and he almost bolts from the car to confront the drunk.

While holding the door open with his boot-heel Baxter rambles in a loud demanding tone to the clerk and points to the back of the store then the street. Josh watches his angry expressions but can't catch what he's saying. A final irate glare covers his face as he searches the parking lot then takes his wallet out of his pocket and approaches the counter, tossing bills at the clerk's face. With an intolerant shake of his head, the clerk bends over and picks up the money then tosses the change over the counter, intentionally making it spill across the floor. Baxter drunkenly points his finger in the clerk's face, his voice getting louder with each shake of his fist. He lifts the case of beer with his other arm, kicks the change under the counter when he turns then leans his back against the door, slowly opening it as he blusters threateningly at the clerk. The clerk just waves and offers a fake smile. Finally he stops berating the clerk, staggers to the driver's door and tosses the box of beer across the car seat. He leans both arms against his roof, bloodshot eyes glowering under his protruding forehead as he searches the street.

Josh hasn't moved—he is beginning to sense what an evil person Baxter is—and is still looking at the fool with a defiant stare when their eyes meet. Baxter slaps his hands on the roof of his car and barks at Josh in a slurring sluggish voice, "What are you looking at, you ugly piece of shit?"

Josh challenges him with his stare. The drunk walks around the hood, stopping beside the driver's side view mirror on Josh's car. Josh is thinking Baxter looks like he can't figure out what year it is when he slobbers, "Did you see a bratty kid out here?"

When Logan hears Baxter's voice so close he tries to curl up as small as possible behind the seat. With his head rammed into the rails under the back seat he flinches every time he hears Baxter's voice.

Josh's respect for Baxter is one notch below a sewer rat. With fire in his voice he declares, "*I'm* a kid."

Frowning in confusion Baxter tries to absorb the response, the wheels slugging slowly through the thickness of years of misuse.

Shaking his head Baxter dumbly tries to explain, "No, there was a kid in the store, he came out here. Did you see him?"

Josh pretends to look around, "Nope. No kids out here."

"You're as useless as a bent dick, just like that damn clerk," Baxter says staggering and falling against Josh's car. Alcohol has been in charge of his small brain and big mouth since he was a young teen; aside from the car crash that knocked out one of his knees, the other was blown out in a bar fight by the business end of a baseball bat when he was in his early twenties. He blames most of his self induced troubles on his inability to get around.

"Why don't you get off my car you stupid drunk," Josh orders sharply.

"Shut your damn pie-hole. You're just a punk," Baxter replies vehemently with an angry frown, drawing up to appear dangerous.

"A punk and a drunk. You should get lost before you get arrested, you piece of human trash," Josh responds tit for tat. He turns his head to take a breath from within the car to avoid the sickening smell of body odor.

The drunk looks at the cars passing on the road then at the clerk as if debating then says with a foolish grinning frown, "This is you're lucky day. I'm not gonna stomp your ass out here on the pavement."

Josh has seen his inability to stand and isn't afraid of Baxter's blusters. With a menacing chuckle he points at Baxter's face, "Just try it. You're about as scary as a pile of turds."

He starts toward Josh but catches his toe under the front wheel, tangles his feet and topples forward next to the driver's door; his face bounces off the greasy asphalt with a resounding clonk. Josh opens the door to get out but stops when Logan whispers, "What happened?"

Josh cracks the door and looks down suspiciously at the drunkard's unmoving body, "I guess I beat him up. He fell on his face right here."

Josh opens the door and pushes the fallen man's leg with his foot. He pushes again and the drunk's leg slowly rolls over.

Josh laughs wonderingly, "He's knocked out."

"Let's go before he gets up!" Logan demands, scrambling to the seat.

The car is already running so Josh backs up but accidently on purpose runs over the drunk's hand with his front tire muttering, "Oops," quietly under his breath.

As they drive he begins to feel a twinge of guilt and admits to Logan what he did, "I feel kind of evil."

Stoney giggles, "He deserved it. He wanted to fight you."

"I know," Josh agrees remorsefully.

Still nervous, Logan blows a big sigh to relax and asks, "Were you going to fight with him?"

"Yeah I was. But I don't think it would have been much of a fight. He's just a drunk and couldn't even stand up."

Logan sits pensively while Stoney giggles and claps Josh on the shoulder excitedly, "You took him out. That was so great."

Josh admits, "In reality, Mister Carl Baxter took himself out. But it felt great anyway."

"How do you know his name?" Stoney asks.

"I just do. Hey, you guys need to keep your mouth shut about all this stuff. We could get in big trouble," Josh knows what his dad would do if he found out. He got in trouble one time freshman year, for smart mouthing a teacher, and he was grounded for a month and his dad made the basketball coach bench him for the entire time. If something like this ever came up there's no telling what kind of hot water he'd be in.

"I swear not to say a word," Logan promises quickly.

Stoney doesn't say anything so Logan slaps his leg, "Well..., what about you?"

"Hey that was really scary. I'm not telling anybody a thing," Stoney pledges with sincerity.

"That *was* scary. But it's not over yet," Josh's voice shakes with determination and anger.

Logan has never seen Josh act so aggressively and never would have believed he would treat an adult like this. He tells himself that it's all right though because Baxter is such a crazed drunken fool and started it anyway, but he doesn't begin to relax until they turn onto their street and there isn't anyone following them.

Fourteen

With the new load of parts delivered this morning Josh has worked hard unpacking and organizing the stores shelves but his mind has been spinning in high gear the entire time. He has tried to focus on his work but no matter how hard he tries to push it from his thoughts, he keeps remembering Lizzy jumping on the seat of the basketball stands holding her fist over her head in triumph and screaming "Go Josh!" her rapturous deep blue eyes meeting his for an instant as he dribbles past, inspiring him to push harder. Like a home movie playing out in his mind, the rush of joy and love he felt at that moment begins to build again then lodges in his heart, twisting into a lump of evil lifelessness that threatens to destroy the fabric of his soul. He'd never even realized that he had such strong emotions until Lizzy was already gone and he can't imagine what life will be like without her. The drive he felt when she was with him feels dead and wilted like the flowers he left on her grave.

Josh lifts the dead battery from the old car, lining it up on the shelf with all the others waiting to be picked up by the battery refurbishing company. Acid has leaked on his hands so he washes them off with detergent and is drying them when Rob asks, "What time do you need to leave today?"

"Since its opening day, the fair doesn't open till six so I'm picking Logan up at five."

"You need to finish up that car and the black Ford parked by the dumpster before you leave."

"What's wrong with the Ford?"

"The water pump or the thermostat is out."

Josh calculates how long it will take him to finish both cars then asks, "Will it be OK if I leave about four-thirty?"

"As long as the work is done right and you've cleaned the tools before you put them up. You left grease all over the torque wrench Monday," Rob reminds him.

"I will," Josh pledges sheepishly.

Rob is rebuilding the carburetor out of a fifty-four Ford pickup. Josh hovers behind him for a minute before Rob realizes he's there. With a glance up he says, "You need to keep an eye on Logan tonight."

"OK."

"You know how he is. He'll run all over the place, not payin' attention to anybody. You could lose them easy in the crowds."

"I'll make sure they don't run off," Josh promises. Last year Josh's family went to the fair together and his parents had asked him to stay with Logan while they watched a show; but he had let Logan take off while he hung out with Lizzy and her friends. Rob had found Logan climbing the scaffolding of the super slide. At four stories high, it's advertised as the biggest drop in the western states, and they luckily stopped Logan and Stoney before they got dangerously high. Josh was grounded for a week after that.

"There's some kind of insane person prowling around. You can't let me down," Rob taps the workbench emphatically.

Josh nods thoughtfully as he remembers the solid sound of Baxter's face bouncing off the asphalt and the sight of LJ flogging through the mud. He is one hundred percent confident that the police are wrong and Logan did see Lizzy riding in their truck and wants to talk to his dad about it but he's not sure how to approach him.

Bending over the carburetor, Rob changes his angle slightly to get at a screw he's adjusting and sees Josh's feet still behind him, "You keep standing around like that and you'll never get the work done."

Josh takes one step away then stops, standing sideways, and blurts out, "You know what dad? I think Logan did see Lizzy in that truck with LJ."

Rob frowns quizzically as he faces Josh, "The police investigated everything already. What makes you think that?"

Josh rubs his hands together anxiously while trying to sound confident, "Logan doesn't lie about important stuff."

"Did he say something to you that he didn't tell me or the police?"

Josh hesitates, knowing that Logan did tell him more, yet he doesn't know how to tell Rob without revealing the things he would prefer to keep secret, "I don't think so."

"Well..., maybe you're right and the police are wrong but there's nothing we can do about it."

"What if we went over, you and me, and talked to them. Like talk to their dad and then talk to LJ?" Josh suggests eager to have his dad involved.

"That's the job of the police not us." Rob takes a deep breath and watches Josh for a moment then continues. "Look Josh, everybody loves Lizzy and I know you miss her. I know it's too soon, but you will have to try to put this behind you at some point."

Josh's cheek twitches and he rubs it with his palm as tears pool in his eyes. His face distorts as he tries to hold back the rush of grief, "Dad, *I can't stand it.*"

Rob leans forward and rubs Josh's back softly with his clean hand. His voice cracks, "I'm sorry Josh." Forehead to forehead they close their eyes until Josh's sobs diminish but not his pain.

"Can't we do anything?" Josh implores, taking a deep breath and drawing away.

"I don't know what we could do. The police already talked to them."

Josh almost tells his dad what he's seen but stops himself and stutters, "I, I wish there was. We could just talk to them to make sure."

"Stay away from them and let the police do their job," Rob orders using a serious tone, aiming his screwdriver at Josh for effect.

Josh nods as Rob bends back over his work. Rob listens to Josh's sighing as he shuffles to the battery rack then watches him select one for the car he is working on. As Josh drops the battery in Rob thinks, *We need to get away for a few days.* He promises himself to talk to Carol about going camping. *Maybe Larry and Ginger would like to go too.*

Fifteen

When Josh parks in the only remaining spot in the row, Logan slams the car door and runs towards the fair entrance. Josh and Stoney are just getting out and he's five rows of cars away when he yells impatiently back, "Will you hurry up, the show starts in fifteen minutes."

Logan's friend, Jesse, told him that he is competing in a comedy contest at six-fifteen. He's not your typical silly class clown and his jokes keep everyone in stitches, even the teachers love him and Logan can't wait to see him on a real stage. The show has already started when they arrive at the amphitheater and Logan is happy to see Jesse still waiting his turn at the side and pushes into the crowd at the front of the audience.

A mime is on the stage pretending to play baseball and runs back and forth playing every position. Her outfit is wild, orange overalls, green over sized tennis shoes and a bright green plastic wig. Spinning a goofy pirouette she falls with her legs crossed and meets Logan's eyes. She pretends to be captured by his gaze and smiles at him sweetly with her interlaced hands under her chin. She waits for his face to turn the darkest shade of red then flickers her eyelashes, blowing him a kiss. Encouraging the audience to applaud for Logan, she dances away leaving him embarrassed. She tortures another boy by tossing him a baseball painted red then playing hot potato. He tries to throw it back to her but she pretends her hands are burning and knocks it back to him, making unbelievably extravagant expressions of pain mixed with happiness. Logan hopes Jesse can be as funny but knows she's a pro. The prize is a twenty dollar gift certificate to the bike shop and Jesse's bike tires are shot. She gets back to her baseball game when the boy's discomfort is at its peak leaving him flabbergasted and holding the ball. She winds up for her pitch then throws in fast motion. Running across the stage in slow motion she holds a ball beside her as she pretends to pass it. Her face is stark white and her lips are painted bright green from ear to ear making her face look wide and flat. She twists her lips from various stages of frightening grimaces to hilarious grins as she swings a plastic bat in slow motion at an imaginary ball. She jumps in the air with each swing and throws her head back in mock exasperation then spins her last swing and drops onto her back in exhaustion. Everyone stands to applaud and Logan plugs his ears to block out the earsplitting cat-call whistles from the boys behind him.

When Jesse takes the stage he is too nervous and stumbles clumsily through his routine. Logan usually laughs at everything that comes out of his mouth but he just isn't that funny today. Jesse's face has flushed bright red and when a boy at the back of the audience boos, he flounders halfway through a joke and walks off the stage. Logan feels sorry for him and watches as he stands next to the mime, shrugging at his mom as if to say, "Sorry." His mom waves her support.

Logan pulls Stoney by his shirt, "C'mon Stoney. That was pretty bad."

They pass the super slide and Stoney notes with intentional irony, "They covered the back with chain link this year. You can't climb it without jumping the fence."

"No way," Josh tugs on Stoney's shirt collar.

Spooky music from the haunted house draws their attention; as they pass Logan stops to take in the ghoulish scene. Next to the fence a worn out mechanism that creates the movement of a flopping ghost rotates slowly, making a decrepit clicking and humming sound as if on its last leg. A witch's arm is supposed to stir a cauldron of smoking brew, but her arm is broken off at the shoulder; hanging below the bottom of the cardboard cauldron it jerks spastically. The painted plywood fascia is dull with greasy dirt, losing the intended effect. He watches the artificial smoke rolling out the entrance and thinks about the disrepair. He wonders how he could have been so scared when they went through it last year. With a quiet, "hmm," he decides it's too cheesy and says, "Let's do that later, after dark. It's not scary during the day."

Stoney stops at a booth and gets change for a dollar then throws dimes at the worthless little plates, hopelessly trying to win one. After he has thrown twenty dimes and hasn't won anything Logan reflects his amusement, "What are you going to do with one of those?"

"My dad can use it for an ashtray," Stoney digs another dollar out of his pocket.

"A two dollar ashtray?" Logan hints.

"I get it," Stoney wads the dollar into his palm as the carnie looks on with interest.

As they walk away she stands on a bucket and teasingly offers to their backs, "Don't leave the best deal in town! Fifteen shots for a dollar."

As if drawn by a magnet Stoney starts back, but Logan drags him away by the shoulder scornfully saying, "You can buy a plate like that at the five and dime for twenty-five cents."

A group of boys are shooting basketballs a few booth's away. Josh stops to talk to them and they wait at his side while he blathers with his friends about work and girls. The bright pictures of snow cones on a crushed ice lemonade stand draw Stoney's attention. He announces, "I'm thirsty."

They get in line and watch as Josh takes his turn shooting the basketball. Josh has made two shots in a row when the food attendant barks out, "You're next. What d'ya want?"

With a patch over one eye and long speckled grey beard that nearly drags the counter he wipes the scratched metal with a rag that looks like it's been used to clean a barn. He grunts at Logan through the greasy window, "Yeah?"

"Popcorn and lemonade," Logan answers, thinking he looks like a retired pirate, a pirate that didn't quite have enough treacherous ability to survive the lifestyle of a real seaman but still wears the outfit as if it is a badge of honor. The pirate leans on the rag and Logan reads a tattoo on his hand, "WOW". He wonders why a person would do that to themselves and is mouthing WOW to Stoney when the pirate slaps a fly out of his face. The tattoo reads MOM from that angle, he grins subtly at Stoney and quietly whispers, "MOM".

Stoney grins back, waving his money over Logan's shoulder, "Me too, popcorn and lemonade."

As the pirate pushes the boxes over the counter Stoney asks, "Can I get butter on mine?"

The pirate reaches through the window and sucks the money out of Stoney's hand with a sour grimace, "They got it already." He slaps the change down and yells over Stoney's head, "You're next. What d'ya want?"

Stoney jambs his popcorn in the crook of his arm and pops a straw between his teeth so he can stuff the change in his pocket, then follows Logan to the basketball stand.

The basketball attendant energetically rings a bell and dangles a small bear over Josh's head while the other boys cheer. The parking lot lights flicker on around the fair, creating dim shadows on the walkway as the attendant hands the bear to Josh and yells for all to hear, "One more try and you get one of the big ones." He slaps one of the big bears hanging overhead to make it swing then holds his palm out to Josh.

One of Josh's' friends tosses a dollar on the table and encourages him, "Do it Josh. Show him."

The attendant picks the dollar up and tries to give it back, "He has to pay for his own turn. Save your money for your turn."

"No he doesn't. I'm not playin. Just let him shoot," the boy pushes the attendants hand away.

Folding the dollar into his roll the attendant looks dumbly at the size of the excited crowd and mutters bitterly, "Just this once. Go ahead and shoot kid."

Spinning the ball in his fingertips Josh smiles and raises his arms to stimulate the crowd. He plays guard on the high school basketball team and knows he can make it every time. When he makes the first shot everyone screams approval and the carnie catches the ball with a shout, "Hey, hey, look at the winner, winner, winner. He's goin for the big prize."

He tosses the ball to Josh who catches it like he's receiving a pass and shoots it without hesitation. The ball drops through the net without touching metal. As the crowd applauds, the attendant uses a long pole to take down a bear then tosses it high in the air as he yells, "A winner. A winner. Everybody look at the winner." He blows a kazoo and takes the little bear from the counter then throws the big bear into the air one last time over Josh's head. Josh catches it with both hands as his friends pat him on the back in overzealous congratulations and crowd around.

The attention makes Josh happy though and he leads Logan and Stoney around the fair passing the booths with a big infectious smile. As he nears another coin tossing game the carnies call out, "Hey winner give it a try over here," but Josh isn't interested in the foolish games. He shakes his head as Stoney, to the delight of the carnie, throws another dollar away and tells him, "You should save your money and play the games you can win. There's better prizes than that anyway."

Stoney protests vigorously, "I'm just having fun. I have fifteen dollars my dad gave me."

Logan stops in front of the house of mirrors and admires the red and blue flashing lights against the dark sky. "Let's do this, it looks cool."

When Josh enters the gate the attendant stops him and motions him to throw the bear to him, "You can't take that in." Josh tosses it over the counter and the man stuffs it on a shelf. He runs after Logan and Stoney, trying to catch them before they disappear. As he turns at the first finger printed corner Logan jumps in his face and yells, "Boo!" He shoves Logan with a loose laugh and they chase Stoney through the warped plastic maze until they reach the exit. When they leave Logan has to remind him, "Get your bear man."

Carrying it on his shoulders like his dad used to carry him; Josh follows them to the next booth where Stoney is already listening to a carnie, as if he's divulging the secrets of the universe. Josh stops behind Stoney and points at his back, smiling spitefully at Logan who nods. Swinging the bear hard by the feet like he's having a pillow fight, he hits Stoney several times. Stoney swings his arm behind to block the blows and yells in an annoyed voice, "Hey! Knock it off."

As Josh swings the bear onto his shoulders a girl taps him on the shoulder timidly, "Josh?"

"Hey Karen."

"Hi Josh. What are you doing?" she makes a poor attempt at seeming surprised to see him.

"Just hanging out with my brother."

"Oh really? I saw him at the pool and he said you were coming to the fair. Did he tell you I was coming?" she asks without looking at Logan.

He shakes his head as they watch Stoney. When he sticks his hand in his pocket for another dollar Josh calls out impatiently, "Stoney. Come over here."

Josh pushes Stoney down the bright midway and orders firmly, "Let's go do something else."

Stoney pulls away, protesting avidly to Logan but when he doesn't receive any sympathy he walks ahead. Josh and Karen follow with her two friends trailing behind.

Karen asks coyly, "What have you been doing lately?"

"Working with my dad and at the store a couple days. What have you been up to?"

"Swimming and being bored. I'm glad the fair finally started."

Karen bumps into his arm with her hand and smiles sweetly at him when he glances down. Logan and Stoney have stopped to talk to a group of boys so Josh sits on the wrought iron fence in front of the haunted house; she stands shyly in front of him while her friends wait off to the side patiently. Her blond hair flows over her shoulders in ringlets reminding Josh of Lizzy's hair. It's a little darker but the cut is exactly the same. He looks in her eyes but while her smiling green eyes are beautiful they aren't Lizzy's. He looks away to conceal his thoughts and watches Jesse animatingly waving his arms as he entertains the group. Stepping back to avoid Jesse's hands, Logan laughs and Josh overhears Jesse say that he locked up on stage because he was scared.

Logan looks around, finds Josh and starts in his direction. Jesse follows, holding out his participant award while exuberantly announcing, "I'm a winner!" When Jesse sees Josh he adopts a deep radio voice and says, "Cool bear man."

"I don't know what I'm going to do with it," Josh flips it over his head by the feet, letting it hang down his back.

"I bet it will barely fit in your car," Jesse says dramatically. When no one laughs he pokes his head forward asking, "Get it? *Bearly*, fit in your car?"

Logan smiles but no one laughs out loud so Jesse points at the bear's duff and says with a big vaudeville grin, "Look! A *bear* bottom."

Logan laughs and claps Jesse on the back but Karen is puzzled, "I don't get it."

Karen's friend explains to her as they start to walk again. Josh still has the memory of Lizzy's eyes dancing in his head. He wishes she were here then an uncontrollable flash of heartache causes him to grimace and shudder. He drops the bear on the pavement next to a cotton candy machine as he mutters crossly in a quiet voice, "I don't need that stupid thing."

Logan picks it up as he passes and runs to catch up, "What'd you do that for?"

"I'm tired of carryin' it," Josh answers casually, turning his head away and wiping the unexpected moisture from his eyes.

"I'd like it," Karen offers trying hard not to sound hopeful.

Logan hands it to Josh who flips it over his shoulder again and asks, "Are you sure? It's heavy."

She looks at it and smiles prettily, "I don't care. It's nice." He hands it to her and she cuddles it, giggling happily. A restrained smile touches Josh's mouth as she shows her friends and they whisper together. A comfortably familiar feeling washes over him and for a few moments his mind swings Lizzy's memory aside. Stepping next to Karen he tries to interrupt and tell her that they're going down the midway but her laughter causes him to stay.

Weary of the romancing, Stoney tugs on Logan with obvious annoyance, "Let's get going."

Logan follows Stoney to another game and is about to tell him what a rip off it is when someone bumps him hard from behind. He tries to step onto the low stand but catches his toe and trips head first over it, landing on the carnie's legs on the other side. The carnie lifts him with one dirty hand, by the elbow and asks, "What are you doing sonny?"

"I didn't do it. He pushed me," Logan responds in an irritated voice as he searches for his assailant.

LJ glares defiantly at him from the other side of the stand, his hands on his hips. Ben smiles greedily over LJ's shoulder, knowing what his brother is up to.

The carnie taps Logan's shoulder, "You running the show now? Or just visiting?"

Stoney follows Logan's glare to the awaiting thugs then grabs his money and jostles away through the crowd to find Josh. Logan steps on the counter and quickly looks over the bobbing heads for Josh before he steps down on the other side to face LJ and Ben.

"I thought you were staying all night. Thought we had some new help. You not stayin' to work?" the carnie continues his worthless incessant jesting.

With one eye on LJ, Logan tries to shuffle into the crowd but LJ grabs his wrist tightly as he greedily commands, "You're staying right here."

Surrounded on both sides Logan knows he's in trouble. He glances around for Stoney's help, "What do you want?"

"Come with us and we'll show you," LJ twists his arm behind his back as Ben grabs his other wrist. Logan drags his feet as they yank him through the crowd then stumbles over someone's foot and his knee cap bangs on a sharp rock. He cries out in pain and hops on one leg, making it easy for them to draw him behind a food vendor's cart. LJ trips him to the ground and Ben intentionally kicks his injured knee. He grabs Ben's heel with one hand and his toe with the other, twisting until Ben falls. With a malicious laugh, LJ kicks his arms and punches the back of his head to break his grip loose.

Mixed distantly within the sounds of the carnie's calls and the crowd's noise Logan hears Stoney yelling his name. He lashes out at LJ with his feet but LJ jumps aside and Ben grabs his arms from behind. LJ kicks his shins and thighs then punches his kidney cruelly before Logan is able to defend himself by blocking with his forearm.

Stoney's voice is getting closer now. Josh and Karen's voices are still further away but calling loudly. He yells, "Help Stoney! Get Josh."

Stoney's face appears behind the window of the food cart. Ben tries to cover Logan's mouth but he squirms and stomps on the arch of Ben's foot yelling, "Get Josh now!"

Stoney's face disappears. Logan hears him calling Josh's name as LJ kicks him with the toe of his boot in the side and Ben brutally twists his arms behind his back. Logan kicks uselessly at LJ then lowers his hips and drives Ben backwards into a light pole. Ben's head bounces off the metal with a satisfactory clang.

Suddenly Josh runs around the cart and sees LJ drawing back to kick Logan's face. Roaring in anger he rushes into LJ before the kick is released. As they roll across the ground Stoney throws Ben off of Logan. Ben crawls away while Stoney and Karen help Logan to his feet. Crouched behind a trash can Ben watches Josh and LJ fight. When he realizes LJ is completely overmatched he runs into the crowd.

LJ fights unfairly and elbows Josh viciously in the head. Surprised by the tactic, Josh punches him then tackles him again. As he blocks the blows from below Josh pushes away and stands, waiting for LJ to get to his feet again.

Crawling backward LJ yells, "I'm gonna get you," then jumps to his feet ready to fight. He charges at Josh and Logan yells, "Take him Josh!" but Josh steps aside, tripping LJ and shoving him on the back so he sprawls to his face.

Ben suddenly appears yelling, "Over here! Over here!" Baxter strides up in a rage and yells, "What the hell is goin on here?"

Josh moves bravely in front of Logan and Stoney while Karen cowers at his side holding his arm fearfully.

When LJ sees Josh's attention is away from him and watching Baxter, he runs in and punches Josh in the ribs then jumps away looking up at his stepdad expectantly. Baxter shoves LJ aside and he bounces off Ben. He points his bandaged hand at LJ, "I asked what's goin' on."

"These guys started a fight with us," LJ lies.

"We didn't start the fight. You grabbed Logan and started beating him up," Stoney yells pointing at LJ.

"You liar! We had an orange fight and you guys lost so you got your brother after us," LJ lies again looking up at his step dad quickly.

Holding his ribs with one hand Josh steps forward while pushing Karen behind him with the other. He contradicts LJ in a weakened voice, "You're a bunch of liars. You threw lemons at my car and then ran off like the criminals you are."

Staring at Josh as if he is trying to recall his face Baxter warns him, "Leave these two alone or you'll find more trouble than you ever thought possible."

"What are you gonna do? You're just a drunken buffoon!" Josh's voice is filled with venom as air returns to his lungs.

Surprise crosses Baxter's face as he rubs the purple knot over his eye, "You're that smart ass kid from the store aren't you?"

Josh nods and mimics him, "You're the drunk who can't stand on his own two feet."

LJ stares at Josh with his mouth agape—he's only back-talked his stepdad one time—and rubs his forearm unconsciously where it had been broken. He steps out of the way, ready to watch Josh go down hard.

As Baxter moves forward Josh tempts him by asking insolently, "What happened to your hand?"

"None of your business you little smart ass," he growls angrily reaching for Josh's face.

"Hey! What's going on here," a policeman shouts out as he unexpectedly steps between them to grab Baxter's raised arm. He twists it behind Baxter back and shoves him away. Baxter starts to retaliate then, through the evil fog that filters his thoughts, somehow realizes who is controlling his arm and lowers his hands placing them on his hips.

Holding his hands up to stop both Josh and Baxter, the policeman demands, "Can someone tell me what is going on?"

Stoney points at LJ and yells, "He started beating up Logan and his dad tried to attack Josh."

Everybody starts talking at once and the policeman shouts aggressively, "Hold on. Everybody be quiet."

He points at Josh and says sternly, "You. Tell me what happened."

"Those guys started beating up my brother when I wasn't there. I ran over to stop them and he," pointing at LJ, "was trying to kick my brother, so I knocked him down. He wouldn't stop fighting when I tried to make him. That's it."

"That's enough. What was going on between you and the man?" the policeman asks.

"I don't know how he got here, he just ran up or something. He was drunk at the store the other day and we had an argument and he was trying to fight me," Josh ignores Baxter's potent glare.

The policeman turns to Baxter as he furrows his eyebrows questioningly and asks, "Well…, what happened?"

"This troublemaker is picking on my step kids here," Baxter answers stupidly, his arms crossed tightly over his chest.

The cop shines his light in Baxter's face and moves closer, "What do you mean?"

"I was rounding up the trash by the farm exhibits and my stepson Ben told me that LJ was getting beat up. So I came over here and this rat bastard was beating up my kid."

"Rat bastard huh? That's probably not the best way to refer to someone's teenage son," the policeman raises one eyebrow thoughtfully.

After a minute of silence he turns to Josh and says, "Well everybody is calmed down now. You boys go enjoy the fair. But…" he warns, "Stay out of trouble. Next time you're outta here."

Josh wraps his arms around Karen and Logan then ushers everyone around the food cart. As he rounds the corner he glances back and hears the policeman asking Baxter, "Are you on the maintenance crew? Have you been drinking?" Baxter eyes track Josh hatefully through the greasy glass of the venders cart as he answers the policeman.

While they jostle through the crowd Stoney keeps asking Josh if he's all right but Josh doesn't answer and directs them half way across the fair before he stops to allow them to talk. Logan sits on a bench and rolls his pants leg up as they gather around him. His shin is dented from the hard toes of LJ's boots. Just above his knee a bruise is already forming where he was kicked several times and blood is oozing where the rock punctured his knee.

Josh kneels to look at his leg, "Are you hurt bad?"

"It hurts a lot but I'm OK," Logan winces as Josh lifts his leg by the heel.

Karen lifts his shirt to look at his side and says compassionately, "Ow. It's all red. That must really hurt."

Logan elbows her hand away and pulls his shirt down. He touches his side gingerly with his fingertips and agrees, "Yeah, stop touching it. It does."

Leaning forward Josh lifts Logan's shirt and his eyes narrow, "Lemme see that." Logan's side has a square red welt surrounding a deep imprint. Josh examines it closely then says in a dumbfounded tone, "Those guys are insane. Metal or something super hard made that mark."

Josh raises his own shirt and asks Karen, "Does my side have that same shape?"

She scrutinizes his side then compares the bruise to Logan's, "It's identical. What it is?"

"I think LJ was using brass knuckles," he replies wryly.

She looks at him then up at Logan curiously, "What are brass knuckles?"

"It's a piece of metal that you hold like this. It covers your knuckles like a metal fist," he slides his fingers over his fist.

Stoney's keyed up and claps his hands together, "I bet that's what it was. Those are bad news."

Logan rubs his head and looks at his fingers, "Hey, my head is bleeding!" He bends forward while Josh inspects his head carefully.

"There's a bump and a small cut that's bleeding. You don't need stitches or anything," Josh says reassuringly, shaking his head in disbelief.

"They must be in a gang," Stoney declares fervently,

Karen slides her arm around Josh's back and touches his chest lightly with the other as she intently watches his face, "You're shaking and really white. You'd better sit down."

He sits next to Logan and leans his head back then bends forward, rubbing his forehead with his fingertips. Karen scratches his back softly as she bends over him. She asks gently, "You want me to get you some ice?"

"I dunno. Maybe. I'm a little dizzy," he replies resting his face in his palms.

"I'll get it," Stoney runs to a food vendor's booth. When he returns Josh is sitting up with Karen on one side and Logan on the other listening to her tell her friends what happened.

Stoney holds the ice out but Josh tells Logan, "Put this on your head to make that knot go down."

After wrapping the ice in a paper napkin Logan holds it on the back of his head and grimaces, "That's really sore."

A group of Josh's basketball friends see them resting on the bench and surround them, asking what happened. Karen tells the story while Stoney interrupts continuously to fill in the details. Boys love to show how tough they are and whenever a friend has been victimized they grow even more loud-mouthed. Several of them vow to find LJ and get revenge for Josh. Josh appreciates their support but is amused because he knows they're just talking big and would only threaten LJ, if they ever caught him. His friends slowly dissipate into the fair leaving their small group alone again.

Karen's friends are getting bored and urge her to leave with them but she delays by asking, "Why don't we all go to the haunted house now?"

Logan tests his knee and announces, "It's a lot better now. I'm ready if you are," he looks questioningly at Josh.

Trying to sound cheerful Josh replies, "Lets do it.'

Stoney runs ahead then stops when he realizes Logan isn't with him. He waits for them to catch up and is about to ask Logan why he is going so slowly when he notices him limping. He asks instead, "I thought you said it was better?"

Bouncing lightly on his toes Logan answers with a short flinch, "Give me a minute to warm it up." By the time they reach the haunted house he feels ready to test it and trots into the entrance with Stoney. Karen's friends are already inside and jump out of the dark scaring them. Logan waits inside the entrance for Josh. When he doesn't come in after a minute Logan sticks his head out and finds Josh sitting at the exit with Karen. With an amused smile he follows Stoney who's screaming like a werewolf on the prowl as he chases the girls.

Even though it's been over an hour since the attack, both Logan and Josh are still subdued and Karen's friends and Stoney are beginning to get tired of waiting for them. Circled around the weight guessing carnie, Stoney just had his weight guessed correctly. Login loves the way the carnie's tempt with their cut-rate prizes but he likes to barter with them to get extra chances even more. When the clown is unable to guess Logan's weight correctly after two tries, he slides a pencil with a cheap star eraser across the counter. Logan would normally barter or make another attempt to get a better prize but he just can't get into it. Josh notices and nudges his side, "Are you ready to go home yet?"

With an apologetic glance at Stoney he replies, "Yeah. I'm kinda tired."

Karen pulls Josh's arm and begs pleadingly, "Not yet."

Josh looks at Logan for assistance but surprisingly Stoney comes to the rescue, "I'd like to go home too."

Relieved, Josh tells Karen, "I have to work early tomorrow."

She holds both his wrists and looks up into his eyes and asks, "Can you come again? Maybe tomorrow? My cousin's band is on the side stage at eight. Could you meet me there?"

Stoney offers, "I've got a lot more tickets at home. My dad said we could use 'em whenever we want."

"Please," Karen bounces her hands on Josh's chest.

"I'll have to ask my dad to make sure."

Karen pulls away from him and says excitedly, "Meet me at seven-thirty in front of the stage. Promise?"

Josh nods, "Let's talk in the afternoon tomorrow to make sure my dad said it's OK."

Her friends are already walking away so she has to run to catch up. She waves at Josh vigorously as she retreats.

During the walk to the car Stoney notes, "That girl really likes you."

Josh just smiles weakly and kicks the can he is following to his car. He pulls the lights on and turns the key but the car doesn't even make a clicking sound. After he tries it again he murmurs in dismay, "Not again."

"I thought dad fixed it already," Logan wonders.

"He put a new starter in but he said the solenoid might cause me problems. I didn't have the money for a new one and forgot to change it," Josh grunts as he opens the hood.

After looking around for any loose wires he orders Logan, "Get me the flash light and screwdriver out of the glove box."

Josh turns the key to the on position and then jumps the solenoid with the screwdriver and sighs with relief when it starts. He slams the hood and drives Stoney home.

Stoney's dad is sitting out front in a lawn chair chain smoking. He waves then walks to the driver's window to ask Josh, "You got another year of high school yet?"

"Yes sir."

"You going to college after that, right?"

Stoney's brother has been in Vietnam for three years. He dropped out of Fossil Community College after one year and got drafted right away. It's almost the only thing Stoney's dad will talk about.

"Yes. My dad wants me to get a business degree."

"Well you stick with it. You don't want to end up in that damn jungle," Stoney's dad's distraught voice trembles.

Unsure what to say, Josh nods as Stoney wraps his arms comfortingly around his dad's waist. When they turn away Josh idles off and rolls his window up then quickly says, "There's something really wrong with LJ and his dad. They're demented or something."

Logan shifts in his seat thinking how much he agrees with Josh.

After he turns the corner Josh stops the car at the curb and shifts to park. Logan looks at him questioningly, "What are you stopping for?"

"I believe you Logan. I know you saw Lizzy with LJ that day. I think LJ and his brother did something awful to Lizzy," Josh says sadly.

"I do too," Logan reaches out to touch his brother's shoulder.

"I wish dad was on our side."

A car passes. The light shines in their eyes forcing them to squint. Logan blocks the light with his hand and notices the pool of tears reflecting in Josh's eyes.

"I want to catch LJ and make him tell me what happened," Josh admits unsteadily.

Logan's body tenses as he thinks about what Josh said.

"Will you help me?" Josh asks. His fist bouncing against the steering wheel makes a dull thumping sound.

"Sure," Logan answers, wondering what he's supposed to do, then asks, "How?"

"Just be there if I need you. And don't tell anyone yet."

"Whatever it takes, I promise," Logan's young voice is strong with solemn grit.

Sixteen

During breakfast Josh tells Rob, "The solenoid's out on my car for sure. I had to jump it last night at the fair."

"Change it this morning. That makes both a new starter and solenoid you owe me for."

"Didn't the work I did on that green Mustang cover the starter?"

"The one that you put a master cylinder in?"

Carol reaches over Rob's shoulder and takes his plate with a warning bump to the back, "If you keep teasing these boys you'll have to eat breakfast at work from now on."

He reaches for it but she slaps his hand, "No way. Not till you stop."

Rob admits, "Yes the Mustang paid for it. Now can I have my food?"

"Play nice," Carol hands him his plate while waving a finger at his nose as though scolding a small child.

"I figured you needed it, so I set the solenoid for your car on top of the fridge at work. It's paid for too," Rob smiles sweetly and twists his finger in his cheek at Carol.

"Are you sure dad? That didn't take me that long," Josh asks.

"Don't worry about it. You've been helping out a lot."

Logan has been listening in; half hoping that Josh might talk to his dad about last nights events. They had agreed to be mum; however, he thought hard on it while tossing in bed. He feels pretty confident that if they tell his dad just a few things, he will agree that the police are wrong too. But so far Josh is letting his parents guide the morning's small talk, answering when spoken to.

Logan wants to direct the conversation to last night's events and is just about to mention the bear Josh won last night when the phone rings.

Carol answers then hands the phone to Josh and says half questioningly, "It's Karen?"

The phone cord is long enough to reach the laundry room so Josh shuts the door and sits on the washing machine. Carol raises an eyebrow and gives Rob a questioning look.

Rob whispers, "It's Lizzy's friend."

"I know who it is, you big galoot. She's just never called here before."

Logan understands their reaction because he felt the same way last night when she was hanging around. Things were going so well with Lizzy and Josh that it's hard to imagine him with another girl so soon, or ever.

Rob starts to speak, "She is…" but Carol shushes him so she can hear Josh better, but he's finishing the conversation already, "I'll call you back in a few minutes." He hangs up the phone and sees everybody looking at him with bated breath as he sits at the table. He explains defensively, "She's going to the fair tonight and wants us to meet her there."

"Who else is going?" Carol asks.

"Some of her friends, me, Logan and Stoney."

Logan unexpectedly aids him, "I'd like to go again. The lines were long last night and we didn't get to do everything."

Rob asks, "Is that why you came home so early?"

With a silencing glance at Logan, Josh answers, "That's part of the reason. I was tired from work too."

"You don't look that chipper this morning," Carol observes.

Rob offers, "The summer isn't that long. You guys should have fun together before school starts and you have to spend all your spare time doing home work and basketball. Help me finish the brakes on that big diesel then you can change your solenoid and rest for a while before you go out."

"You're feeling generous," Carol kisses Rob fondly on top of the head.

"I'm having a good day," Rob banters as Josh jumps up and dials the phone. Rob winks at him as he takes the phone into the laundry room again.

Rob and Carol's eyes are glued together unblinking, as they listen to Josh tell Karen that he'll meet her at the fair between seven and seven-thirty then pause and say, "Logan has to do his route. He'll probably finish at five. I can't get there before five-thirty no matter what." Another pause then, "Uh huh. It won't be later than six-thirty. At the stage by the slide. Cool." He drops the phone into the cradle leaving the cord wrapped around the door handle, avoids their eyes and digs into his breakfast without a word.

A few silent minutes pass then Rob begins to ask Josh about Karen, "So this girl..." but Carol is ready and kicks his foot breaking in and changing the subject, "Speaking of basketball. Are you going to that camp next week?"

Rob smirks to himself thinking, *she never wants to talk about basketball.*

"Yeah it's only for two afternoons. The coach just wants to make sure everyone will still be playin'," Josh answers through a mouthful of pancakes.

Logan is about to bust because he wants to talk about last night so bad, so he blurts out, "You know what? Josh won a big fuzzy bear at the fair last night."

"Oh? What did you do with it?" Carol asks.

"He gave it to Karen," Logan answers for him.

Josh glances at him with a subtle—what are you doing look—then slides his chair away from the table, "How long before you're ready dad?"

"I'm ready. I'll meet you down there in a few minutes," Rob replies joining him at the door.

Josh watches his dad kick off his slippers, search for his work boots and start down the hall in his socks with Carol following.

He touches Logan's shoulder, "You be ready by five-thirty. Got it?"

"I will."

"And don't forget. Whatever it takes," he quotes Logan.

Logan turns sideways, his elbow resting on the chair back and somberly faces Josh with a short nod, "I promised."

After the Chieftain rumbles off, Rob and Carol return to the kitchen. Rob pulls one work boot on and laces it up as he notes, "He's been pretty hooked on Lizzy for a long time."

"Yeah I know. I didn't expect him to…"

Rob broke her off, "Exactly. He talks about her at work all day. Yesterday he asked me if I would go talk to those boys Logan said he saw with Lizzy."

Stretching across the table on her elbows Carol gives Rob a loud kiss on the forehead, "Really? That's strange. But at least he's acting more normal."

"What's normal for a seventeen-year-old?" Rob snorts wonderingly.

"You're quiet this morning," Carol notes skimming her palm lightly over Logan's shoulders on her way to the pantry.

"I'm just eatin'," he responds plainly.

"Just eating? You're never *just* eating. My wallet would be a lot fatter if that were the case," Rob jokes as he adjusts his pants legs over his boots.

"The lawn is getting too tall. Run the mower over the side yard by the garage before you run off today," Rob orders as he leaves.

Logan watches him pass by the front window, whistling and checking the lawn out front. Carol opens a bag of beans; sits in the chair next to him and starts sorting them, dropping the bad ones in the trash and the good ones in a cooking pan.

Logan asks her, "What are you makin'?"

"We're having chili tonight. What are you boys doing today?"

"Ball.., Robert and Stoney are probably coming over."

"Is Karen nice?" she asks conversationally.

"Sure. She hangs on Josh's arm like a leach though," he answers, rising to get out of the discussion.

"Do you think he likes her?"

"He likes Lizzy," he blushes when he realizes what he said, and then explains, "He still talks about Lizzy all the time."

"Mow the yard like your dad wants," her distressed tone evidence of Lizzy's laughter echoing from her memories.

Seventeen

Logan uses the living room phone to call and tell Stoney that he has to mow. Bummed out by the news, Stoney tells him that he will call Ballsac and they'll come over in a couple hours.

Logan grumbles as he battles the stacked trash cans apart. Bent and rusty from the trash man's abuse; Logan has pounded out the dents so many times that the cracks have to be folded over on each other to prevent the grass from leaking out. He carries two of them to the drive in front of the garage and lines them up, dropping the lids behind each one with a clatter.

Their mower is an old leftover from his grandpa. His dad rebuilt it but it's still finicky to start. The starter handle broke off the cord the last time he used it; the new handle is smaller and harder to grip and slips from his hand several times before the engine catches. While it warms up he takes the gas cap off and finds the tank is almost empty. Leaving it idling, he runs into the garage for the gas can his brother keeps filled. He starts to fill the tank without shutting it off but spills gas on the front of the engine. As steam rises he quickly shuts it off when he realizes that he'd almost started a fire. He frowns with chagrin as he recalls when his dad warned him about shutting it off first. He fills it up and is yanking on the starter when Stoney and Ballsac ride up.

"Pull, Pull!" Ballsac yells and giggles as the mower resists his tugs.

"What're you guys doing here already?" Logan breathes heavily as he wipes the sweat from his eyes with his shirt sleeve.

"There's nothing to do so we came over to swim," Ballsac replies.

"You should have brought your mowers," Logan says wishfully.

Ballsac hangs his towel on the pool wall, "I would've but I tried to make money with my dad's mower and it broke. He won't let me use it for anything but our house anymore."

"You ran over a tire iron and broke the blade in half," Stoney reveals, clapping him on the back.

Smiling sheepishly, Ballsac dives into the pool without a word.

The motor finally cooperates and breaks into an even idle. Logan catches his breath, hangs the grass catcher on the side and pushes it down the driveway to start mowing at the front by the street. He spins it around a tree, hears a honk and Lizzy's dad waves as he drives by. Logan stops and watches the car drive away. His vision fades as he remembers Lizzy's face waving at him out the back window; *Rusty tugging on her hair and Lizzy slugging him in return. They both disappear as she wrestles him to the seat.* He shakes off the uncomfortable tightening in his chest and lifts the mower's rear wheel away from the tree.

He works fast as he can but the mower is heavy and he's just one hundred ten pounds and has to rest after every pass. The grass is longer than he usually allows it to get, making it harder to roll the mower and he has to constantly let the engine recover when he cuts into a thick section. His leg cramps a little and he rubs the bruise where he was kicked last night. It makes him thinks about LJ and his family, wondering how people can become so mean. It seems like every time he sees them they are doing something awful. Almost as if they live for it, like they were born wicked.

He dumps the grass catcher, leaves the mower idling and takes off his shoes then jumps in the pool to cool off. He's dripping wet when he puts his shoes on, and has difficulty sliding his heel in and painfully pinches his thumb. When his mower sticks in a rut he knocks his shin on the handle in the same spot that LJ's boot gouged in. He cries out, "Agh," then crouches and runs his palm over the lump. As the pain subsides he curses silently, thinking about how unfairly he was attacked. LJ is a lot bigger than him and *both* LJ and Ben were beating him up. He doesn't realize how angry he is until he rises and gets a little head rush. Bent over and leaning on his knees he blows air between his teeth in a long whoosh as he commits again to helping Josh find out what they did to Lizzy then squeezes the mower handle and shoves it forward hard. His bruised side aches from the exertion and he clamps his teeth together in resolve.

Ballsac is jumping off the shed when he finishes. Stoney watches him sweep the drive and shouts sarcastically, "What's taking you so long? It's almost lunch time."

He lifts his leg into the can and smashes the grass down with his foot, wincing as the rim of the can digs into the back of his knee. Filled to the rim with grass trimmings, the trash cans are too heavy for him to lift. He calls out, "C'mon, help me move these into the alley."

Ballsac drags one, while he and Stoney carry the other. They run to the pool while he walks back, slowly rubbing his sore side. When he dives in Ballsac tries to wrestle with him but Logan cries out in pain. Ballsac lets him go and looks at him with a puzzled expression, "I wasn't hardly touching you."

"My side is really sore," Logan growls as he climbs onto the deck and looks down at the deep contusion.

"What did you do? Crash your bike?"

"LJ and his brother beat me up again," he answers, recoiling at the touch of his own fingers.

"I told you. They hit him with brass knuckles or a stick," Stoney admonishes.

"Yeah I know. But look at that," Ballsac voice is filled with astonishment as he tilts his head to get a closer look. Deep purple, the bruise is bigger than the palm of his hand.

"It's hurts bad. Look at my shin too," Logan lifts his foot on a chair.

"The war victim's are arriving at the hospital," Stoney voice gets deeper as he tries to sound like a radio announcer.

"It's like a war isn't it," Logan says wonderingly, "We're just not fighting back very good." A frown covers his face as he remembers the trapped feeling he had while Ben held his arms behind his back and LJ leered in his face.

Ballsac rolls over a lawn chair shooting a pretend machine gun in the air. They laugh together then Stoney proclaims, "I'm getting hungry."

Logan leads them into the kitchen and is digging through the fridge when Carol asks, "What are you looking for?"

"Something for lunch."

"Well shut the door, I'll make it," she says, shooing him out of the kitchen. The boys turn on the television and get absorbed in a Deputy Dog cartoon. She brings their lunch and they sit glued to the silliness for the next couple hours.

The show is over and the boys are getting restless when Carol interrupts Stoney and Ballsac's wrestling match, "Its past three Logan. You better go do your route."

Logan jumps to his feet, "I thought Josh was coming home early. I wanted him to drive me."

"Your dad said he's been messing with his car all afternoon. He was washing it the last time I talked to them. You'd better not wait," she cautions.

"You guy's wanna help me?" Logan asks hopefully.

"Only if you buy me an RC," Ballsac offers.

"Deal," Logan knows he can get them all the free RC they can stomach at the convenience market.

While they deliver his route Stoney tells Ballsac some of the things that he wasn't part of. When he starts to tell him that Josh went inside LJ's house Logan cuts him off by intentionally bumping his front tire into his leg and announcing, "I've only got about six more papers to go. We'll all take two and whoever delivers them fastest wins a candy bar."

Stoney has helped Logan enough times that he already knows the nearest customers houses. He grabs two papers and races off. Ballsac yells, "Cheater!" as he stacks his papers on his handlebars. They meet at the corner and Logan recognizes Stoney as the winner but contests the result with a page from Stoney's playbook, "On review, because you cheated, he is eliminated and you are the official winner," and points at Ballsac with a grin.

Ballsac enthusiastically yells, "Yeah," and races towards the store. They follow him across a field, jumping their bikes over the little mounds of dirt until they reach the street in front of the store. As they wait for a break in the traffic Stoney yells, "Look!"

Following his gaze they see LJ and his dad enter the store. Logan whispers "Hide," and drags his bike behind a creosote tree.

Ben's leaning out the back window on the driver's side, drumming on the door with his hands and singing. They watch LJ's head bouncing along behind the racks of food as he follows Baxter to the beer freezer, then over to the register. They're both carrying a case of beer when his dad kicks the door open and follows LJ out. As they cross the threshold Baxter slaps him in the back of the head and yells crossly, "I'm *not* buyin you *shit!* You can stop asking all ready." Ben disappears in the back seat.

LJ stumbles forward, trips over the step off the sidewalk and falls face first onto the case of beer. Baxter kicks him in the rear, rolling him face first over the beer. His chin bounces off the asphalt but Baxter only screeches "Get off the beer you damn retard."

As LJ stands the case breaks open and cans roll across the lot. He scrambles after the cans, piling them on the case but is shoved violently off his feet again when Baxter yells, "Dipshit, get away from it before you break it all."

Baxter opens the back door and drops the case he carries in the back seat then feints a punch towards LJ, but only stoops to pick up the beer. He snickers evilly, "You're just a scared little dumb-shit like that old bag of a mom you've got."

Unsure what to do LJ dodges out of reach and nervously watches Baxter pile the beer in the back seat.

Leaving the back door open, Baxter drops in the driver's seat, slams the driver's door and starts the engine then waves his arm out the window at LJ. When LJ backs away he lowers his voice trying to sound gentle. It comes out like a surreptitious viper, "I'm not gonna hurt ya. Just get in the car *before I run outta gas.*"

LJ skirts around the door and slams it behind as he jumps over the beer. As they drive out of the parking lot, Baxter's hoarse yells reach Logan's ears over the chugging engine and he can almost feel the blows, and even winces himself when he sees Baxter's free arm whipping brutally over the back seat, the bobbing top of LJ's head just visible over the door as the driver's side wheels weave over the centerline.

When the roar of the engine subsides Ballsac utters incredulously, "Whoa that is a really bad man!"

Logan listens carefully to the retreating sound of the engine then tells them, "We're OK. Let's go in now."

The clerk waves at Logan, "What's up groovy dude?"

Ballsac asks him, "Did you see that man beating his kids?"

The clerk nods and leans his elbows on the counter as Logan takes his cup from behind the fountain machine. Logan asks him, "Do you mind if my friends have some RC too?"

"No problem. We have fifty bottles of the stuff out back," the clerk exaggerates, brushing his pony tail over his shoulder and sliding two plastic cups over the counter, "just wash 'em out in the sink."

As Logan waits for hot water to arrive at the spigot he smiles gratefully at the clerk, "Thanks. These are my best friends."

"If they're your friends, they're mine too," the clerk gives Stoney a friendly grin.

Ballsac's thoughts haven't been able to leave the cruel beating he'd just witnessed, "I'd hate to have him for a dad."

The clerk shakes his head in pity, "I feel sorry for those kids."

Stoney declares, "I feel sorta sorry for them but they're just as bad as him."

Logan listens, thinking, "*How could anyone feel sorry for them? I can't stand them,*" but only asks evenly, "Do they come in here much?"

"He buys beer here pretty much every day, but I don't see his kids much. I don't think they have much money."

The ice machine door sticks and the glasses slip from Logan's hand bouncing across the ground. He starts to chase them but Stoney catches the glasses and hands one to Ballsac. They fill them with ice and RC while Logan searches the rack for the western comic's. He doesn't find the latest release so he flips through the covers until he finds last months Hulk and slides his back down the counter until he's sitting on the ground with the comic resting on his thighs.

Ballsac is contentedly blowing bubbles through his straw when he suddenly stops tilts his head and indignantly pushes Logan, "*Hey!* You cheated. You were supposed to *buy* me an RC."

Logan grins at him, "Just drink it. I don't have to *pay* money." Suddenly he remembers that he's supposed to meet Josh and twists his head up to see the clock. It's already past five.

"We gotta go. Josh is gonna kill me," Logan dumps his RC into the fountain's drain.

"What for?" Stoney asks.

"He's pickin' us up for the fair at five-thirty."

Logan shouts at the clerk, "Thanks I'll see ya later," as he runs out the door. He gets on his bike and Stoney asks, "Where's Ballsac?"

Standing on his pedals to see over the magazine rack Logan's jaw drops, "He's chuggin his pop." Logan bangs on the thick glass and Ballsac tips his glass to get the last drop then dumps the ice and runs outside yelling, "Thanks," as the door swings behind.

When they get to Logan's the smell of the spicy chili hits them at the front door. Stoney takes a deep breath, "That smells great. My mom never makes chili."

Charmed by the compliment, Carol smiles at him, "Help yourself."

A stack of bowls, grated cheese and diced onions sit on the counter next to the pan of chili. Ballsac eagerly layers the cheese in his chili. He spoons the bowl full then piles cheese and a generous scoop of onions on the top and smiles maliciously, "You guys will hate me later."

Stoney giggles, "Payback, my dad says payback is deadly."

Shaking his head at their foolishness, Logan notices a dirty bowl in the sink and asks, "Who ate already?"

"Josh, he's been here for a while," Carol replies.

"Where is he?"

"In his room getting ready."

From down the hall Josh asks loudly, "Why are you so late?"

Everybody looks at Logan but he stuffs a cracker in his mouth and just shrugs then starts to fill his bowl. When he doesn't get an answer Josh walks to the kitchen doorway and stares at Logan. He's brushing his teeth and his crinkled eyes convey his annoyance to Logan. When he turns to walk down the hall Logan says lightly, "You're not so tough."

Stoney slides his chair away from Logan, raises his hands and says incredulously, "My brother would kill me for that."

Confident that his mom will protect him Logan shakes his head, "He knows better." But his back is to the door and Josh pokes him in the kidney before she can intervene. He grabs his side with both hands and cries out loudly at the sharp pain.

Realizing that he'd just jabbed Logan's injured side Josh puts his hand on his back and exclaims compassionately, "Oh, I'm sorry."

Carol looks on concerned, "What did you do to him?"

Josh's face turns a light pink as he stutters, "I, I hit him too hard."

"You shouldn't be hitting him at all."

"I'm all right mom. It didn't really hurt that bad," Logan musters the pain away and makes his tone strong.

"You sure acted like it did," she rubs his side as she slides past. He starts to wince and turns his head while clearing his throat so she won't notice. She organizes the napkins on the counter and says serenely, "I talked to Steve's mom this morning. She said she overheard him talking about some kind of fight at the fair last night."

Josh stiffens and glances briefly at Logan, "What'd she say?"

"She didn't know any details. That's why I asked. She said he mentioned your name though," Carol meets Josh's eyes questioningly.

The room is silent for a brief second then Ballsac's chair screeches as he slides it back and stands to get more chili. Logan scoots his chair in to let Ballsac pass. Josh allows him to sidle by, wishing he could hide in a crack or was somewhere else.

She continues eye contact with Josh, "Well?"

"I had a fight with that kid that keeps hassling Logan," Josh admits reluctantly.

"What's he doing to Logan?"

"It's that kid he had a fight with before," Josh answers shortly.

Logan adds with emphasis, "The one I saw driving *Lizzy* when she disappeared."

Crossing her arms pensively she remarks, "I didn't *know* that was the same boy."

Josh offers, "Yeah, but I don't think he'll bother Logan anymore."

"Why? Did you beat him up or something?" she uncrosses one arm and tugs her ear lightly.

"No. I just told him to stay away. We had a little fight," Josh lies poorly.

She watches him twist his shoulders uncomfortably then suggests, "Maybe you shouldn't go to the fair tonight."

Josh huffs then gripes, "That's not right mom. I didn't start anything."

The other boys are watching silently, each of them has experienced her wrath before and are happy that they aren't under her thumb but remain ready to jump in if she tells them to stay home.

She stares at him for a long second debating his incomplete answers then orders Logan, "Tell me what happened. *Now!*"

Ballsac sits down with his second helping and Logan searches his empty bowl briefly before saying, "LJ and his brother kinda ambushed me and Josh made them stop."

"How did he do that?" she demands.

"He knocked LJ down and made him leave me alone."

"Then what?"

"The cop came and told us to split up and go have fun," he tries to sound buoyant.

"Did anybody get hurt?"

All the boys look at Logan but he shakes his head and mutters, "Not really."

"Are you sure? Is there something wrong with your side?" she asks doubtfully as she slides around the table to check.

"C'mon mom. I'm fine," Logan pleads.

She tries to pull up his shirt but he scoots out of his chair and stands with his arms holding the tail down and gripes with a whine, "Mom, my friends are here."

Her eyes flash from Logan to Josh and back. She finally sighs resentfully and warns them, "Against my better judgment—I'm going to let you go tonight, only 'cause I know you promised to meet Karen though, but there'd better not be any more trouble."

The boys nod assent and she asks, as if talking to three year olds, "Well…, are you promising to stay out of trouble?"

Logan glances at Josh then answers softly, "Yes."

The room has an uncomfortable silence broken only by the sound of Ballsac crunching on a cracker. Logan kicks him under the table and he starts eating faster. With a knowing glance at Stoney Logan gathers Stoney's empty bowl under his, rinses them off in the sink then leans against it watching Ballsac devour his chili.

Josh has been trying to find a decent reason to get out of the house but can only come up with a lame excuse, "I need to clean out my back seat. I'll be outside when you're ready." In his hurry to leave he twists the door handle but the door sticks and it slips from his hand with a loud snap. He grins apologetically at his mom as the door swings shut behind.

Logan wets the washcloth, wipes the table where he and Stoney sat, then swipes Ballsac's nearly empty bowl and cleans his mess. Ballsac raises his elbows off the table and holds his spoon up while making a comical expression of disappointment, but Logan ignores him and snatches the spoon from his fingers.

It's almost six when Logan checks the clock on the stove. As they head out the back door he says cautiously, "Thanks for dinner mom. We're goin' now."

She waits for Stoney and Ballsac to go out then tells Logan quietly, "Don't forget what I said."

With one foot outside he smiles at her searching eyes, "We'll be good."

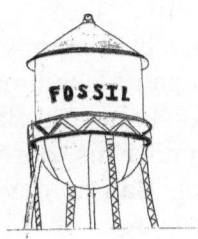

Eighteen

Josh is leaning under the open hood of the Chieftain when the boys exit the house. Logan asks, "Is something wrong?"

"Nope. Just making sure my starter wires didn't come loose," Josh closes the hood with a clank.

The reverse gears whine as Josh backs out of the drive, relieved that his mom is still letting them go out. When he shifts to drive he notices her leaning on the front door watching them with her arms crossed, and gives her an apprehensive wave as he drives slowly away. She waves back without uncrossing her arms.

"Turn on the radio," Stoney demands from the back seat.

Logan reaches for it but Josh blocks his hand observing, "Mom is pretty mad."

"She'll probably tell dad too."

Ballsac bursts out, "They started it. You shouldn't be in trouble."

Josh rolls his eyes at Ballsac, "That's not the point Ballsac. What took you guys so long? We were *supposed* to leave at five-thirty."

"We saw LJ's dad whipping him at the store," Ballsac chortles.

"Wha...?" Josh starts before Stoney breaks in.

"Yeah, it was messed up. His dad totally slapped the crap out of him," Stoney slaps the back of the front seat with his palm next to Logan's head. The sharp sound makes Logan's ear ring.

"Why?"

"He dropped his dad's beer. That was it I think."

"I hate that old drunk so much," Josh face crunches up sourly.

The busy traffic near the fair has caused backups on all the main streets so Josh pulls onto a side street muttering to himself, "I don't want to wait in *that* line." The small road dead ends after a few hundred feet however a dirt road is gouged across the field to the side entrance of the fair. Josh turns onto the dirt exclaiming disappointedly, "I just washed this thing an hour ago."

A small water tower with *Fossil* boldly printed on the side is lit up by the twinkling lights of the fair; a rope that dangles from the walkway swings in big circles around the supports drawing Logan's attention.

He cranks his window down as he looks on with interest, "Look at that."

Josh lifts his foot from the gas pedal and Logan asks curiously, "Why's it spinning around like that?"

"There's somebody hanging from it down there," Stoney points towards the tower base.

Josh turns the car slowly so the headlights flash across the supports where Stoney pointed. He softly says, "Oh," then jabs the brakes causing Logan to jerk forward. He punches the gas and Logan is pressed against the seat.

Ballsac hands grip the seatback as he pushes off the floor from his knees where he fell. Stoney chuckles at Ballsac's inconvenience, "He drives like that all the time."

As the headlights circle back onto the road Logan asks, "What are you doing?"

"LJ's brother is over there," Josh exclaims as if electrified. He turns off the lights then the engine, allowing the car to coast silently to a stop in the dark. Lifting his knee on the seat so he faces Logan, Josh explains quietly, "Look. I want to talk to them. You guys stay in the car while I go over there."

"No way!" Logan protests with a pinched look of fear.

Stoney jumps in loudly, "I'm not waitin' here either."

Josh recants quickly, "Shhh! OK fine. But keep your mouths shut."

They huddle by the driver's door peering into the dark. The rope flips against the tower creating a thin wave of colored light streaking into the sky. Josh crouches as he trots towards the origin of the ropes motion with the others tagging behind. Logan slides one hand on his brothers back so he is easier to follow. Tucked against Josh's back he debates if this is a good idea.

Crouched low, they run along behind a retaining wall. Josh pokes his head up every few steps then whispers. "He's still there. You guys stick close and help me catch him if tries to run off."

Josh jumps over the low block fence, waits for the others then sprints up to Ben. Ben doesn't hear them until their right on top of him. He spins around to get away but is caught against the water tower support beams. He backs up until he's leaning on the metal beam. Josh moves quickly and clasps Ben's elbow while Logan stays back in the darkness. Ben doesn't recognize them at first and asks Josh apprehensively, "What do you want?"

"Where's LJ?" Josh demands.

Pointing his thumb up the tower ladder Ben answers, "Up there."

Josh yanks his arm roughly, "You know Lizzy Camber?"

"No," Ben leans away from Josh.

"Did you ever see a girl named Lizzy?"

Ben starts to jump over the beam but Josh grabs his shoulder spinning him around. He drops to the ground with his hands raised defensively and yells, "LJ! Help. Hurry!"

Backing away so that he can see up the ladder, Josh keeps one eye on Ben. When LJ starts down the ladder he orders Stoney, "Don't let him get away." Stoney tugs Ballsac and they surround Ben.

Positioning himself so LJ will be trapped between him and the beams Josh readies at the bottom rung. But rather than climbing all the way to the bottom LJ steps off the ladder onto a platform and challenges, "Who are you?"

"Josh. Come down here. I need to talk to you."

"Josh who? I don't know you," LJ says suspiciously.

Josh picks up a fist sized rock and threatens him, "Come down here or I'll clock you with this."

LJ weighs his options as he searches for an escape route then agrees, "All right. Just don't hit me on the way down."

"I won't. I just want to talk," Josh promises, alert for any tricks.

As he climbs down LJ unexpectedly drops from the third rung then lunges at Josh's legs but Josh is ready. Sticking out his foot, Josh trips him grabbing his back as he falls. LJ swings wildly behind his head striking a painful glancing blow on Josh's shoulder. Josh slides lower to avoid the flailing fist when he realizes that he was hit with the brass knuckles again. He spins sideways, trapping LJ's arm in his legs and tears at his fingers until he rips the metal from his hand. He throws them aside and straddles LJ on the ground absorbing several punches to the face before he controls him with his knees, but LJ won't give up and arches his back, tossing Josh off his arm. About to take more blows Josh rabbit punches LJ in the face three times then pushes his arms under his legs yelling, "Stop fighting." But LJ is a confident street fighter and drives his knee into Josh's thigh. Josh is much stronger than LJ and wrenches his arms around his back, punches him then turns him over and smashes his face into the dirt with an elbow to the neck. With a muffled scream LJ finally stops struggling.

Logan has been worriedly circling them. When Josh has control of LJ, Logan's foot rests on the brass knuckles. He picks them up putting them in his pocket so LJ can't get them again.

With his mouth next to LJ's ear Josh asks, "Do you know a girl named Lizzy?"

"Kiss my butt," LJ snarls defiantly.

Trembling with grief, pent up anger and frustration, Josh is sick of the whole thing and drives his knee in LJ's ribs. Grunting in pain LJ tries to curl into a ball. Josh lifts his hips off the ground, slamming his knee continuously into LJ's ribs with his full weight until Logan cries out in fear, "Josh hang on."

Ben pushes Stoney away and tries to escape but Stoney tackles him and Ballsac wraps his arms around his neck. Holding Ben tightly they watch Josh twist LJ's arms and punch his neck.

His face stuffed in the dirt and wheezing like his ribs are broken, the fight is completely out of LJ. He's in so much pain that he can't even cry. Josh turns him on his back and shoves his knuckles into his throat and barks furiously, "Tell me what you assholes did with Lizzy!"

The breath beaten from him, LJ screeches like a beaten donkey, "We just gave her a ride."

"I - don't - believe - you," Josh's voice emphasizes each word. He jams his thumb into LJ's throat and leans his full weight on it. LJ twists his head so Josh elbows his stomach, "What did you do?"

"We took her to the river," LJ admits miserably.

"Then what," Josh pressures with another thumping blow to the ribs.

"We took my stepdad's truck to the river and Lizzy went with us. He caught us and made us go home."

"You're not telling me anything. Who did that shit to her?" Josh's voice chokes uncontrollably.

"I don't know. My dad strapped us and we ran off. She was fine when we left," LJ cringes.

Josh places his forehead forcefully against LJ's and asks, "What do you think happened to her?"

LJ flinches and replies fearfully, "She was alone with my stepdad. That's all I know."

Josh knees him in the gut and punches him again then motions to Stoney, "Bring Ben over here. Logan, don't let this turd get up."

Logan stands over LJ while Josh grabs Ben by the arms and twists them cruelly, "Tell me what you guys did."

Ben has seen his dad beat his brother so many times that he caves instantly, confessing in a single fading breath, "She was walking by the pool so we gave her a ride. We went to the river and had some whiskey then went swimming. She didn't want to go or drink or nothin' but LJ made her. We were going home and got caught with the truck. He started beatin' us with his belt so we ran off. She was hiding in our kitchen when I ran down the alley."

Josh lifts him off the ground and slams him on his back next to his brother. He glares down at them explaining in a harsh seething voice, "I'm telling the police and you'd better not lie when they come and ask you. If you do I'll kick your teeth in again. Understand?"

Josh's voice thickens to a gruff tone as he bends over LJ's face and informs him, "You'll catch the same treatment if you low life garbage collectors bother my brother or his friends again."

Barely in control of himself, Josh looks around for something to smash their heads with but can't find anything in the darkness and slams his fist into Ben's kidney. He stands over them fighting his emotions for control over his body. His head trembles with rage, grief and a disgusting sickness as the truth of Lizzy's destiny sinks in. He is about to attack them again when suddenly he makes a decision and turns. "Let's go," Josh pushes Logan ahead of him.

Stoney and Ballsac tag after Josh as he strides to his car. He slams the door then waits for them to get in, pounding his steering wheel with his palm while he waits. He races into the parking lot then slows to an idle, the gravel ticking against the undercarriage in the sudden quiet. All three boys stare at Josh but he is tightlipped as he searches for a parking spot.

When Logan shuts the door with his hip his skin pinches between the door handle and the brass knuckles in his pocket. He pulls them from his pocket and examines them as he follows Josh to the entrance. Sliding his fingers through the rings he makes a fist and holds it out for Stoney to see.

Stoney admires them, "Those are wicked."

Josh glances back and orders in a shaky voice, "If you get caught with those you'll be in so much trouble. Give 'em here," then stuffs them into his pocket.

They stand at the gate in a circle while Stoney hands them their tickets. Logan notices Josh's trembling body and asks him, "Do you want to wait a minute before we go in?"

"Yeah, I need to cool off," Josh leans his hands on his knees and blows long slow breathes.

They watch the distant rides in uncomfortable silence, shuffling their feet in the gravel. Finally Stoney acknowledges, "That was totally insane man."

Ballsac looks at Josh respectfully, "You're really strong."

Josh grins weakly at him, "They're just a bunch of out of shape losers."

"I don't know about that, he beat me up," Ballsac admits.

"He's two years older than you," Stoney defends him.

"Do you think they'll really tell the police the truth?" Logan asks Josh revealing his thoughts.

"They'd better. Look guys. Either them or their stepdad did something..., something terrible to Lizzy. They admitted it. I'm going to make sure they pay and pay big time. They're probably going to tell the police I beat them up too. So you need to back me and make sure the truth is told," Josh asks for their commitment.

They nod their unity and Ballsac says, "I'll tell my dad tonight."

"That's cool. You do that too Stoney. I'm telling my dad when we get home and if he doesn't believe me I'm calling the police anyway," Josh announces.

Logan has always admired his brother and his pride swells while he watches Josh's broad back spin through the turnstiles.

Nineteen

Carol waits restlessly for Rob to get home. She's been contemplating her discussion with the boys and is anxious to fill Rob in. When his tire's thump over the curb she darts out the front door and follows his car up the drive. She bends and waves at his eyes in the rear view mirror and he lifts his hand to acknowledge her. He parks and pushes his shoulder into the door as he lifts his papers from the passenger seat but she is standing in the way and blocks it with her hands to avoid being bumped when it opens. Smiling questioningly through the window he waits for her to swing it open.

His smile weakens when he notices her serious face, "What's the rush? Is everyone OK?"

"Yes. Everything's fine. I'm just worried about the boys."

"Why? What did they do?" his smile disappears in sudden concern.

"Let's go inside," she says seriously, pleased that he's finally home.

As she starts in he takes her hand and says evenly, "Tell me if something's wrong with my sons."

She wraps her hand around his waist reassuringly and soothes him, "They're fine. Nothing happened. I just want to make sure that they're still safe and nothing *does* happen. I want to talk to you about that."

After setting his papers on the counter he kicks his knee over a stool and rubs his thighs with his palms, "Tell me what's going on now."

"Well…, the boys had some trouble at the fair last night."

"Like what?" he asks suddenly exasperated.

"They didn't make it exactly clear. But that LJ boy was bothering Logan again, and Josh had some sort of scuffle with him," she explains with a feeling of guilt for telling on the boys.

"You mean Josh had a fight with this kid LJ?" he asks, the creases in his forehead becoming obvious.

"I don't know if it was an actual fight or not. But Logan said that the police had to get involved."

"Hey neighbors!" they are both startled to find Carol's dad peeking through the screen door.

Carol put her hand to her chest, drawing a sharp intake of air, "Oh. Hi Dad."

"Can I come in?" he asks, completely unaware that he had snuck up and shocked them.

"Sure," she says shushing Rob with her fingers to her lips.

"It smells good. What are you having?" her dad asks hopefully.

"Chili. Want some?" She already knows why he knocked. If there's nothing on the stove at home he shows up over here, but it's usually not such an inconvenience.

"You bet. We never have chili," he states disappointedly, dropping on the couch and kicking his loafers off.

Rob rises to help and her lips tighten flatly as she opens a box of Saltines. She arranges the crackers on the plate around the bowl of chili then hands them to her dad with a welcoming smile, "Here ya go pop."

"You never call me that anymore. I like it," he thanks her with his eyes.

"Mom doesn't make chili for a reason," she hugs him quickly.

"A man's gotta have a little fun," he happily scoops into the chili with a cracker.

Rob sets his bowl on the table as he motions her into the bedroom with his eyes. He shuts the door quietly and asks, "So the police got involved last night? What do you want me to do?"

"Yeah, that worries me. Just go check on the boys. After dinner, please go down to the fair and see if you can find them," she says anxiously.

"They seemed OK last night."

"You don't get it. The boy they were fighting with is the *same* boy that Logan said he saw Lizzy riding with," she spouts in a rapid stream as she clutches his elbows.

"Really? That's bizarre. I wonder why they're fighting with him?" Rob frowns and grasps her shoulders supportively.

"*That's what I thought.* Do you remember the fight Logan had a week or so two ago?"

"Yes," he waits for her explanation.

"It was with the same kid," her whispering voice explodes.

"How do you know that?" he asks uneasily.

Beginning to feel annoyed she asks, "How many LJ's are there?"

He ponders for a moment then promises, "Right..., I'll go to the fair after I eat and finish my bills."

"Can't you do the bills later?" she suggests.

"They're supposed to be mailed in the morning...."

"*Listen to me.* Their story sounded like a bunch of cock-n-bull and I think they're in more trouble than they know," she uses one of her dad's stock phrases.

Rob can't stop the corners of his mouth from turning up in a slight smile as he grasps the door knob and commits, "I'll eat dinner with your dad then go see what they're up to. OK?"

As he opens the door she stops him with her hand on his shoulder, "I was thinking...., maybe Logan *was* telling the truth and those boys tricked the police somehow."

Her dad interrupts from the living room, "My chili's getting cold."

"Be right there dad," she rolls her eyes at Rob then continues in a whisper, "Before you leave can you call the policeman and ask him something for me?"

"Sure."

"Ask him if he knew about the fight Logan had with LJ last week," she is relieved that he has agreed to go to the fair but still feels ill at ease.

"Why?" Rob asks, confused with this new request.

"I was thinking that maybe Logan really did see Lizzy riding with LJ, but maybe LJ lied and told the police that Logan was trying to get revenge on him."

"Really? Revenge for what?" he asks incredulously.

"For *fighting*," she insists in a serious tone," Lizzy told me that LJ beat up Logan and Robert."

"I see. So you think there's a lot more to this than just a couple kids having a pushing match," he looks as if a firecracker of knowledge has exploded in his head.

"*Exactly*!"

"I'll call after we eat and your dad leaves. Then I'll go find the boys and bring them home. I'll get the whole story out of them," Rob commits briskly as he opens the door.

When they appear in the hall her dad tries to make her feel guilty, "Are you eating with me or leaving me here by myself?"

"We're planning something special for the boys," she carefully lies.

"Well let me know if I can chip in. Can you refresh my chili?" he asks with a mischievous grin as he holds out his bowl.

Before Rob leaves, he calls the number Dixon left but he's off for the night so Rob leaves a message. Carol is disappointed but pushes Rob anxiously out the door before grandpa has even made it the short walk home.

Twenty

Tonight is the big crash-em-up derby. They race on a quarter mile oval dirt track next to the north parking lot. Metal stands line both straight-away's and they are full of fans eating vein stiffening food, Indian fry bread, hot dogs, pretzels and chili fries. The first elimination heat starts as the boys walk past and they line up on the fence to watch the cars roar past. The five clunkers bang around the track for four laps to the crowd's thunderous cheers, until the winner finally limps across the finish line.

When Josh pushes off the fence he notices blood running between his fingers. He rubs his knuckles and finds the blood is already clotting in the small cuts. As they pass a hot dog stand he wets a napkin and cleans the blood from his fingers and palms. Logan sees the bloody napkins and asks, "Are you hurt?"

"No. These are just little scrapes," Josh holds his hands in the light for Logan to see.

Go carts buzzing behind the administrative building draw Stoney's attention and he reads the sign out loud, "Go Carts Schmo Carts. I want to ride that." Ballsac follows him to the line and Stoney sorts his money then buys the tickets.

While dropping the red tissues in the trash Josh remembers his promise to Karen and tells Logan, "I was supposed to meet Karen a half hour ago. We should head over there now."

Logan tells Stoney they need to go, however Stoney shakes his head insisting, "There's no line, everybody's watching the races. It will be crowded later. Let's ride now."

Josh reluctantly nods and sits on the chain link fence to watch. Open wheel carts with a top speed of almost twenty they seem a little dangerous to Logan. He apprehensively buckles the safety belt but when the light turns green and Stoney streaks away a smile instantly covers his face.

The brass knuckles are digging into Josh so he drops off the fence and pulls them from his pocket. He slides his fingers through the circles. They're obviously designed for an adult's hand and he wonders if LJ stole them from Baxter. He tests them with a light punch to the chain link then with a shake of his head, shoves them in his back pocket and watches the carts rattle around. Logan is about to catch the leaders when the red light flashes and a man flags them off the track.

Stoney begs to have another go but Josh shakes his head and walks off ignoring his complaints. They follow Josh and the noise from the race cars fades as they reach the midway. Josh turns at the blue ribbon picnic park and checks the clock over the tables. It's after seven-thirty. A twinge of guilt makes him increase his pace. A comedian from the Wild West comedy show is performing handgun tricks in the middle of the path to attract attendance to his next show. Josh passes by quickly but when he turns at the next corner he looks back to find Stoney and Ballsac being handcuffed together by the comedian. Logan, stopped halfway to the corner, is spellbound as well. Josh slaps his hand on his thigh, waits for a second then returns to Logan and asks in a cross voice, "Are you coming or not?'

"I'm just waitin on those guys," Logan complains but he's really thinking about the cowboy's shirt. It's exactly like the one his hero wears in the comic book. Logan's working up the courage to ask him where he got it.

"Stoney. Let's go!" Josh yells impatiently.

Stoney glances up but doesn't come immediately so Josh tells Logan, "I'll meet you over there. Just hurry up."

Logan nods and makes his way back to the cowboy.

A band is playing an almost unlistenable version of Surfin Safari on the stage. Josh stands on the last row of benches behind the crowd on the outside of the amphitheater looking for Karen.

When the song is over the singer dances crazily at the left side of the stage and announces that they have two more songs. A group of girls scream in enthusiasm as they start into Surfer Girl. Karen is right in the middle of the bobbing girls, waving her arms over her head.

The music is way too loud for her to hear Josh and the crowd is too thick for him to reach her, so he makes his way to the side of the stage, grateful to not be in front of the speakers any longer. The entire band is wearing surfer clothes and works the audience for all their worth. Josh can't hold back his laughter when the singer dances across the stage backwards then trips and slides headfirst off the edge into the girls. He climbs back on the stage before the songs is over but misses half the lyrics and the song ends in a clunking train wreck. The guitar player starts right into Surfing USA and the crowd of girls screams enthusiastically while the other half of the audience laughs at their antics. When the song is over Josh thinks, *that wasn't half bad, they must have saved the best for last.* The crowd flushes through the exit while Josh keeps an eye on Karen. The singer is sitting on the front of the stage joking with Karen and her friends, signing autographs for a line of small kids. When the last one is signed he jumps down and hugs Karen then leads her to the side of the stage near Josh. They're both looking around as if trying to find somebody and stand on a bench to see over the heads of the crowd. When Karen spots Josh she waves, grabs the singers hand and pulls him through the herd.

"Whew, this is my cousin Charles. This..., is my friend Josh," she swooshes her hands ladylike to introduce them.

"Hi, Josh. What'd you think?" Charles asks.

"About the band?" Josh thinks quickly, "I really liked the last song."

Charles nods in agreement, "Yes. That's one of our best ones. Sorry I fell off the stage."

Josh wonders why he's apologizing and nods as Logan and his friends arrive, talking excitedly about the upcoming Wild West show.

Charles asks Karen, "Hey, have you seen my sister yet?"

"No. She's probably around here somewhere though," Karen stands on her tiptoes to look over the crowds.

"She was here about six but had to go over to the exhibits. Her church has a booth and she was supposed to check in with them before the show. I don't think she had to work until eight-thirty. What time is it?"

"About eight twenty-five," Josh replies.

"I know she wanted to see my show. I wonder where she is?" Charles asks bemused.

"You know his sister, Wendy. She was with me last night," Karen reminds Josh.

"Oh yeah, she's only with you half the time," Josh says with a sarcastic smile. Wendy is the third wheel to Lizzy and Karen's friendship.

"I hafta take our equipment off the stage now. Can you find her for me?" Charles asks Karen hopefully.

"I'll go to the church booth. She's probably over there. Will you go with me?" Karen asks Josh, tugging on his hand.

Logan follows them, complaining when they pass the cowboy comedian again, "We want to go in and watch the cowboy show."

"That's fine. Just stay here and we'll come get you after we find Wendy," Josh starts away then stops and returns, pointing his finger at Logan, "Look. You guys stick together and don't go anywhere without each other. Better yet, stay at the cowboy show until I get back."

As they walk Josh tells Karen what he learned from LJ. She listens quietly, enthralled with his attention until she realizes what he is saying and stops in front of the cuckoo house staring at him. She doesn't say anything as she ponders his words and the colored lights create a sparkling in her eye that Josh is unable to miss. He looks away uncomfortable with his unexpected admiration and the conflict it creates, waiting for her to say something.

Finally she admonishes him, "You have to tell the police."

The tension broken he replies, "I'm going to call them in the morning. I want to tell my dad first."

She sighs softly, "That's so sad," then starts down the midway towards the exhibits.

"Keep an eye out for Wendy. We don't want to miss her," she says as they near the exhibits. The noise of the fair subsides as they enter the exhibits mall; they walk quietly side by side looking for Wendy both of them reflecting on the new facts.

When they reach the booth it is eight forty-five. Three girls are sitting on the wooden box next to the church display. Karen asks them, "Where's Wendy?"

One of the girls answers in a pouting tone, "She went to see her brother's band about two hours ago. She should've been here to take over for me fifteen minutes ago."

"Two hours ago? She was here and left already?" Karen asks in surprise.

"Yes. And she hasn't come back so I'm stuck here," the girl indignantly shakes her blond curly bangs out of her eyes.

Josh asks the other girls, "Did you see her too?"

The youngest looks at her friend as if to say, "Didn't he hear you?" then nods at Josh, "We were jumping rope when she was here. She was swinging the rope while we played three feet in."

"She really left at like six-thirty?" Josh asks the first girl.

"Yes. If you see her, tell her I have all the tickets," she answers holding them out for proof.

"Are there any adults around? Like her parents." Josh asks.

"No. They went to the car derby already."

Josh looks at Karen as he thinks out loud, "I don't think that ends till ten-thirty or later."

Karen sits on the box next to the other girls, "Let's wait here until nine and if she's not here then lets go back to the band stand."

Trying not to alarm the other girls Josh shushes Karen and they wait impatiently until eight fifty-five. Sitting in the dirt at

Karen's feet he nudges her ankle and asks, "Shouldn't we go now?"

"Yes." The girls are jumping rope again so Karen waits for the girl to trip on the rope. When she doesn't Karen asks, "If you see Wendy tell her to stay here?"

Counting out loud one of the girls replies without looking over, "Forty-one, OK. We will, forty-three…"

The crowd in the midway has grown and it is difficult to get anywhere quickly. Josh pulls Karen along and they are ruffled and hot by the time they reach the cowboy show. Logan is on the stage and the comedian is using him for a prop. While waving a magic wand over Logan's head, the comedian fluffs his hair with the other. It stands on end, following the wand as he waves it over his head and utters the magic phrase, "Allamazacky kazoo!" Ballsac's eyes are watering and Stoney is laughing so loud that Ballsac has to cover his ears.

Josh interrupts them for a second to tell them to stay put until he gets back; Logan is being led around the stage by the comedian's assistant while the comedian indiscreetly points to the donkey tail he stuck to the back of Logan's pants.

Charles is done loading his equipment and is sitting at the side of the stage with his group watching a doo wop band. Karen pulls him aside and asks, "Did Wendy ever show up?"

"No. Wasn't she with the church?" Charles asks uneasily.

With a shake of her head she told him what they had found out.

"My mom and dad are at the car races. I'll never find them."

Karen offers, "Maybe she went with them. We'll help you look for her."

Charles rounds up his band and they quickly decide to split up into four search teams of two persons. With the map on top of an old barrel they divide the fair into four sections and assign one to each team. As they start to split up Josh raises his hands and yells, "Hang on. Let's meet at ten at the church booth. If we haven't found Wendy by then, we'll tell the police."

Josh and Karen's section includes the lost and found so they plan to stop by there after he tells Logan what he is doing.

Washboard Wally is on the stage and the boys are sitting in the middle of the front row. Josh crouches as he crosses to them but Wally won't let him interrupt his show without a fight and points to Josh playfully, "Hey you. We gotta good show goin' on here. Why don't you sit down and put a load on your brains," with a crash of the cymbal mounted on a strap to his head.

Plugging one ear Josh tells Logan what his plans are and points out where he's searching on the map then says, "If I'm not back here by ten. Meet me at the church booth in the exhibits at ten. Got it?"

Logan studies the map to identify the booth and points at it questioningly. Josh nods and whispers loudly, "Ten o'clock. Don't forget. There's a clock right over there."

Logan watches Josh run to Karen and lead her away. He jumps up to follow as he fully absorbs what Josh said but by the time he reaches the exits they've disappeared in the chaos. He sits back between Stoney and the fat man that occupies the two seats next to him, thinking about the day's events. He tries to watch the show but his mind keeps wandering to Josh and he is unable to follow the jokes any longer. To track the time he has to lean far backwards and strain to see the clock over the man's bulging neck fat. Time slows for Logan and his mind begins to play tricks on him as he worries about Josh. Every crash of the comedian's cymbals or kick on his floor drum causes Logan to flinch and check the time again. The fat man gets tired of his shuffling and frowns discouragingly at him while stuffing cotton candy into his pursed lips. The blue dye has stained his teeth and mouth around his lips in a filthy ring and Logan is unable to stop staring at the gooey disaster or to resist the feelings of disgust.

Twenty-one

Lost and found is on the far side of the midway. As they make their way through the throng Karen looks forlornly at the Ferris wheel and tells Josh sweetly, "I really *really* want to ride that with you tonight."

"We'll have time after we find Wendy. The line may not be so long later anyway," he tries to sound casual. He isn't ready for her fascination and his discomfort is obvious, at least to him.

The Trash Can Gang is playing in the middle of the street at the end of the midway and a huge group of people are rocking to the clanking rhythm. Pushing his way around the edge Josh bops his head to the beat making Karen smile in return. A path through the crowd suddenly opens in front of them and they start through but a drummer with trash can lids strapped all over his body spins in front of them and shanghai's Karen by the hands. He pulls her into the center of the circle and shoves a trash can lid and hammer into her hands. Embarrassment covers her face as she tries to push them away but he jumps back and encouragingly pounds the lids hanging from his knees. She plays along with a shy shrug at Josh, until a break occurs in the music then drops them to the ground. The drummer chases her, feigning a mixture of anger and humor for the crowd. She looks behind her, giggling easily as she follows Josh away.

When they enter the lost and found office a thin man sits with his back to the door smoking a pipe and watching a rerun of Gilligan's Island. A little boy behind the entry door rises to his feet momentarily and catches his breath, then lowers himself back to the chair, sniffling and crying quietly.

Josh tells the thin man's back, "Hi. We're trying to find our friend."

"Ain't everbody," the thin man absently hands Josh a clipboard. "Fill this here out."

"Can you tell us if she has been here?" Karen asks.

The thin man nods while pointing at the boy with his pipe, "Course I can. That little feller there is the only person missing so far today. He's waitin' for his mom right now."

"We're looking for a sixteen year old girl named Wendy," Karen tries to explain.

"Like *I* said. He's the only one today. Just fill that out."

"She's been gone for over two hours and," Karen begins but the thin man interrupts rudely.

"*Don't git all panicky.* We usually lose three or four people every night. If I were to hazard a guess, I'd bet she'll be by here anytime now. If you fill that out, when she shows up we'll keep her right here until someone comes to pick her up," he pokes interestingly in his pipe with his thumb.

A short wide woman swings the door in with a bang and the little boy jumps into her arms wailing. She engulfs his tiny body, crushing him to her enormous bosoms then wipes the tears off his ruddy cheeks with his shirt.

The thin man rolls his eyes as he watches their reunion then claps his hands together and waves them in front of his eyes as he says expansively, "See what I told ya. It's like magic, it happens all night long."

Josh fills out the paper with Karen's help as the woman signs for the release of the little boy and thanks the thin man. He smiles weakly at her as she leaves. After the door shuts he mimics the woman's voice, "Everybody's *so* grateful when they find a loved one."

Changing tone in a complete turnaround, he asks Josh colorlessly, "You want us to send her over to the churches booth or just keep her here?"

Karen answers, "Keep her here. That will make it easier."

"You got it little lady," he absently drops the sheet into a folder and turns back to the television. They start to leave but he knocks on the counter and adds, without taking his eyes off Mary Ann's thighs, "Oh. I almost forgot. Check across the way at emergency services. Sometimes they show up over there too."

When the door shuts behind them Karen giggles and Josh asks pointedly, "What's so funny?"

"What a strange icky person," she exclaims in an amused voice pointing over her shoulder with her thumb. Josh smiles lightly and looks for the emergency services building. He's wondering if the police will be there so he can divulge the news.

A small sign over a double door on the block building across the street declares 'Emergency Service.' Josh opens the door for Karen as he belatedly agrees, "Yup, he wasn't much use."

They enter a tiny room with two old wooden school desks along the wall. A low sliding window with a wooden counter faces them on the other side. Josh stoops and pokes his head through the window, looks around and finds a woman in a green nurse's uniform. He calls out, "Hi. We're looking for a friend of ours."

She looks up from her magazine and asks indifferently, "Who?"

"A girl named Wendy," Josh answers as Karen tip-toes to lean her head around his shoulder.

The nurse smiles with her eyes at Karen and says somewhat derisively, "Well as you can see…, she's not here."

Josh taps the counter while looking down at his hands trying to maintain his patience. He lets out a small relaxing breath then asks nicely as he can muster, "Has she been here tonight? She's been missing a while."

"Nope. I've been here all night. You should check at lost and found," the nurse flips her magazine over with a slight huff.

"Thanks," Josh steps backwards, almost tipping Karen over but catches her by the wrist before they tumble to the ground. She giggles as they leave, "This place is full of useless people."

Josh holds his map up in the light, "Where do we go next?"

She traces the map with her finger and says questioningly, "The historic exhibits?"

"Why would she be there?"

"Who knows? I thought she wouldn't miss her brother's concert either. Maybe she's with some boys."

Josh thinks about the rational for a second then leads her into the exhibit. They make their way past the old tractors and farming equipment until they reach the black smith's shop at the back of the exhibit where Josh asks doubtfully, "Have you seen *anyone* you know yet?" He's sure his friends would be on the midway.

"No. My friends wouldn't be caught dead in here," she answers sounding sort of out of touch. She's content to be with Josh and had been thinking about him more than looking for Wendy.

"Why are we looking here then?" Josh asks slightly miffed.

She pretends to pout, "I thought we had to cover our whole area."

"Sorry. I just…" he begins to apologize then breaks off and unfolds his map. "Where do you think you would find your friends in our area?"

"I'm not really into farming or work stuff. I'd be at the rides," she offers hopefully.

"We already went down the midway. There's more rides over here before the cows and horses." Josh folds his map and starts in the direction of the rides. She tugs on his elbow timidly, "You're not mad are you?"

He shakes his head and attempts to reassure her with a joke. "You should make up your mind. My dad says all you girls are too fickle," he grins to let her know he's fooling around. Confidence restored, she tags along at his side.

When they reach the rides Josh watches the flipping, soaring Tilt-a-Whirl and points at the chattering mob, "Look through the lines. Maybe she's on a ride and forgot about church."

The long line for the old wooden Crooked Coaster takes them a few minutes to search. Josh stretches his neck to check the time by looking at the watch of a man in line and informs her, "It's after nine-thirty. We'd better keep going."

The Punkin Swing is across from the little kids Lollipop Swing so Josh says nicely trying not to offend her again, "Let's try to go faster. Since these are kitty-corner you check over there. I'll check the Punkins and meet you at the Dragon slide line."

She looks at him curiously and squeezes his bicep. As they separate she gives him a longing glance over her shoulder and says, "Don't take too long."

The Punkin Swing spins in a circle, swinging the rider's feet close to the ground then sailing them high above the heads of the people in line. Josh searches the faces of the riders as they spin round, laughing easily and kicking at the chairs of the other riders; trying to twist around while at the same time trying not to get caught by the carnie. When it stops he checks every girl getting on then walks over to the Dragon slide to meet Karen. She is already waiting and asks, "Did you see her?"

"Nope. Did you?" when she shakes her head he sighs in exasperation, "I guess we need to check the barn yard now."

A dark road behind Hillbilly Village leads to the barn yard. They're entering the darkest section when Josh suddenly grabs her by the wrist and urgently whispers, "Shhh, Stop!"

"Wha..." she begins but he shushes her again while pulling her against a building. She follows his glare but can't tell what he's looking for. At a loss she whispers, "What is it?"

"It's Baxter," Josh clacks his teeth angrily.

"Who?"

"LJ's dad. Remember I told you. LJ said she was alone with him when she died," he hisses.

"I didn't know his name," she admits hunching next to him.

Baxter unlocks the maintenance building door and attempts to shove a cart of garbage cans inside. The sharp impact with the high threshold causes the cans to tip off the cart and debris spills in front of the door. He kicks and rocks the cart several times until it disappears in the room then hurriedly sweeps the garbage into a pile in front of the door. Several trash cans have rolled across the sidewalk into the grass.

Karen can hear his rude grumbling and whispers, "He sure is mad about something. Why's he making such a mess?"

He lifts the metal trash cans over his head then tosses them through the door where they clang across the floor. He rams his shoulder into the door to force the pile of rubble into the room but his broom falls before it closes and the wooden handle sticks under the door. He curses and yanks the door; the bent broom drags across the concrete until it jams in a crack and the door suddenly stops; the door handle slips from his hand and he stumbles backwards, flailing his arms in a circle to maintain his balance. The middle of the broom is lodged under the door; the end of the handle is stuck in the crack and the bristles hung on the threshold. He stoops and pulls on the bristle end but the broom doesn't budge. Throwing his hands up in frustration he punches the door then kicks it open, breaking the broom handle with a loud crack. He bends down and snatches the two pieces then tosses them into the room over the cart. The trash skitters into the room as he rams his shoulder against the door with a grunt. It finally closes tight and allows him to lock it.

Huffing with exertion, he lights a cigarette. The matches glow reveals his sullen eyes, making him appear dark and dangerous in the dim light. The lit match sticks to his thumb. He flaps his hand furiously as it burns his skin then tosses it into the grass, stomps it out with a loud grumble and sticks his thumb in his mouth.

Karen shudders as she whispers, "He's scary. There's something really wrong with him."

As if he'd had heard her Baxter peers suspiciously in their direction then quickly crosses the grass and disappears behind another building.

Josh squeezes her hand, "I'm following him. Do you want to go meet Logan for me?"

"*No*. I want to go with you," she replies right away.

Josh nods and rashly follows Baxter around the building, towing Karen behind. Baxter scurries along the unlit sidewalk then enters a door. Josh waits restlessly for him to appear again then tells Karen, "Wait here I want to see where that goes." She huddles against a tree while he runs to the door and reads the sign then runs back, standing with his hands on his hips.

"It's a maintenance office. I don't think there's another way out," he informs her quietly.

The door suddenly bursts open with a bang and Baxter exits. Josh drops to his knees and pulls Karen behind a small bush as Baxter trots towards them. He turns to cross the grass; his cigarette passes in front of their eyes in a bright red streak, trailing a foul odor.

Josh rises to follow however, Karen pulls on his hand until Baxter rounds the other building. "C'mon," Josh whispers, wriggling his hand free to follow. She tries to keep pace with him as he sprints across the grass and peeks around the corner.

"He took off his work uniform. Why's he going so fast?" Josh wonders out loud.

Baxter is trotting between the buildings, his arms flopping in an ungainly balancing act. He stops at the edge of the darkness and crouches against a chain link fence then slinks along it towards the horse barns.

Josh runs after him with Karen hanging on his shoulder. When they reach the fence she admits in a small voice, "This is scaring me Josh."

"You can go back if you want. Just go through that street there and you'll be on the midway again," Josh urges her.

"Can't you go with me? We need to find Wendy," she argues impatiently.

"In a minute. Are you going back or with me?" he asks, absorbed in tracking Baxter's lumbering figure. His question unanswered, he starts off again. She runs after him, troubled by his demeanor.

Baxter hobbles across the field in his unsteady pace, crouching when the occasional light passes over him. A row of horse trailers line the parking lot behind the horse barns. Baxter enters the parking lot and ducks behind the first horse trailer; looks around quickly then rushes to the next trailer. He climbs on the wheel well and peers over the trailer then dashes to the next trailer until he is crouched on his knees in the parking lot, in front of the horse stalls. Josh and Karen watch his distant bobbing head from behind a short sign at the end of the fence.

Karen observes and says instinctively, "He's crazy or something. He's acting like my cat."

Suddenly, with a new demonstration of speed he sprints in a zigzag to the barn. He leans his head against the building as he unlocks a tack room door, then slips in. Rumbles from the race track almost a mile away momentarily override the quieter sounds of the parking lot. Josh looks back at the midway lights over the buildings. The Ferris wheel turns slowly, the lights blinking in a circle at the middle then working their way outward in an increasing circle until the outer ring is reached and it blinks rapidly before starting a new pattern. Next to it the hammer slings wildly and the screams of the riders cut through the growling of the distant race cars. The lights dance appealingly in Karen's curls, forcing Josh to consider taking her back to the midway but he tells himself that Baxter would probably disappear and it may be impossible to find him again.

Josh trots through the field to the west end of the horse barn then leads Karen to the south corner so he can see the doors. With all the exciting activity on the other side of the fair, it is relatively quiet here and he doesn't want to take Karen any closer. The horse in the first stall hears their steps and thumps his hooves in anticipation. The tack room is ten or more doors away.

"Can you wait here?" Josh asks Karen.

1

84   *Tyler Anderson*

"What for? I don't want to be alone out here," she confesses, frightened by the isolation.

"I'm going to go in the horse stalls and climb down to the tack room to see what he's doing," he plans out loud.

"Who cares? Just call the police tomorrow," she urges desperately.

"I will call them. But he's acting so suspicious. Maybe he's stealing something," Josh guesses with another glance around the corner.

"What? Like a horse shoe?"

Her sarcastic tone makes Josh pause and search her curious eyes. "I don't know. Maybe a saddle," he tries to explain. He looks away guiltily then takes her by the hands. "Look, I want to talk to him about Lizzy," Josh admits his voice suddenly morose.

"That's crazy," Karen cries with angry trepidation and pushes Josh away.

Josh doesn't answer, but instead trots to the tack room door and listens with his ear against the jamb then runs back faster, sliding around the corner on one knee. He whispers, "He's yelling at someone, maybe a woman. It's too muffled to hear what they're saying."

"Let's just go now. Who cares what he's doing," Karen pleads uselessly.

"Stay here, I'll be right back," Josh whispers. He unlatches the first horse stall and shuts it softly behind.

"*Josh wait!*" Karen implores. When he doesn't reappear, she leans her back to the wall and kicks it angrily with the sole of her shoe. She watches the sparkling lights of the midway and questions her situation—*What am I doing here? Why is he doing this? Does he really love Lizzy that much? Will he ever like me? Maybe I should go back by myself?* Cheerful sounds are carried to her. The loud loose laughter of a group of happy kids, the joyful screams as the Whizzer spins, the screechy rock music just reaching her ears in the breeze. The solitude is about to overwhelm her when she hears fast footsteps approaching from the stalls.

Certain that she will regret it, she starts to turn around the corner to tell Josh that she is leaving when Baxter thuds past the end of her nose. Flinching in surprise she slides down the wall to the ground and holds her breath, watching his feet slap in the dirt to the offbeat rhythm caused by his klutzy running gate. She gasps for air as the smell of severe body odor mixed with alcohol and cigarette smoke lingers on the weak breeze; her nostrils flair at the revolting funk. Suddenly she hears thumping from the stall but can only sit fearfully on her heels against the wall with her eyes closed. The stall door bumps shut and Josh asks breathlessly, "Did you see him?"

A small sob escapes her as she clutches his arm, "Yes. He *really* scared me."

"What did he do?"

"He just ran by and went over there. But I thought it was you for a second," her voice trembles.

The glow of Baxter's cigarette ember bops across the darkened parking lot towards the maintenance buildings.

She pulls Josh close and pleads, "Can we go back to the fair now?"

He hugs her briefly then says, "No." With a shake of his head he clarifies his meaning gently, "I mean *I* can't. I need to talk to him," then squeezes her shoulders as he asks, "Will you go back to the church booth and tell my brother to wait for me there? I'm sure it's after ten and he'll be waiting."

"Come with me. Please?" she asks hopefully, wiping away a tear that tickles down her cheek.

"I'll be there in a minute. I promise," he replies trying to make his voice sound convincing. Baxter clods behind the maintenance building out of sight, and Josh feels a jolt of energy as he turns to pursue him. "I'll meet you at the church soon," he calls back loudly as he jogs away. Karen waits for him to round a building then looks for the shortest way back to the midway.

Afraid that he won't be able to find Baxter again Josh takes a shortcut through the corner of the fair. The line for the Shaker reaches across the road so he splits through the middle, apologizing as he bumps people out of his way. He turns to run and stumbles into a Stilt-walker—bowling the entertainer over onto his back—but he doesn't stop to help and angry protests ring in his ears as he disappears. He's feeling frantic and slides along the buildings to avoid the crowds until he reaches the path to the maintenance building. He sprints across the grass beginning to wonder what his own intentions are, *What will I say to him? What will I do if he admits what he did?* He fantasizes about dragging him forcefully to the police.

But Baxter is nowhere to be found. Keyed up, Josh rubs his hands together anxiously then runs to the far side of the maintenance complex. In an unlit area of the parking lot he spots Baxter's bouncing head and bends low to use the weak street lights to improve his view. Baxter is shuffle running toward a row of cars parked by the exit. Josh starts after him but it is several hundred yards away and Baxter gets in a car and drives around the outside of the parking lot before Josh reaches him. Josh is used to running for hours and his breath is even but he feels aggravated that he can't catch the fiend. He walks slowly towards the maintenance buildings while he watches the car's dust rising through the outskirts of the lot. When it reaches the farthest corner, instead of exiting, it turns and follows the lane toward the horse lots. Josh utters, "Unbelievable" under his breath then takes a couple skipping steps to see over the roofs of the cars. Sprinting again, he follows the tail lights reflecting in the dust, as he runs to the corner of the maintenance buildings. The car speeds by two rows away, and he can hear the gravel crunching under the tires and clanking when it bounces off the parked cars. Josh gives chase but the car is going over forty miles an hour and pulls away quickly. Josh runs silently, his eyes squinted to block the dust as the car grinds to a stop in front of the tack room.

Josh is still several hundred yards away when Baxter gets out of the car, opens the trunk and unlocks the tack room. He leans his arms on the roof of the car, takes a pull of whisky then sets the bottle on the roof, the dark bottle outlined by a light behind. He bends over to reach in the driver's window and starts the car again. Chugging greedily out of the bottle, he tosses it through the window and is hastily heading into the tack room when he hears Josh and stops in his tracks with a stiffening jolt. He turns quickly as if heading back to his car then instantly recognizes Josh and faces him with an evil grin. Scrunching his eyes into narrow slits as if it means something, he takes a last drag on his cigarette then flicks the butt at Josh and demands acidly, "What do you want boy?"

Josh knocks the sparks out the air reactively. His eyes widen in return as he steps closer knowing that he's confronting one of the most revolting vermin that walk the earth.

Twenty-two

At nine forty-five Washboard Wally and Cowboy Bob take the stage together. They search the audience for everyone that has contributed to the show throughout the night and bring them on the stage for the grand finale. Of course, Logan is in the front row and the comedian's assistant drops a floppy donkey hat onto his head. It hangs down his back into a silly tail that trails the ground behind his feet. She escorts him onto the stage then dramatically swooshes her arms and announces him as the winner of the night's beauty contest. But when she asks him to bray Logan refuses in embarrassment. She recruits the audience's applause and he finally agrees. The comedians shush the audience until it is almost totally silent then Washboard Wally aims the microphone at Logan while closing one eye and pretending to be afraid of the sound that Logan may produce. Logan rolls his eyes, unknowingly adding to the drama and the crowd chuckles lightly. When he finally bray's, his silly honking interpretation of a donkey leaves Ballsac in shambles. Stoney stomps his feet and elbows Ballsac as he doubles up in laughter.

The comedian's line their victims across the front of the stage and everyone bows randomly as the comedians pretend to kick their lower half. Just when the audience thinks the show is over, a mini cannon fires confetti over the bowed heads with an unexpected boom. The audience flinches and Logan cowers, dropping to his knees and covering his ears until he sees the confetti fluttering over the seats. He gives Stoney a sheepish look as Wally helps him to his feet with a flourishing wave. Stoney throws ice at Logan and covers his mouth with his hands to hold back his giggles.

For the moment Logan has forgotten about Josh, his worries have subsided and he smiles grandly as Wally lifts his arm and forces him to wave to the applause. As each participant steps off the stage Cowboy Bob gives them a magic wand and says with a jesting but business like deep voice, "Thank you, for your valued assistance."

"You were awesome," Stoney exclaims clapping Logan's shoulder.

"I've never seen anything so funny. Jesse would be jealous," Ballsac adds with a silly laugh.

Stoney grabs the magic wand from his hand and bonks his head, "I dub thee Sir Logan Donkalot."

They are pushing their way toward the midway with Stoney waving the wand in passerby's faces making magic spells, when Logan reminds them, "I have to go to the exhibits and meet my brother."

"Man I wanted to ride the Yo Yo," Ballsac argues forlornly.

"After we get my brother," Logan insists over the Yo Yo's blasting music.

They stop to watch John the Stilt-walker juggle basketballs, but one of his arms is wrapped in an ace bandage from the elbow to the wrist and he keeps dropping them. He abandons his attempts to perform the feat and tosses two balls to his assistant then bounces the last ball over his head in giant arcs. His assistant directs people to walk between his legs and Stoney stops in the middle while looking up and yells, "He's really tall. He should be on Josh's basketball team."

Logan begins to jog through the thinning crowd near the exhibits, "Hurry up and we'll get to ride more rides." He stops at the entrance to review Stoney's map then leads them to the church booth. A girl sits by herself watching the crowd, Logan says, "Hi. I'm supposed to meet my brother Josh here at ten."

She looks at him quizzically, "I'm the only one here."

Logan checks the clock over the mattress booth. It's ten-twenty. He asks the girl, "Has he been here?"

"There were a bunch of people here. They're looking for Wendy and left a couple minutes ago."

"They never found Wendy?" Logan asks in a startled tone then continues, "My brother is kinda tall. He was with Karen too. Did you see him?"

"Sure, *I know* Karen. She was here a while ago with a big guy, like maybe eight or nine," the girl recalls confidently.

A salesman is barking a commercial a few booths down. Stoney tells Logan, "We'll be back in a minute. I want to see what that is."

Logan sits on the box next to the girl and waits for Josh—hoping that Josh didn't run into LJ and Ben again but confident that he could take both of them by himself if he had to. The girl scoots away and turns sideways so she can see Logan better. He looks away uncomfortably so she doesn't think he's trying to be weird. Stoney has pushed his way to the front of the crowd gathered around the salesman. The salesman tosses out sample towels at the end of his show but Ballsac catches one behind the crowd and Stoney doesn't. They fight for it as they make their way back and Logan thinks that they look like a couple dorks. Stoney has the towel wrapped around Ballsac's neck and is choking him when Ballsac gives in. Stoney folds the towel and beams happily, "My mom will love this stupid thing."

"I didn't want it anyway," Ballsac replies sourly.

Logan is sick of watching the clock and is concerned about Josh. He slides off the box and asks the girl, "Will you tell my brother we'll come back by eleven-thirty?"

"What's his name again?"

"Josh"

"Josh," she repeats. "I will if I see him," she waves her fingers in a folding motion as they leave.

When they reach the midway Logan climbs onto an upside down trash barrel and notes incredulously, "There's a thousand people here."

"There's a lot more than that," Stoney corrects in agreement.

"Why are there so many all of a sudden?"

"The races let out at ten-thirty," Stoney points at a group of boys wearing racing t-shirts and hats.

Ballsac yells up to Logan, "Hey somebody's calling your name."

"Where?"

"Over there somewhere," Ballsac points over the crowd across the street.

Rob is waving his arms over his head and jumping up and down. Logan waves back and drops off the barrel wondering, *Why is he here?* They fight through the throng, finding Rob pacing between the screams from the Sizzler and music blasting from the Scorpion. Rob yells, "Where's Josh?"

"I can't find him," Logan explains with his mouth against Rob's ear that Josh is searching for Wendy. "We were supposed to meet him at ten, but he never showed up. I was standing on that barrel to look for him."

Rob checks his watch, "Where do you think he went?"

Logan smacks his head with his palm, "*Oh yeah.* He showed me on the map." Logan holds his hand out to Stoney for the map then crouches over it on the ground outlining Josh's search area with his finger, "He told me he was going to be out here somewhere."

"You boys stick with me and we'll find him together," Rob orders as he folds the map under his arm.

"Why are you here dad?" Logan asks when he suddenly remembers that his dad had shown up unexpectedly.

"I came to get you boys. Your mom told me you had a fight again last night. Now keep your eyes open for Josh."

Logan quietly says, "Oh,' then follows silently, trying to keep pace as Stoney and Ballsac exchange knowing looks.

Every ride is packed as if the entire city has arrived. The lines feeding the rides form around the unsteady fences then curl into the street blocking the pathways. Rob's frustration is obvious as they press on. He sighs and tugs Logan through breaks in the lines, by the shirt sleeve. With so many bodies bumping and elbowing each other Logan is warming up and rubs the dampness from his eyebrow with his shirt sleeve.

Stoney whispers to Logan, "It's gettin hot with all these people."

Logan nods and suddenly spots Karen at the edge of the crowd. She is leaning on her knee's panting, as if she has been running. Logan yells, "Karen, Karen." Then he shouts at Rob and sticks his finger through his belt loop and tugs to get his attention, "Dad, they're over here." He leads Rob to Karen who is still gasping for air with her back to a building. She leans forward and looks around the side of the building hoping it will provide a shortcut to the exhibits. She is about to start into the hallway between the buildings when she hears Logan calling and turns around with her searching eyes opened wide. When she sees Logan she smiles weakly and falls against the wall with her eyes closed in relief.

"What's the matter?" Logan asks her flushed face.

"I've been looking everywhere for you," she explains breathlessly.

"Where's Josh?"

"He's chasin' that man Baxter," her voice is filled with heavy emotional angst, her eyes dancing between Logan's and Rob's.

Rob grabs her shoulder, "What do you mean? Chasing Baxter?"

"Yeah, he's a trash man. Josh followed him out to the horse barn," she answers, frightened by his tight grip, she brushes his hand away.

"You mean Baxter works here? But why would Josh do that?" Rob demands.

"Uh huh," Karen nods. "Josh saw him pushing a garbage cart and told me he's the man that did something awful to Lizzy. He said he wants to talk to him but I think he is going to do something bad, something…" her voice trails off and her eyes fall to her feet.

Rob drops on one knee, grips both of her elbows and says evenly, "Listen to me carefully. Can you take me to Josh?"

"I think so," she snivels lightly.

Rounding everyone into a circle Rob orders, "Let's stick together. I don't want to lose anyone else." He waits for their nods then tells Karen, "You lead the way."

They press against the building until they reach the fence around the Zipper. Ignoring the loud protests of the carnie, they slip around the back side of the fence to the next building. The next two rides share a fence and they are forced to snake through the massive crowd waiting to be spun like a ragdoll. A burrito vendor's cart blocks half the street at the corner so Karen takes Rob by the hand and splits the food line, getting snarled at by an angry short fat bald man anxious for his taco, probably his kangaroo meat taco, *everybody says fair food tastes better…*

"There. There's the Punkin swings, that's the right way," Karen's eyes shift with uncertainty. Even though she's following the same route they did earlier she is beginning to think that she's totally lost when they enter the maintenance complex. She bursts out in elation, "This is it! This is where we followed him."

A maintenance man is cleaning up the mess that Baxter made earlier. She inspects him interestedly for a second then says, "That's not him. He went over to the stables down this way," as she leads them into the dark.

They reach the chain link fence and Rob puts his hand on her shoulder, "Hang on a sec. I want to talk to that worker. Stay right here I'll be right back." Striding across the grass he approaches and calls out so the man isn't startled, "Hello?"

Trash skids out of the room then his head pokes out of the door, "Hello yourself. You're not supposed to be in this area."

"Sorry. I'm looking for a person that works here. A guy named Baxter," Rob explains quickly, hoping that he would know where to look.

"You and me both. He's left a damn mess and cut out early for some reason. Didn't tell nobody either," he says in a raspy pissed of voice.

Hoping for more useful information Rob asks, "Do you have an idea where he may have gone?"

"Nope. If you find him tell him I'm sick of doing his job for him," he dismisses Rob as he returns to work.

Rob watches him work, wondering if he can get any further information then gives up and trots back to the fence. "They're not here. Where are the stables?" Rob asks Karen patiently.

"This way," she is grateful that he came back so quickly.

"C'mon boys. Don't get lost," Rob follows her into the ever increasing quiet. When they reach the parking lot at the end of the chain link fence she points at the barns across the field and explains softly, "That's where Josh was when I left."

"In the parking lot?" Rob asks wonderingly?

"Yes. *Sort of.* He was going to follow the man over that way," she points the opposite direction. "But we were right there by the barn."

Rob searches the dark parking lot for any signs of Josh or Baxter. Unsure of which direction to go, he sighs in irritation and murmurs to himself, *We shouldn't have let them go out tonight.* He strides into the parking lot and steps onto the rear bumper of the nearest truck so he can see over the tops of the trailers. Slapping his thigh in annoyance he steps down to ask Karen what Josh was doing at the barn when he hears distant angry voices from that direction.

Karen listens carefully then cries in a high sharp voice, "I think that's where Josh is! It's coming from the other side of the barn where we followed that man."

Logan breaks away towards the barn, sprinting as fast as he can get his legs to move, terrified his brother is in serious trouble. He hears Rob shouting to the others, "Stay here. We'll be right back." He glances back and sees Rob following but running backwards and pointing at Karen.

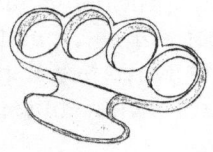

Twenty-three

"What did you do to Lizzy?" Josh demands sternly. He had thought of a million questions he wanted answered in the last few hours but he wants this answered first.

Baxter's eyes shift awkwardly as his mind slugs along searching for an easy lie. "Git out of here before something bad happens to you," he warns when he is unable to craft a reasonable response, trying to dismiss Josh.

"Stop threatening me you filthy pig. You don't have any power over me," Josh barks aggressively, involuntarily crossing his arms.

"I don't have time for this shit. Get lost!" Baxter orders, his voice reaching a whining tone.

"LJ told me Lizzy was at your house, alone with you. You'd better tell me quick," Josh grits his teeth in uncontrollable anger as the image of Lizzy's soft hair mixed with Baxter's sickening face bounces off his skull.

Too lost in his own doings to realize that Josh means business—used to being able to manhandle his own boys—his confidence is unshaken, "I've got things to do. *Git* your sorry ass *outta* here boy."

Baxter starts toward the open door of the tack room but Josh unyieldingly blocks his path spreading his feet wide and raising his hands in anticipation. Baxter's eyes open widely as confusion crosses his face. He studies Josh's posture then begins to realize that this isn't a terrified little boy he's dealing with. Josh is several inches taller than him and may even outweigh him. He backs away a step putting his hands on his hips and stutters seriously, "LJ, LJ told you something? What did that shitpoke say?"

"Lizzy was at your house," Josh presses powerfully, "What did you do to her?"

Baxter searches his pockets quickly as he turns his feet in a half circle. His cheek twitches with the effort of making his brain push through the years of foggy drunken stupidity. He measures the distance to his car, flexing his knees slightly as if preparing to take flight. Josh slides his front foot forward anticipating the next move as the rank smell of his enemy invades his senses.

As he comes to grips with the fact that he will have to deal with Josh one way or the other Baxter delays with a hiss, "What sorta hogwash did that piece of shit LJ tell you?"

Josh is growing impatient and growls in an uncompromising tone, "*You're* the piece of shit. Lizzy was killed and tortured by you. I know it and you know it."

Suddenly from within the tack room a weak frightened girl's voice calls out despairingly, "Help! Please help me!"

Josh backs into the doorway but a quick glance into the darkness doesn't reveal anything. He runs his hand along the wall but can't find a light switch and doesn't want to risk taking his eyes off of Baxter. As he starts to step back out the door the chain of a ceiling light brushes over his shoulder. Baxter shuffles his feet nervously as he watches Josh's face. Josh tugs the chain—as the light illuminates the room a girl cries out in fear, "Don't!" Baxter takes advantage of the disruption in Josh's focus and lunges towards his car cursing loudly.

Josh squints in the sudden brightness, his brain whirling in astonishment and turmoil when he sees Wendy lying on her side. Stuffed under several saddles her arms and legs are hogtied together; tape circles her head but she has chewed it in two where it covered her mouth. Their eyes meet briefly, hers desperate and pleading in violated terror, his wide in horror.

He leaps through the doorway silently pursuing Baxter with deadly intent. But Baxter's engine was already running and he drops it into gear, spinning the tires in the gravel. The engine races and the car moves forward slowly; Josh hurdles against the driver's door, grabbing Baxter's head through the open window with one arm and the steering wheel with the other. The car gains speed and Josh yanks at the wheel, his feet taking giant steps and skipping over the gravel; as they fight for control the car slews sideways, slamming into a trailer, tipping it up on two wheels. Thrown from the car, Josh flies briefly, spinning like a top; the air rockets from his lungs when his ribs thud against the trailer axle. The wheels bounce back to the dirt, narrowly missing his hand.

Curling into a ball on his side Josh wraps his arms around his ribs and gathers his wits. As he recovers from the sharp pain he rolls up on his knees, leaning one elbow on the front bumper of the car. Baxter is flopped against the steering wheel holding his face. Hot water suddenly burns Josh knees from the punctured radiator. With a grunt he lifts himself to his feet.

Baxter spots Josh through the crazed basketball size dent in the windshield. He mutters to himself then leans over and digs under the passenger seat with one hand as he watches Josh approach the window. Josh yanks the door open and grabs Baxter's arm with both hands but Baxter's fingers are clutched tightly around the steering wheel and his other arm clings under the seat bottom.

Baxter leans over further, his arm rattling through the jumbled papers under the seat. When Josh wrenches his grip from the steering wheel he kicks Josh's chest but Josh catches his leg and twists Baxter onto his stomach on the seat. Baxter screams hysterically as he wraps his left arm further under the seat and stretches for the passenger door handle with his right hand.

Locking elbows around Baxter's shins Josh heaves, lifting him halfway from the car. Baxter grunts and kicks one leg loose trying to pull back into the car with the steering wheel. Josh squeezes the other leg in his armpit but Baxter's shoe slips off allowing him to twist his leg loose. Baxter shoves off the steering wheel tumbling backwards over Josh. They fall across the gravel in a tangle; Baxter's cussing raises to a paralyzing shriek. Josh spins under Baxter's weight, holding his breath as the nauseating stench of body odor and pure filth envelopes him.

As they scramble to their feet, Josh wraps Baxter's knee in both arms and thrusts the point of his shoulder into Baxter's larynx. The sudden pain causes Baxter to twist away so Josh continues to lift, flipping him on his back with a thump. Baxter tries to crawl away but Josh drops one knee across his calf and smashes Baxter's face with his forearm tossing him to his back again.

Swinging upward at Josh's face Baxter hits him in the side of the head above the eye. Josh turns his head away from the sharp pain as he realizes what Baxter was reaching for under the seat. Baxter has a weapon in his fist. He grabs Baxter's wrist with both hands and pushes away.

Josh circles Baxter as he climbs to his feet. Clapping his hands together Baxter flips his switchblade forward and clicks the blade out, grinning grossly through his snaggeled teeth as he goads, "Didn't know what you were gettin into, did ya boy?"

On the offensive now, Baxter's confidence swells as he mimics Josh's backward steps. Josh quickly creates a safe distance then slides his hand into the brass knuckles and faces his enemy warily. Baxter flicks the knife at Josh's face grinning crazily and limps closer. Josh feints a swing, grabs Baxter's wrist then rabbit punches his side twice and pushes away as Baxter tries to cover with his elbow. Wincing heavily, Baxter's expression changes to confusion so Josh feints another punch then steps on his foot and trips him; punching his forehead twice when he reaches behind to break the fall.

Rolling to his knee's Baxter swings the knife in defensive arcs and bawls in frustrated fury, "I'll kill you, you little bastard!" He dives at Josh's ankles but Josh sidesteps and knees his face while dropping two violent punches into the back of his neck.

Flopping to his back, Baxter kicks at Josh, slicing the knife as if it were a sword; then reaches over his shoulder and arches his back, rotating his head and grunting in pain as he gets to his feet again. His hands tremble with unfamiliar fear—fear he's never faced when he callously beat his wife and step children. He faces Josh again, unclear how to get the advantage, then backs slowly, looking for an escape route. Years of self abuse have dampened his reactions and he has the endurance of a hundred pound slug; panting, he leans heavily on one knee with the knife pointed defensively at Josh.

Blood runs from the deep gouges in Baxter's forehead, dripping into his eye. He tries to clear it away by rubbing with his wrist; only creating a more gruesome effect to his nasty expression. His dirty sock is slipping from his shoeless foot as his feet slide backwards over the loose pebbles. He feels the wetness on his wrist and takes account of his face with his free hand and screams ferociously, "I'm gonna stick this where the sun don't shine!"

He abruptly rushes Josh but his stocking foot loses traction and he trips to his knees without coming within a mile of Josh's retreating legs. Josh blocks behind Baxter's arm and runs a short circle around his back and kicks him to his face. As he falls forward Baxter's hands slide through the gravel; the knife rolls free under his palm; he tries to grab it in a panic but it stabs clear through the muscle between his thumb and index finger. Frustration and fear covers his face as he howls in pain and tears the blade from his hand. He sits on one leg and flips his hand over, squeezing the gushing wounds where the knife penetrated both sides of his hand. He grimaces at Josh as he clutches for the knife on his lap with his weakened hand then switches it to the other hand when he finds he can't grasp with the wounded hand any longer. The pouring wound leaves a bloody hand print in the dirt as he struggles unsteadily to his feet.

Josh watches Baxter's pain with terrible indifference while he crouches in anticipation of the next attack. He knows revenge isn't the right path but he's unable stop himself. Lizzy's happy voice; her hair; the touch of her hand; her enchanting eyes all vibrate incessantly in his mind directing his actions; he's fighting for Wendy too; he's fighting a life and death battle for himself. He's breathing heavily, not from exertion, but within the uncontrollable raging storm and anguish that clenches his heart like a tightening steel band.

Unable to pursue any longer, Baxter hunkers defensively over his knee. Waving the knife at eye level his face contorts in pain as blood drips from the blade, reminding Josh of his appalling history.

Josh circles now, looking for an opening. A jolting shudder runs into his neck causing his vision to blur briefly. He dances on his toes to shake out the weak trembling in his legs. He feints a punch then pauses for Baxter's reaction and trips him while at the same instant reaching for the knife hand. Baxter strikes at him but Josh blocks wrist to wrist and shoves him to his back. Unable to catch his balance Baxter's head bounces off the dirt. Josh seizes his wrist with both hands and twists Baxter's arm under his knee then brutally jams all his body weight into the tendons of the snared wrist.

Baxter punches and claws uselessly at Josh's back with his free hand; leaving bloody finger tracks across the back of Josh's shirt as blood sprays from the knife wound. He rotates the knife in his trapped hand and tries uselessly to cut Josh.

Josh continues to fight silently, bouncing his body and grinding his knee into Baxter's arm, ignoring the pathetic blows to his back. Baxter screeches like a skunk in a trap but Josh doesn't hear him, his neck muscles are drawn so tight his hearing has completely gone away.

Baxter tries to bite Josh's thigh and receives a sharp elbow to the eye, causing him to jolt flat on his back in pain. He drops the knife and yelps in a panicky howl when Josh kicks it away.

Keeping Baxter's arm pinned with his knee, Josh spins to face Baxter. Baxter claws at Josh's eyes, leaving a streak of blood from his hairline to his chin. He shoves his bloody hand against Josh's chin and squeezes his jaw.

Josh props his chin on Baxter's wounded hand and rains blows to his face and head until his arms fall stiffly to the ground. Suddenly Josh realizes that he isn't fighting back any longer and pauses to look into his half open eyes then slams him in the temple while looking for any reaction, but Baxter's head only lolls to the side.

His chest heaving, Josh tosses the brass knuckles aside and stands over his enemy then kicks his ribs and screams in pent up agony as tears begin to rush down his face, leaving tracks of heartbreak grooved in the bloody dirt. He turns away from the nauseating human scum and leans on his knees with both hands while his hearing slowly returns. Faintly he hears Wendy desperately calling for help and stumbles through the tack room door.

She cringes and cries out in fear when he throws the saddles aside and bends over her to untie her bonds. Unaware of the blood covering his face and confused by her reaction, he tries to calm her with a weak froggy voice, "You'll be all right. Let me get you loose."

She struggles to talk clearly through the tape, so he carefully pulls it off of her face and is untangling it from her hair when she stutters with quivering lips, "What happ..., are you OK?"

"Yeah. I don't know. Let's get you loose," he answers, grimly fumbling with the ropes again. His heart is thundering in his chest, creating a strange throbbing sensation in his head that he's never felt before.

He frees her hands and is struggling with the ropes around her ankle when he hears Baxter's car starting. He watches the door as he continues to work on the ropes and orders in a whisper, "When I get these off, you run for help. Run for your life!"

Her whole body is shaking with shock, fear has locked her into a knotted muscle, her teeth clack together as she hysterically tries to answer him, "I'll try."

When he unties one leg, she can't stand on her own so he lifts her and half carries her to the door, the cotton rope dragging behind from one ankle. As they cross the door jamb they run into Logan. He skids to a stop, his head bounces off Josh's chest knocking him to his butt. Rob is just behind and cries out in fear and disbelief when he sees Josh's bloody face.

The car is tearing across the lot leaving a plume of dust behind, the open trunk flaps wildly as it bounces over the ruts. It slides onto the main parking lot artery and accelerates towards the exit; the engine rattling in dissent at the abuse. The dull interior light is on and Josh spots Baxter's head briefly as it groans past a row of parked trailers.

The headlights blink on as it nears the street, but it doesn't slow when it approaches the red light at the exit. The car has reached over sixty miles per hour when Baxter tries to make the turn. The sliding tires screech angrily over the pavement and the car makes a slight turn but drifts almost directly across the street, bouncing over the curb into the dirt. A truck spins in a slow circle as it avoids the out of control car. The car is entering a sideways slide when it launches into the air off of a small dirt mound. It makes a half spin before it hits the ground upside down then rolls sideways once and crashes into the low metal fence in front of the canal. With a screech of protesting metal it bounds into the air end over end, landing with a huge whumping splash, upside down in the muddy canal water.

Rob involuntarily raises his palms toward the dusty crash as if to block it from his sight and screams at Josh in a panic, "What is happening?"

Josh carries Wendy to Rob and they fall emotionally exhausted in his arms. Rob hugs them to his chest, terrible anguish covering his face. Dropping to one knee he cries in despair, "Oh my. Oh my! Where are you hurt?"

Josh's face and neck are streaked with blood where Baxter defended with his injured hand. The front of his shirt is blotched strawberry as though it has sopped up a gallon of cherry Koolaid while the back is covered with dark red handprints like an oil covered wipe cloth. Logan bends over Josh with his hand to his forehead in fright. Karen throws her arms around Logan's body, restraining him to give Rob room. Stoney and Ballsac are staring at the blood in amazement.

"I'm not hurt. I'm not hurt at all," Josh shouts with regret when he realizes the pain Rob is in. Rising to his feet, he takes stock of his shirt then pulls it off over his head to prove that he's not injured. "Look dad I'm fine," he says trying to show composure as he runs his hands over his chest.

"Your face is all bloody," Rob exclaims running his shaking fingers over Josh's chin and examining his face.

"Is it? But I'm not hurt. See?" Josh lifts his chin and turns his head to show Rob.

Wendy pulls away from Rob, latches her arms around Karen's neck and sobs hysterically into her hair. Karen does her best to console her but at the same time doesn't know exactly what happened to her and watches Josh intently.

Rob wipes Josh's face with a handkerchief, dumb-founded that he's uninjured and says in a barely audible strangled voice, "Tell me what's been going on here."

"Let me think a second," Josh looks toward the accident. The trail of dust left by the fleeing car hovers over the lot and partially obscures their view. The haze above the crash is illuminated as rubbernecking motorists park in the dirt along the edge of the canal with their lights aimed toward the accident. Josh watches the flickering forms of the people running through the headlights and the dark cloud as he tries to think where to begin.

"I'll try," he rubs his neck with both hands to calm his agitated nerves. He watches Rob rinse his now pink handkerchief in the melted ice water from Ballsac's drink, takes a deep breath then begins.

"We were trying to find Wendy. I saw Baxter and chased him. I followed him here and we started arguing," he looks uneasily away from Rob's stern gaze as he catches his breath. "Then I heard Wendy yelling for help and when I saw her tied up, he tried to get away and we started fighting."

Josh looks down at his bloody arms as he recalls the battle then points, "He crashed his car into that trailer and then we had another fight. He had a knife. I punched him out and came in to help Wendy and he took off..., over there," he points at the growing crowd across the parking lot.

"Who tied you up?" Rob asks Wendy as rage covers his face.

Wendy's voice is a thin tense whisper as if she can't force her body to utter a sound, "The stinky garbage man grabbed me in the bathroom and choked me really bad. He tied me up too," Wendy's small voice falters to silence as she shows Rob the bruises on the back of her arms and neck.

She closes her eyes to keep the sobs at bay then stammers faintly, "He cov..., covered me up in a box of trash then put me in that room, a *long* time. He came back a couple times to twist my arms and tie me up tighter. He said the worst things I ever heard. He just got back when Josh started fighting with him." She pauses as if to catch her breath then moans and begins to say something else but is unable to speak as soft tearful sobs wrack her shoulders. Karen hugs her consolingly as she rubs the muddy tears from her cheeks with her arms.

"This is unreal," Rob mutters, shaking his head and wiping his face with both hands as if trying to wake himself. "When did he tie you up?"

"It was still light outside. Like six or seven maybe?" she answers questioningly, pulling Karen down with her as she collapses in the dirt with her back against the barn. "Do you know where my dad is?" she begins to weep softly with her face between her knees.

Rob sighs sadly then looks around trying to decide what to do. He doesn't want to leave any of the children behind to get lost again. The few people in sight are hurrying to the accident but there's no one near to provide assistance. He looks at the blue and red emergency lights spinning round in the intersection, jumbled with the background flashing of the fairs lights. "Let's go over there and talk to the police," he says with a frown after he considers the ugly option of going into the fair and searching for help.

"Can you walk?" Rob asks Wendy compassionately as he kneels at her feet with his hand lifting her chin. She doesn't answer so he carefully lifts her slight delicate body in his arms.

Logan puts his arm around Josh's waist to help him walk. Josh smiles down at him thankful for the comfort, and they begin to follow Rob the several hundred yards to the exit. Karen wraps her arm in the crook of Josh's, staring up at him with revere and dedication.

Stoney finds the weapons in the dirt and picks them up, exploring them quietly with Ballsac as they trail behind. Rob hears the click of the blade and glances behind to make sure they're following close, so Stoney covers them with his hand then shoves them into his pocket.

Josh starts to tell Rob why he was following Baxter but Rob shushes him saying earnestly, "We'll talk later son. Let's get her to the police."

There are three police cars but one of the policemen is holding the crowd away while the others search the canal with flashlights. When they cross the street and approach the policeman that is restraining the crowd he looks at them with astonishment and says broadly, "Everything always happens at the same time."

Sirens of an arriving ambulance blast over the crowds wondering chatter and Rob rushes Wendy to the ambulance without waiting for the policeman's direction. The emergency team steers him to the back door and pushes everyone aside as they direct him to set her down. Josh stands shirtless with Logan and

Karen, worriedly watching over the team's shoulders as they lay her on the stretcher.

Stoney and Ballsac watch for a minute then go the edge of the canal to see if the police have found Baxter. Except for one corner of a bumper that the water swirls around, the car is completely submerged. Stoney crouches over a deep gouge in the ground that the car made with its last roll. He calls Ballsac over to point it out marveling, "There's *no way* they're gonna find him."

The police are returning from the quarter mile trek to the gateway in the canal searching along their way. One of them is saying to the other, "If somebody floated under that, they'd be stuck till spring. We found a body under one of those gates last year that was at least a month old."

Stoney raises his eyebrows at Ballsac and they move out of the way of the arriving tow truck. The policeman directs the tow truck with his flashlight as it backs to the bank then asks the driver. "Can you hook onto that bumper there?"

"We'll try," the driver presses the button to feed out the cable. His helper drags the cable to the bank and waits. Like an experienced cowboy, the driver slings a rope over his head looping around the bumper after the first try. The helper catches the end trailing in the water with a pole and then ties it to the cable; they feed out more cable securing it around the bumper to a loop on the back of the tow truck. The police whisk the crowd back as the driver revs the truck engine and reels the cable in. When the slack is gone the truck engine revs higher and the car slowly drags up the bank; the flowing water trying to suck the backend around. When both front tires are above the water the cable slips off the bumper, bouncing off the bank with a thump. The helper fixes it securely to the frame and they watch as the smashed windshield appears; then a man's forearm, dangling limply through the crack between the dashboard and the crushed roof.

When the wrecked car finally sits across the canal road the driver turns off the winch and a policeman bends to the ground to peek through the crack between the smashed roof and the top of the door. "Yup. There's somebody in there all right. And it ain't purty," he tries to use a business like tone but sounds appalled as he brushes his pants off.

Stoney and Ballsac return to the ambulance where Stoney repeats the grim news to Logan with emphasis on, "It ain't purty."

Terrified for her friend, Karen is coiled under Josh's shoulder watching them roll Wendy's stretcher into the bright lights inside the ambulance. A fire truck has honked its way next to the ambulance and the firemen are gathering behind the ambulance. Rob asks them to look at Josh and they sit him on the steps of the ambulance as the medical team cares for Wendy inside. Logan sits on the bumper at Josh's side with Karen squeezing against him. Rob leans over Logan and watches a fireman cleaning the blood off of Josh's face and the cut in his hairline.

"You need to go to the hospital too," the fireman tells Josh firmly as he glances up at Rob. He lifts Josh by the elbow, leads him into the ambulance then sits him on the bench next to Wendy. "This boy probably needs stitches in his head," he says to the paramedic on the other side of Wendy. Wendy smiles weakly at Josh and taps his knee then slides her hand into his.

As the fireman climbs down Rob puts his hand on Logan's shoulder and says confidently, "Logan, I have to go with Josh. You need to take Karen back to the fair so she can meet her mom and dad, they'll be worried sick. You boys stay together and I'll have your mom pick you up at the church booth."

"My dad can drive them home," Karen offers through her pools of tears.

Rob thinks for a second, "Yeah, that's better." The fireman shuts the door and slaps it with his hand. The ambulance turns onto the street and speeds away with the siren blaring.

When Logan starts to lead them away the fireman asks unbelievingly, "Were all of you in that car when it crashed?"

Logan shakes his head at the crumpled wreck and answers, "No. Just a drunken crazy man."

"What happened to that girl and boy then? Did he hit them with the car?"

"He attacked them, at the fair. My brother chased him off," Logan responds proudly, pointing towards the spinning lights of the ambulance.

The fireman lowers his eyebrows in confusion at Logan, "You wait here. The police will want to talk to you." He walks towards the two policeman working on the car but is interrupted by another fireman who leads him to the other side of the fire truck.

"Let's just go. I want to find my dad," Karen whispers to Logan.

Logan grabs her hand and the four of them run across the street, disappearing into the darkness before the fireman returns. Using the trailers for cover they quickly reach the barns and make their way into the thinning crowds and to the exhibits.

A huge crowd is gathered at the church booth planning a search when Logan leads them under the awning. Karen's mom spies her first and cries out as she stumbles over to them. Karen and Logan do their best to quickly relate the story as a million questions fly; helping each other when they run into a question that they can't answer. Wendy's dad interrupts early in the questioning, demanding in a weakened voice to know where she is. When Logan says she's at the hospital, they don't ask any more questions but flee from the fair as though from a forest fire.

When everyone is satisfied that they have an understanding of what happened they begin to give Logan and Karen breathing room and break into small groups of shocked parents, hugging their own children when they realize the evil and destructive monster that has been in their midst. To Logan's relief, Karen's dad finally ushers them to the parking lot leaving the speculating crowd behind.

Logan checks Karen's dad's watch and finds it's after twelve and asks him if he can get a ride home. He wonders if his mom knows yet and hopes to get home quickly to reassure her. Ballsac is spending the night at Stoney's so they drop them off first. Stoney's dad is waiting out front as usual. He already has one son in jeopardy and is ecstatic when Stoney climbs out. Logan almost smiles as they drive away and he hears Stoney finally talking a mile a minute again. Carol is waiting at the door too. She rushes to the car then smothers Logan with love as she leads Karen's family into the house. Carol calls Rob at the hospital several times to get reassurance that Josh is actually doing well and it's four in the morning before Karen's family leaves. Logan is still taut when she tries to put him to bed. He begs her to call Josh but she soothes him and they drift to restless sleep on the couch desperately holding each other.

Twenty-four

Logan and Carol wake at eight. She starts to call the hospital but decides to wait, just in case Josh is still resting. She thinks it would be best to let him get as much sleep as a hospital room will allow. She knows his day will be a busy one.

Even though he didn't get much rest either, Logan is ready to go before she is and waits with the door propped open while she ties her Keds. They are starting to accelerate down the street when Logan sees Lizzy's mom, Christy Camber, running out her front door and gesturing for them to stop. He turns around to watch her and says sleepily, "Stop mom. Lizzy's mom wants to talk to us."

He rolls down his window and Carol leans over looking harried, almost frantic, "Hi, we're on our way to the hospital."

Mrs. Camber's eyes are tear filled already. She compassionately explains, "I'm so sorry, I heard what happened last night. We want to go with you."

Mr. Camber slams out the door and they slide in the back seat, shutting the door after Carol releases the brake and zips off. During the short drive Logan tells them the bits and pieces he is sure of. Lizzy's dad is barely able to contain himself and pounds the seat in grief driven frustration with his fist crying, "I *knew* it. I knew you were right Logan."

Mrs. Camber's holds her hands to her mouth barely able to breathe, unable to utter another word.

Logan has been sitting sideways in the front seat watching them as he answered their questions and decides not to say anymore as he sees them crumpling together under the horrible knowledge.

Carol parks at the emergency entrance and they follow her to Josh's room. Josh is already awake and talking to Officer Dixon and Rob. Carol tells everyone to wait in the hall then shuts the door as she shoves Dixon out of the room.

Dixon leads Logan and the Cambers down the hall to the waiting room and sits in front of them and admits awkwardly, "I'm sorry. I just didn't know everything. I was tricked."

Whether they understand him clearly or not, Lizzy's parents don't say anything, they just hold each other and stare like he has three fish eyes or is speaking another language, the news too fresh in their minds.

Logan shifts uncomfortably, looks Dixon in the eye and replies plainly, "That's OK. It doesn't matter, my brother believed me." Dixon mouth opens as if he is going to speak, then rises and paces in front of them for a minute, finally leaving without a word.

Logan watches him leave then stands, "Let's go see if Josh is all right." He takes Lizzy's mom by the hand and they follow him back to Josh's room. He knocks on the door and Carol cracks the door to let them in. Josh is sitting on the side of the bed putting his shoes on.

With a worried expression glued to his face Josh asks, "Did you guys check on Wendy yet?"

Rob answers in a calming voice, "She's still sleeping. They told me she's going to be fine but needs to rest now."

Josh drops his shoe and lies back on the pillows looking up at Mrs. Camber's. His eyes begin to puddle with tears and he raises his hand to draw her near. She sits on the side of his bed and runs her hand over his cheek and says softly through her matching tears, "You did a brave thing last night, the right thing."

Josh shakes his head unable to speak for the moment. Carol sits on the other side of the bed near his feet and Rob stands behind. Mr. Camber puts his hands on Logan's shoulders at the foot of the bed.

Wiping his eyes with his fists Josh clears his throat, then his face twists in torment as he sobs, "I miss her so much."

Clutching him to her chest Mrs. Camber moans over and over, "We'll be with her again someday. We'll be with her. We'll be with her."

Josh's voice trembles with dark sorrow as he holds her at arms length needing to be heard, "I wish I could have saved her too. I didn't do enough. I can't go on without her!"

The room is filled with the weeping of the terrible tears of unspeakable loss and words of comfort are futile.

Twenty-five

"Hey Woody! You're driving me crazy," Karen yells at Logan amid the hoots and hollers of his crowd of friends in the pool. He swims to the side of the pool and their shocked eyes meet. She's sipping on her coke and blinks over the rim of the glass at his thoughtful stare. She walks close, reaches over the side of the pool and tugs his head then whispers gently into his ear, "Do you remember?"

Pulling her tight so their cheeks are pressed together he starts to talk but his voice catches, "Liz…" He clears his throat, closes his eyes and whispers, "Lizzy? I remember. She used to call me that."

"At the pool huh?" she squeezes his neck cozily.

"Uh huh," he says not wanting to talk any longer.

"What are you two doing?" Wendy asks from her lawn chair as they separate.

To hide the rush of sad emotions covering his face Logan dunks his head under the water then leans on his elbows over the edge of the pool with a forced smile tugging at the corners of his mouth. "Talkin 'bout you," he declares.

"You're not either! What were you doing," Wendy asks Karen dubiously.

Karen bows down to wipe her eyes with her towel and sits on the side of her lawn chair then takes another sip as she stares at Logan's wide eyes. Leaning over to Wendy she gives her a hug, their unblinking eyes meeting Logan's. Unspoken words of love pass between the three of them.

From the other side of the pool Josh throws a sopping wet foam football. It bounces off the back of Logan's head and slops onto Karen's stomach. "Hey!" she yells, playfully throwing it back. Logan swims after it then chases Josh out of the pool faking throws at his head.

Rob is grilling steaks and listening to Larry telling Wendy's dad how he loves the deep throaty sound of the new exhaust Rob put on his Corvette. Carol walks up behind Rob, rubs his back briefly then runs one arm over his shoulder and the other under around his side clasping her hands together at his chest. Affectionately digging her chin into his neck she admits, "I'm so glad you went down there that night." They watch Logan slam Josh in the neck with the ball and run away, Carol giggles, "Look at them now." Logan runs up the stairs screaming for help and dives in the pool with Josh on his tail.

Every family has brought a picnic table. They are formed into a huge horseshoe under the trees to the south of the house. Larry hung strings of white tinkling Christmas lights in the tree's and under the tables creating a magical setting for the dinner. Ginger has created unique centerpieces for each table from arrangements of red, yellow and pink tulips. She is setting silverware at the picnic tables with the assistance of Wendy's mom. Karen's mom is assisting Logan's grandpa with his seat selection, with some difficulty. He is committed to sitting next to Josh but Karen and Wendy have already reserved both sides. After testing several seats he reluctantly agrees to sit next to Stoney's parents. It's only a minute or two before he and Stoney's dad are in the midst of a discussion of World War Two as though they had been friends forever.

Ginger interrupts Larry's dreams of a new camshaft in his Corvette by asking him to move the tables closer together. Wendy's dad takes advantage of the break from car talk and sidles up to Rob asking quietly, "So why do you think the cops didn't catch this lunatic before?"

Rob flips a steak to check its doneness and speaks softly, "They stopped by yesterday to let us know how sorry they were. They apologized to Logan and Josh. Dixon seemed pretty embarrassed."

"What went wrong?" Wendy's dad presses.

After a brief glance at his face Rob thought about his discussions with Dixon then shrugs, "I guess the first thing was, they didn't believe Logan's story. Then they listened to that bastard's lies and got themselves all tied up in a confused fix."

Grandpa hollers, interrupting Rob, "I learned you good Rob. That smells wonderful."

Rob waves at him with his spatula, "Thanks dad," then continues. "Baxter and his wife told him they weren't even in town the day Lizzy disappeared. Logan wasn't sure about the truck either so..., it was some kinda pickle," Rob shrugs again.

"Thank God, Wendy's starting to feel better. Your boys saved my daughter's life and..," Wendy's dad began then broke off when Larry came back hiking his pants up.

Larry raps his knuckles on the grill and asks Rob interestedly, "What are your kids up to now?"

Logan and Josh are standing in a small circle in the darkest area of the yard behind the shed with Stoney and Ballsac. Stoney opens a bag and dumps out the switchblade and brass knuckles onto the grass. Josh digs a hole and kicks the weapons in the bottom then quickly buries it. Logan says gravely, "Don't tell anyone this stuff is here, ever."

"Why would anyone care?" Stone asks too lightly for Logan's comfort.

"I don't know. Me and Josh just want it to be buried forever," Logan answers bluntly before he briefly wraps his arm around Josh's waist. When they had remembered the weapons Josh wanted to turn them over to the police, but Logan didn't want to face any more questioning and Josh quickly agreed. They finally agreed to bury them so they could never be used again. As Josh fills in the dirt Logan is thankful for the strong rush of finality.

Although Logan tries to disguise his feelings Josh notices his strained expression. He messes Logan's hair and adds, "It's just best this way." He tosses the shovel against the shed as they enter the light and smiles at Karen and Wendy who have been watching his every move.

Larry asks Rob with a good natured tone, "Well what do think that was all about? Boys just being boys again?"

"*I'll* raise my boys. *You* just worry about getting your car souped up, and someday we'll have that drag race you keep asking for," Rob aggressively chases him away with his spatula. Josh is talking to the girls while running his hands through his hair. Rob looks at the bruise on his side then looks for the bruises on Logan's side. They are slowly fading from the deep purples and reds they were at first to a dull brown. A small section of Josh's hair had been shaved for the stitches and Rob wonders if the hair will grow back where the scar will be. He cracks his knuckles and makes a mental note to make sure to ask the doctor when they are removed next week.

"Carol, the steaks are done," Rob announces as he wraps the last one in aluminum foil.

Larry blares in his most annoying loudspeaker voice, "Grub's on. Let's go."

Ginger and Wendy's mom direct everyone to their designated chairs. Josh has the center seat with Wendy and Karen on each side, Logan, Stoney and Ballsac on his right and Rob and Wendy's family on the left. Carol, Ginger and Wendy's mom wait for everyone to be seated then circle the tables, dishing up the steak, salad and potatoes.

Wendy's dad raises his glass and clicks it until everyone gives him their attention. "Before we eat I'd like to have another moment of silence in prayer for Lizzy."

While the evenings talk has mostly been on Josh and Logan's timely yet somewhat lucky actions, everyone's inner thoughts are still with Lizzy. After a minute of silence he continues in a choked voice, "I'll be brief so this wonderful food doesn't get cold. He stands to face Josh and looks solemnly in his eyes then begins, "Josh, first off. Thank you. Thank you. I can't say it enough. You know, we don't have a lot of money, but I'm going to contribute half of the money needed for your college fund, on the off-chance you don't get that basketball scholarship," he smiles and holds his hands up again as Rob protests. "You can't stop me. From now till the end of time you are a part of our family. I expect you at our house every holiday from now on, and I think…, Karen expects you at hers every day." He lowers slowly to his chair amid the laughter and blush that rushes over Josh's face.

To Josh's chagrin Karen's dad holds his hands up to stop the clapping then says, "Josh, you're welcome in our house day and night. I haven't prepared anything, but if you ever need anything and I mean *anything*, just say the word and it's yours. The world is blessed with your presence."

Rob is surprised when Josh stands and clears is throat then coughs into his hand. His voice wavers at first but gets stronger as he speaks, "Thanks for all the kindness. I only did what I thought was right." He looks at Logan then continues, "To be honest though, I wouldn't have done anything if Logan hadn't kept telling me the truth. He's the one you should all thank." Logan puts his hands over his face as Karen hugs him and everyone applauds.

Dinner begins and clicks of silverware and small talk fill in the voids between the silence; everyone doing their best to move forward together.

Lizzy's parents are sitting with Rusty at Grandpa's table. Lizzy's mother continually wiping tears; she can't resist the strong pangs of envy when she sees Wendy and Karen happily doting over Josh. Seeing her pain, Logan sits across from her on his way to get a piece of cake. He takes her hand, squeezes lightly and smiles with his eyes, trying to share in her grief and relieve her aching heart. She tries to smile in return but only her mouth responds, her eyes ruled by the truth of her loss.

Logan waits his turn in line, and while Ginger cuts his cake he reads a handwritten note hung over the table.

Josh
You may not know what you've done for us
It might always seem a mystery
So we set aside a few moments to let you know
You'll always be our hero
Love Charles & Wendy

PS. Sorry it doesn't rhyme

He smiles and points at it with his fork. Ginger nods agreeably, "Pretty nice huh?"

During the cake fest Rob and Carol stand together munching, happier, but concerned about their family and friends. Rob takes a deep breath and talks through a mouthful of cake, "This cake is good. You know what…" he hesitates as he swallows, "Let's take the boys camping next weekend. Get away for a few days."

Carol adds supportively, "They sure need a break."

He nods as he chews, "We *all* need a break."

Larry puts his hands on the table next to Josh wanting to lighten things up, and asks him like a juvenile, "So…., tell me, were you *trying* to get that guy?"

Josh rubs his hands together and thinks hard for a minute before he answers. He continues looking away into the darkness of the backyard, the serious expression getting deeper as he replies, "I really don't know what I was doing." Then surprises himself when he blurts out questioningly, "Maybe I wanted to kill him?" Shocked by his response Larry is awkwardly stunned and doesn't know what to say for once and moves away to leave him alone with the girls.

Stoney throws his paper plate into the trash and asks Logan, "Did you hear what happened to LJ?"

"I heard the police arrested them and took them to the station. They arrested his mom and brother too?" Logan answers with a question in his voice.

"I didn't know all that. Billy said they moved away to Flagstaff," Stoney adds with surprise.

"They're just criminals I hope I never see them again," Logan voice is filled with venom as he follows Josh to the pool.

Wendy folds her towel into a small square on the pool stairs then sits on it. Karen diligently hangs on Josh's arm while Wendy shows them her fading bruises on her arms and wrists where Baxter twisted them. "They were worse a few days ago," she looks closely and rubs them lightly with her finger tips.

Stoney and Ballsac are already swimming, impatiently waiting for Logan. Ballsac sneaks onto the shed's roof and crouches low so the adults can't see him then whoops as he soars over Stoney, landing with a big splash. With a quick peak towards the picnic tables Logan holds his finger to his lips and tiptoes onto the shed then cannonballs into the pool, soaking Wendy and Karen. Josh dives in and dunks him with vengeful laughter. The girls follow Josh into the pool, even getting their hair wet for once.

Stoney begins to swim circles around the pool, "We can create a really fast whirlpool with this many."

"Let's do it," Josh shouts, dunking Karen and chasing after Wendy.

It's not long before they're all floating in a circle with their parents watching, content and grateful for their safety as they sip cold beers.

"You know what?" Stoney asks Logan.

"I know a lot of what's," Logan banters, relaxing on his back.

"No. Quit it. Do you think there's such thing as a million dollar bill?" Stoney asks seriously.

"There *are* real millionaires, they probably have 'em," Ballsac supplies.

Josh splashes him and laughs, "Don't be stupid."

Larry tosses the football to Logan, "They *are* real, I have one at home."

Logan catches the ball with one hand and squeezes the water out thinking about the things he would do if he had a million dollars. He could forget about that new Rollfast and buy his own airplane, maybe buy Josh a brand new car, one faster than Larry's....

Thanks for stopping by
FOSSIL
Hope to see ya soon!

7/8/2009
8/11/2009

About the Author

Tyler Anderson grew up in Phoenix Arizona, spending his childhood and adult life there. He and his wife Jody have two children, Chelsea and Mason.

Tyler will soon be releasing The Green House and further tales featuring the town of Fossil and its residents.

Look for them at your local bookstore or check the website TheCannonBallKing.com.